The Oranges of Valencia

by

Arthur StJames

Joel Chapter 1

^{1}*The word of the LORD that came to Joel the son of Pethuel.*

^{2}*Hear this, ye old men, and give ear, all ye inhabitants of the land. Hath this been in your days, or even in the days of your fathers?*

^{3}*Tell ye your children of it, and let your children tell their children, and their children another generation.*

^{4}*That which the palmerworm hath left hath the locust eaten; and that which the locust hath left hath the cankerworm eaten; and that which the cankerworm hath left hath the caterpillar eaten.*

^{5}*Awake, ye drunkards, and weep; and howl, all ye drinkers of wine, because of the new wine; for it is cut off from your mouth.*

^{6}*For a nation is come up upon my land, strong, and without number, whose teeth the teeth of a lion, and he hath the cheek teeth of a great lion.*

^{7}*He hath laid my vine waste, and barked my fig tree: he hath made it clean bare, and cast away; the branches thereof are made white.*

Chapter One

On the outskirts of a small city in Asia Minor known as Jerusalem, resided a Jew named Saul who lived a life now barren of family and very much alone in his makeshift home. He rises, as always, early from his night's slumber to begin his morning prayers. He wears a black robe along with a blue tunic. His prayers are heavy with grief for his departed wife, Rachel. As he prays prostrate on his floor, Saul rises to his knees with the look of distress apparent upon his face.

Hearing a knock at the door he says, "Enter!" Saul notices his old friend Joseph who recognizes immediately and works quickly to greet him with a smile. Joseph is dressed almost identical to Saul and is the shorter of the two.

"How are you feeling today?" inquires Joseph.

"Well enough," replies Saul. "What ugly mess has the Sanhedrin made for us today?"

"Be careful Saul, and pick your words wisely my friend," warns Joseph; "you don't want to end up on a cross like that peasant do you?"

Saul chuckles and says, "well, alright then, as you wish."

Joseph begins to grumble about this Christ, and the whole Christian movement. "It will bring all of Rome down upon our heads and be the end of us all," declares Joseph. "What was that peasant (Jesus) thinking anyway?" he continues. "Son of David indeed..... and their numbers grow daily?"

"You have to admit that his attempt, though ill conceived, was creative, Joseph.

"What do you mean, Saul?"

"Well, my brother, this peasant, Jesus, had his government almost in place and his followers already calling him the Hosanna, Hosanna in the Highest. First, this kingship he most certainly claimed by being a descendent of David. Second was his cousin, John (the Baptist), who was of the line of Aaron; he would have established him over the Levi class. And third were his twelve followers, who would surely laid claim to representing each of the original twelve tribes of Israel, Joseph. All in all, not a bad attempt if you ask me brother," Saul ended.

"But, he could have never have hoped to have overthrown the Roman Empire by the use of force?" questions Joseph.

"Quite the contrary, my friend, from all I heard about Jesus, he was anything but violent."

"Tell that to the money changers in the temple," laughs Joseph.

"Quite true Joseph, and later when one of his followers drew a sword one of the temple guards, it was this same Jesus that told his follower to put his sword away. And didn't he go as far as to tell the follower that if he lived by the sword that he would surely die by the sword? exclaimed Joseph.

"He hardly sounds like a descendant of King David, Saul. Perhaps his father was a Roman soldier as some rumors might suggest, Saul. All that matters not as his mother was a Hebrew, and as to the identity of his father this late in the game is of no consequence as he is still a Jew," responds Saul. "And with his death on the Roman cross, any claim of being the messiah died with him, Joseph."

Both men then reflect quietly while sitting in the room with the only sounds being heard were those of their own breathing.

"The people yearn for a savior in times such as these, Saul, and what with all of the crucifying and the raping going on by the Romans."

"And the taxes; all of those ungodly taxes these Romans require!", interjects Saul.

"Taxes for their emperor, for their armies, their senators, and worst of all their pagan gods," grumbled Joseph. "Too bad Israel did not have such an army like Rome's to carry the message of the Lord of Hosts, that would have made the ushering in of a new messiah rather easy wouldn't you say, Saul?"

Saul smiles momentarily and says, "Another thing to consider, as you well know, is that any arrival of a savior brings hope to the people."

"For the scriptures tell us that without hope, the people perish," replies Joseph. Pausing thoughtfully, he then asks the daring question of Saul, "Perhaps now is time for a messiah?"

Saul says nothing for a few moments, then says, "Damned Sanhedrin, they should have worked with this Jesus; found and accommodation of some kind."

"I guess they (Sanhedrin) fear losing what little power they have left," utters Joseph.

"Spoken like a true Levite, but what were they doing turning Jesus over to the Romans - of all people," demand Saul? "I mean after all he was a Jew, heretic or not, Jesus was still a Jew," Saul continued. "And even if this Jesus was an Essene, what could have the High Priests have been thinking, Joseph? Then the Levite quietly grumbles, for that grievance alone the whole Sanhedrin should have been taken to the edge of town and been stoned. They are a self righteous lot, the whole bunch of them," states Saul. "Parading around in their fine robes, making long, public prayers; preposterous. Now who could take them seriously?" Saul asks Joseph quietly. "Least of all, God, Saul thinks to himself."

"More like theater than worship if you ask me", quips Joseph as Saul chuckles.

Quickly changing the subject, Joseph says, "How long has it been since you lost your wife, Saul? Four, five years is it now is it?"

"It's closer to five," replies Saul.

"Does she still visit you in your dreams?" questions Joseph.

Saul begins to look a little angered by Joseph's query. "You know, Joseph, the Lord would never introduce his Messiah to the people in the way this Jesus did – but rather God would have raised up a learned man, a man educated thoroughly in the intricacies of Midrashim. The Lord would have anointed someone who practices what he preaches, not like one of those pretenders who preside over us now."

"Again brother," replies Joseph, "I caution you, as surely the Sanhedrin has ears everywhere."

Saul continues," I am very well aware of my position, thank you. I will never become high priest and I will most assuredly never see an end to Roman rule in my life time, these things I am sure of, Joseph. Just as I am certain that it seems like the only thing I am good for is doing the Sanhedrin's dirty work."

"Dirty work, as in bringing Jewish justice to this rabble, this cult of saints?" quips Joseph.

"Quite right, Joseph;" says Saul, "and whether saint or sinner, they are still Jews (at least most of them are) and they cannot be allowed to flaunt the Law."

"Do you ever feel any guilt over putting these, these people to death, Saul?"

"Guilty, whatever for, Joseph? I have not lost any sleep over the likes of them to in the near future," admits Saul.

"There is nothing like a good stoning to set things right," replies Joseph half jokingly. "Yes, that is what I always say... like that one a few days ago – what was his name, Saul?"

"Stephen", I believe was his name, suggests Saul.

"Now that really put the fear of God into them," laughs Joseph cynically.

"Well perhaps, Joseph, perhaps not?"

"Perhaps?" questions Joseph. "Jesus might have had something there by defusing the situation where the crowd wanted to stone that poor, pathetic prostitute, Saul?"

"But she did break the law, as did those who were accusing her, Joseph."

"I mean how do you suppose they caught her in this act of adultery anyway?" questions Joseph.

"If Jews are stoning Jews and killing one another, then the real enemy goes unpunished," suggests Saul.

"But the law, Saul, it must be upheld or we are nothing... nothing."

"Of course brother," replies Saul as he smiles reassuringly.

"You know that they are ignorant for the most and are tired of Roman rule."

"Our brethren? says Saul.

"I cannot help but wonder if we should not have tried harder to explain things to these peasants," Joseph utters softly?

"I believe they have followed this Jesus out of primarily frustration, and most had good intentions, of that I am sure," snaps Saul.

"Pity you never met this Jesus," suggests Joseph.

"I would have liked to have clashed wits with him", continued Saul; "oh the questions I would have liked to have asked him."

"It is not every day you get the chance to interrogate the Messiah," Joseph replies.

"Perhaps all they really needed was a good rabbi rather than a peasant messiah," contends Joseph.

"Perhaps", replied Saul, "perhaps."

"Imagine what things might have been like had they (peasants) had a good rabbi to lead them and then who knows?" queries Joseph.

"Maybe even an end to Roman rule," Saul replies quickly with a gleam in his eye.

"Those thoughts will remain within these walls if you know what is good for you," cautions Joseph quietly.

Saul laughs loudly and then asks, "Do you see yourself as this rabbi?"

Joseph replies, "Who me, the Messiah? Oh heavens no, Brother Saul. I have neither the learning nor the where withal take on such an undertaking. But perhaps you, Saul, do you see yourself their Messiah, as the next King Saul?" Joseph smiles at Saul and Saul smiles back in kind.

Then Saul says, "Now back to the business at hand."

"Damascus, is it this time?" asks Joseph.

"Yes, to do more of God's work," Saul answers sarcastically.

"What of the gentiles," Saul?

"Well now, Joseph, that is an interesting question. Maybe I shall convert them?"

"Would you actually go as far as to dine with them, Saul?"

"Why not?" replies Saul. "Plenty of swords for circumcision." Saul laughs again and says, "Imagine me, some sort gentile persuader so to speak, that'll be the day."

"You may make high priest yet, Saul." Both men laugh.

"Perhaps when I was married, like my father, I might have had a chance at becoming high priest, but never now as a widower, Joseph, they just would not hear of it."

"Have you ever considered remarrying, Saul?"

"Not while I am still in love with my wife. It just would not be fair to another now would it, Joseph?"

"You can still grieve for her even after five years, Saul?"

"The heart does pick who it loves in life;" replied Saul, "it just knows to love is all."

"It is not like you are her bond servant, Saul."

"No?" questioned Saul. "Are you most certain?"

"Do you still blame these Christians for her; their death, Saul?"

"No brother, not any longer," replies Saul. "At least I am not blaming the Christians so much anymore, nor do I blame their Jesus. It was not their fault that my wife died in child birth on the same night the High Priests decided to arrest this, this Messiah. With all of the commotion going on in Jerusalem that night, the people were in fear of arrests and would not leave their homes. Those temple guards were running around and trying to arrest so many Jews that night."

"The guards seemed to be finding Christians where none existed before if you ask me," cried Joseph. "And they scared one of his (Jesus) followers so much that not only did he deny his messiah, but he did it at least three times that very night, or so I heard, Saul. One of them was so distraught that he hung himself."

"Good, serves him right," Saul quickly replied, "And who betrays a friend like that anyway? Thirty pieces of silver, indeed."

"Well the guards behaved more like Samaritans than anything else, Saul."

Then Saul stops for a moment, looks at Joseph and says sadly, "You know that there was no midwife was to be found that night. I only wanted my son to be born here in Jerusalem, and how was I to know that Rachel would give birth on that exact night, Joseph? Surely it was God's will that I be alone, Joseph. Now I will truly be devote my time left fully to the tending of the Lord's work. And if I no longer have my work, then what am I, Joseph, moreover, who am I?"

Joseph just listens quietly and his face soon begins to reflect the pain that he sees present in his friend Saul's face as well.

"Surely, I will see her again the bosom of Abraham," whispers Saul. "But I must be off now, Joseph, and I have a long ride ahead of me."

"May the Lord be with you, Saul," says Joseph.

"And with you," replies Saul.

Saul opens the outer door and begins to exit when to his surprise, finds his wife standing before him, yet appearing at a younger age than he had remembered her. She takes his hand and leads him to a nearby place where he finds himself standing under a large shade tree and looking at his lost love with complete abandon. Rachel is a woman who appears to be in her late teens and has beautiful, long, raven hair, and most of all is noticeably pregnant. She is modestly dressed in a black garb and she seems quite pleased to see her husband. The shade protects both of them day's sun, as Saul looks around as if stunned and asks the question, "Rachel, where did you come from?"

She replies lovingly, "From the hills, of course, where I have been gathering flowers." Paul looks in disbelief and just stares at her.

Rachel continues, "You know that my parents have been working feverishly helping me prepare our home for the upcoming arrival of their first grandchild."

"I am sure that they are very excited, Rachel."

"And the thought that our child will be born in Jerusalem pleases me so. Thank you for making this journey possible, my husband." Saul smiles with compassion.

"And you do of course know that both my and our mothers believe that the baby will be a boy."

"Is that so? Saul questions with a big smile on his face. "I see that I will have to work even harder to be able to give our son all the things in life that he will need to succeed, like an education.

"I know how hard you have laborer doing God's work, Saul. One day Saul, you will be a very great man. Your mother saw it in you and I see it too, my husband; a great man, God willing."

"I am hardly great, Rachel, the most I can possibly hope for is to become more learned in the Torah and then maybe one day wise. All in the service of God, my dear wife, praise God."

"You are far too modest my husband, for God surely has his hand upon your life."

"Some days I am not so certain of God's blessing, Rachel."

"You are just tired, my husband. Rest a little and I know, let us sing like we did as children."

"I can see your mother now, Saul, comforting you when you felt discouraged after one of your encounters with your father. I remember her singing one of David's Psalms and how you would join in. How did it go, Saul? *'I will sing unto the Lord for he has triumphed gloriously, the horse and the rider thrown into the sea...'*" Then both Rachel and Saul begin to sing the song again and this time in unison.

"Remember Saul, how you then pretended to be riding a horse and you would fall to the ground and laugh and laugh? How your mother would beam as she watched you, Saul? Oh how proud she was of her little boy. And how your father would arrive home and with a very strict voice call to you, Saul!"

"Yes, Rachel, I still remember."

"And how your father would scold you for wasting such precious time on trivial things when there was work to be done, prayers to be read and memorized, Saul. He would show up suddenly, standing there in the garden in his best robes and look me square in the eye, toss out a scripture and expect me to immediately know its origin. I can hear him now Saul, 'Spare the rod and spoil the child.'"

"The proverbs of King Solomon," Saul retorts quickly.

"I also remember how you quoted a scripture condemning the use of strong drink and how he then how he slapped you across the face."

"Yes, it was from Leviticus, Rachel."

"Yet, you never retaliated against his cruelty."

"The fifth commandment given by God through his servant Moses," calmly replies Saul.

"Honor him then if you must, Saul, I may not have."

"It is God that I honor by obeying his command, my beautiful wife to be."

"What most I remember most of all is how all the joy and life ran from your face and when he struck you;, you only kept quiet and smiled, almost a smile of quiet defiance, Saul."

"He was just trying to prepare me for later life, Rachel."

"Preparing you by getting drunk and beating you for not living up to his standards, Saul, standards that he himself never lived up to?"

"He was not drunk, just a little over worked," protested Saul.

"I remember those beatings, Saul, and how your mother would later find you after your father's rage had passed and would pull you to her side and how she then sang to you."

Saul hugs Rachel and then begins to laugh with great joy as his courage is renewed as before. "He is long dead, my wife, no need to fear him anymore. Now he is God's problem." They both laugh briefly and then sit together quietly looking into each other's eyes.

As Rachel smiles at Saul, Paul awakens to only find himself in prison. He moves the chains that bind him in hopes of getting some comfort and further adjusts himself on the hard, stone dungeon floor. Paul notices a thunderstorm as it flashes and booms through a small window high above his head. He tries to get his eyes to focus on the periodic flashes of lightning in hopes of getting his bearings. The sweat seemed to roll down his forehead and into his eyes which made them his burn in the night air which hung heavy with humidity. The stench in the air was almost unbearable and try as he could, Paul was not able find much relief from his misery.

Paul laughs as realizes that he had not just been visiting with his old friend Joseph (now Barnabas), or his beloved Rachel, but rather that he has been dreaming. He looks around the prison hoping that his eyes might make out anything recognizable in the light provided by the storm. In near pitch darkness, Paul whispers to himself, "Not exactly a great man now. This is surely God's punishment for my putting all those Christians to death while in the service of the Sanhedrin." Then Paul cries out, "Why Lord? Have I recently offended you? Have I not served you faithfully? Show me the error of my ways, oh Lord, and I shall repent, cries Paul!"

Another prisoner begins to grumble as Paul begins to sing one of King David's Psalms. *"I will sing unto the Lord for he has triumphed gloriously, the horse and the rider thrown into the sea"*, sings Paul almost in desperation. A Roman guard notices the noise coming from the cell and orders the prisoners to be quiet or he will have their heads.

"No way to talk to a citizen," Paul quickly responds.

"A citizen?" the guard questions Paul.

"Yes, I was born Saul of Tarsus and became a Roman citizen shortly after my birth as was my father before me and I,

Paul, am now a prisoner in chains for preaching the message that the Lord, Jesus Christ lives and offers salvation not only to the Jew but to the gentile as well. What is your name my good man?" asks Paul.

"I am Titus and I will slit your throat should you dare to cross me," declares the guard.

Paul chuckles. Then Titus walks away quietly thinking Paul to either be crazy or some political prisoner who may possibly have powerful friends in Rome, even in the Senate itself. Either way Titus figures that either way it would be more trouble than it was worth to deal with this prisoner.

Slowly, Paul sings quieter and quieter and then begins to nod off to sleep and later echoes, for it is written, your young men shall dreams and your old men shall see visions. Then quietly Paul whispers to himself, "Tomorrow, Rome," and then soon he falls back to sleep.

Chapter Two

It is early morning just shortly before sunrise in the town of San Gimignano, in the hillside of what was known as Tuscany. Inside the monastery the morning light is beginning to peak through shutters of a nearby window. Just a hint of a distant fire lingers in the air and the sound of wood being chopped can be heard off in the near distance.

"Father Thaddeus, Father Thaddeus, it will soon be time for morning prayers," the abbot announces quietly.

Father Thaddeus is a man in his early twenties, above average height and average weight, with black, semi curly hair and brown eyes, as well as a big, friendly smile. The room is small and almost Spartan in appearance in this mid fourteenth century monastic structure known as Bella Vista Abbey. The Abbot, Beauvais, is a middle-aged man of French extraction; he is balding and is a tad bit rounded in his middle, but he seems to be a pleasant enough man. Beauvais' large smile, (which discloses his yellow tinted, half rotten teeth), are only over shadowed by his even larger than life nose and is ever present bad breath.

Father Thaddeus opens his eyes and asks, "have the klaxons sounded already"

"No father, but I know that you have a long journey ahead of you today on your way to Rome, and I did not want you to be late for morning prayers."

"I hope it will be worth the trip with the Papal father being in Avignon," retorts Thaddeus.

"Most assuredly, father, and I envy you making such a voyage, starting work at a new post, where as I truly love San Gimignano, what I wouldn't give to see Rome just once. So, so many pilgrims come through on their way to Rome and there are many days that I consider joining them," comments Beauvais.

"From where do you hail, father?" inquires Beauvais.

"I am from a small place in the lower Alps, just beyond Milan," replies Thaddeus.

"*Beauvais*, is that French, father?"

"That is correct, Father Thaddeus, as I was born along the coast in a small, French fishing village known as Nice."

"Ah yes", replies Father Thaddeus noticing a very prominent French accent in the abbot's voice, "I see, father. My grandmother was of French linage," replies Thaddeus, as he smiles and tries to escape the stench of Beauvais lingering breath.

"Father Thaddeus, I do implore you to please stay a few days and rest here in our humble abode and regain your strength. The trip to Rome has been a bit overwhelming especially with all of the excitement and anticipation of starting my new position," replied Father Thaddeus.

"I am sure though that the bishop is most eager for me to begin my duties in Rome, so I must decline your most gracious offer," replies Thaddeus.

"The Sisters of San Francesco will be very disappointed if they do not get a chance to at least greet you, and you do know how hard they have worked here in the town caring for the poor, Father Thaddeus"

"I am of course at your service Father Beauvais," replies Thaddeus.

"So, then you will be staying, at least for awhile."

"Yes if you order it," Father Beauvais.

"Order is such a harsh word, Father Thaddeus; let us refer to it as a request, shall we?"

"How could I not accept your hospitality Abbot Beauvais, Thaddeus?" replies submissively.

"Excellent, Father Thaddeus, as I have already sent word to the Holy Father that I am in need of your services and request that you be immediately reassigned (at least temporarily) to this abbey, under my care and supervision of course."

"Of course your Eminence," retorts Thaddeus.

"So, shall we go down stairs, father?" Beauvais announces quickly.

The abbot pours some water into a large bowl and Thaddeus washes his face and the two men depart the room.

Outside of the bedroom door is an open air piazza with steps descending down one wall to the cobblestones below. A well for drawing water rests in the center of the piazza, which is surrounded by more cobblestone and frescos. Thaddeus notices a few more frescos line the walls near the cobblestone supports which extend up to the roof and short overhang as they begin to descend the stairs. As light rain begins to fall but it is not unusual for this time of year. At the bottom of the steps stands a man of short stature, slightly hunch backed, with a noticeable limp, awaits them.

"How may I be of service, Eminence?"

"Ah, Friar Gennaro, it is so good to see you this morning," replies the abbot. "Allow me to introduce Father Thaddeus, as he only arrived here last night but has graciously offered to stay with us and work on a little project I have which needs attention." Gennaro nods towards the priests and says, "Welcome father."

"Thank you, brother," Thaddeus responds cheerfully.

"Father Thaddeus, like you brother Gennero is new to our monastery and has only served here the last three years. He comes to us from the City of Volterra by way of Fiesole. He will assist you while you are getting settled in, and he is at your disposal," continued the abbot. "Also, I have no room for you here in the abbey, but I do have the use of a room just a short walk from here above the Florence Gate, continues Beauvais. The room is near a small bell tower and it will be part of your duties to ring it on occasion, Father Thaddeus."

"Surely, there is room somewhere in the monastery for me?" asks Thaddeus. "Perhaps even the room where I slept last night?"

"That room is for the sole purpose of accommodating visitors, Father, surely you can understand the importance of that," explains Beauvais. "Shall we continue to morning prayers then?" Beauvais suggests sounding more like an order than a question.

All three men turn the corner to hear a loud noise coming from the room ahead; it was the klaxons calling the monks to morning prayers. Soon breakfast would be served and of course eaten in total silence.

For the next few weeks, Father Thaddeus found boredom to be his primary adversary in the small village he found himself stranded in. The towers were plentiful and the people were in general very kind to him, but after all he was a priest and most people were polite to the priest because they feared the Lord's wrath otherwise. This made it very difficult for Thaddeus to gauge people for their honesty and sincerity, because whatever they might have been talking about when he enters a room will soon stop abruptly and the niceties soon begin. It was of somewhat importance to the young priest to be liked for who he was, not just necessarily for who he represented, yet there was little Thaddeus could do with that and decided then and there not to concern himself with the whole notion. He decided that he would be liked both for his goodness for heart as well as the final vows he took in seminary just a few short weeks ago. The life of a priest could be full of excitement and new friends, but friends that would rarely invite him to spend time with them or their families except upon a special occasion here and there. He surmised that it would for the most, be a very, very lonely job for the most, he thought to himself. Yet he had made his bed and now he must lie in it, for better or worse, it was what he had chosen and it was what felt honor bound to do. He was a priest and he could live with that, even if it did mean his first assignment was filled mostly with boredom.

San Gimigano was not without its charge though, for there visitor coming through on the way to and from Rome, or stopping in to buy goods to take back to their homes, and there were the town's people, Thaddeus thought, "Surely some of them have to lead interesting lives." Perhaps this would be only a short detour in the road of life and soon he would be on his way to Rome and most of all the excitement of starting his first assignment. This project for that he had been given might be an interesting one as well and perhaps if he did well there might be a promotion in for him, thought the neophyte priest.

Later that afternoon, Gennero, along with another monk, came and gathered up Father Thaddeus's belongings, such as they were and moved them to his new abode. Beauvais instructed Thaddeus to take a leisurely stroll about the town and introduce himself to some of the local parishioners he might meet along the way; that his work could wait until time allowed the abbot to show him the tasks at hand.

"There is no need to rush, my son" said Beauvais, "we will have plenty of time for work after you get settled in. I would also like for you to lead mass tomorrow as well, Father Thaddeus."

"Of course, father, as you wish," said Thaddeus with a forced smile.

"Excellent," replied Beauvais, then it is all settled. "Now I will leave you to your exploring," states Beauvais, as he walks away with a large smile on his face revealing once again his crooked and mostly rotten teeth.

"At least the streets are paved with cobblestone, not like the dirt ones as he had back in his home town," thought Thaddeus. The towers were everywhere; it seemed as if they were almost tall enough to touch the sky, or so he wondered. Thaddeus could hear conversations coming from some of them, and could even make out part of the conversations if he tried hard enough, but he did not like the thought of his eves dropping, so he decided against it. Soon he began to see people, mostly poorer day laborers moving about the lanes and most would smile and nod at him as he did in return to them. Some would stop and inquire if he was a new priest there to take up residence, or whether he might be on some pilgrimage perhaps just back from the Holy Land. All were polite, most were shy, but none seemed to frighten him in the least. As Thaddeus approached the city square, he could smell the aroma of food cooking and eventually followed his nose to a small osteria where he decided to stop in and check out the local fare. And after a pleasant lunch, which was on the house of course, the young priest went back to his exploring and decided that life here might not be all that bad after all. He knew he would see

Rome soon enough, but perhaps this could be a sort of sabbatical, or at least he decided for now to look at it that way.

Now on the other side of the Appemine Mountains to the west, in the port city-state of Genoa, a modest sized Spanish ship, transporting passengers and goods, slowly enters the harbor and moors along the boardwalk. A young man disembarks the ship, attempts to get his bearings, and soon looks for a place to purchase supplies for his journey ahead. He seems to get his land legs much quicker than he was able to acquire his sea legs as he walks shakily down the pier. Sailors going to and from distant ports pass him on the streets without so much as a word eager to get to their destination. Women walking near the water wait in anticipation, hoping to get his attention as well as any money he might be carrying. The young man does not stop to entertain any of these enchantresses, yet he does manage an occasional smile for them as he passes by; after all he is not made of stone. After carefully checking to make sure that none of his money had unexpectedly been left in the crowd, Diego proceeds up the street and away from the sea to a small shop marked mercantile and then soon enters. Genoa can be a fascinating city with most every type of people dwelling there, mostly traders, or sailor, from almost walk of life who have come to this most serene republic to of course seek their fortune.

As Diego makes his way out of the city and down the road towards San Gimignano, the days are primarily free of any rain which pleased him immensely. The thought of walking in the rain for days on end was not what Diego considered to be enjoyable. He also feared the possibility of bandits along the road, but just the sight of his sword would dissuade all but the ardent of criminal. He had purchased sufficient food to see him through his journey, just as long as he was careful to eat sparingly. Diego knew that there would be other travelers along the way who were most likely making a pilgrimage to Rome and wondered if perhaps he might ally with one of them long enough to reach his destination. No more had he thought of this possibility when he happened across a small caravan of merchants heading east as well. They were all too happy to hire Diego and of course his sword once they realized that he was no threat to them. Now not only did he have enough to eat, but even better he did not have to gather any firewood, nor cook along the way. And on one occasion, Diego got to ride in one of the wagons as well. What a great way to make a little money for his time, he thought, after all what could be better? The sound that the draft horses made as they plodded along sounded much different to Diego than the Arabian horses he had been used to seeing back in his own village. The draft horses were of course much larger in build and nearly twice the size as the ones at home. Diego thought how beautiful they were, but even more how could a man pay to feed them unless he was quite wealthy, although some of the Arabian horses were more valuable than the income that a man might make in his entire life. "Perhaps one of these wealthy merchants might have an eligible daughter that he might romance and one day marry, and thus inheriting many of these fine horses and the means to care for them as well," Diego thought to himself. Yet on the other hand she could be quite homely, a consideration which had escaped him until now. No, he decided, he would be content with just admiring the draft horses from afar and leave all that cost of upkeep to someone else.

Eventually Diego sees a town up on a large knoll and he is told that this was the place he had been asking about, San Gimgnano. With that, Diego separated himself from them and accepting his pay in the form of silver, with the exception of a new pair of boots, purchased at a very fair price I might add, that he had seen in merchant's wares. The merchant was eager to do business with him and the boots, Diego had to admit, did fit like a glove. The caravan bypassed the town and made way for Rome while the day was yet young. Diego looked toward one of the gates controlling one of the many entrances to the town. There he noticed a priest walking back and forth on the wall above the gate near a small bell tower. The wall and the guards did look formidable, and Diego wondered if he had made the right decision to stop here, but he would have to eventually find out? So, up towards the gate he walked and with that he called out the priest who was walking on the wall above him, to which he got no immediate answer.

Chapter Three

"Get in he...re you fo....ol, get in here im....mediately!"

In the early hours of the morning and a slave enters the bed chamber of the palace and drops down to one knee. With head bowed and a fearful look in his face the servant asks, yes, my lord?

"Send for my phy....sician at once!"

The servant exists quickly and soon the physician enters the room. Caesar's face is pale and his breathing is short and fast, for he has had another dream, the same dream he's had the past three nights. The palace walls are dark and gloomy. A set of six oil lamps suspended from the ceiling burns and flickers from the slight breeze which slipped quietly through the hallways.

"Has the dream revisited, sire?"

"Ye....s, that aw...ful, awful dream has returned, and how do... you plan to make it sto...?" Caesar snaps back quickly.

"This is a matter for the spirit world and best resolved by the temple priests."

"Dam...n it all, man, I be...g of you, make this nightmare fle....e my presence and I shall reward you hand....somely."

"I will endeavor to try, Caesar. Can you please tell me again the exact details of this terror in the night and I will do my best to interpret your dream," he then hands Caesar a potion that he has been mixing from him to drink.

"What is thi....s, a bit of dried leaves again in bit...ter waters?" asks Caesar.

"It will help calm your nerves sire, please drink it all quickly."

"Oh ver....y well," Caesar replies and downs it all in one gulp.

"There now, isn't that better, my lord?"

Caesar grimaces, and begins his tale of woe." The last three nigh...ts I rest normally through...out most the nigh...t until short...ly before the sun is to rise and then a voi...ce, or sp...irit, or inva...des my sl..eep and says in a very fright...ening voice, "d...o no har...m to this m...an, P...aul, for he is a servant of the Mo...st High or sure...ly you shall per..ish". Ne...xt, I see the fa...ce of a man who I do not rec..ognize wea..ring the cha...ins of a prisoner and then I look down to find myself com...pletely covered in sores and boils. Then I wa...ke up in nothing more than cold sweat."

"Please, sire, allow me to send for Jupiter's priests and ..."

"Fra...uds, they are all fra..uds!" Caesar interrupts loudly. "Now you want me to tr...ust my care to those fo...ols? Never!"

"Perhaps we could call upon the priests from the Temple of Minerva, or Mars, possibly Julius Caesar if it please you, my lord?"

"I, the great Emperor Claudius, afraid of the terrors that come in the night," Caesar reflects quietly; my enemies the senate will smell blood should they ever learn of this. "You may go, doc...tor, your serv...ices are no longer re..quired. And not a wo...rd of this to any...one it will sur...ely be you....r last."

The morning light was beginning to break through the small, barred windows of the prison cell. A few of the prisoners bound for Rome began to stir, with one of them being Paul.

"Do they not know that they have most certainly made a mistake with me?" one of the prisoners announced suddenly. "Guard, guard, I demand to see a representative of the senate immediately!" he continued while attempting to stand up.

"Shut up dog, or I'll cut your tongue out!" replied Julius.

"Then at least give me some water..."

With that the centurion responded, "Here's your water," as he threw a dipper of water from a wooden bucket into the prisoners face. Laughingly, Julius then mocks the prisoner as he struggles to get a little of water from his face into his mouth.

Dropping back down to the floor the prisoner weeps and says, "All I wanted was a little water."

"If its water you want my friend, then its water you shall have," said Paul.

"But how you give me water when you yourself are in chains", the prisoner asks?

"It is not I but the one I serve who will give you living water, and you will never thirst again," replies Paul.

With that Julius hearing the conversation interrupts Paul and replies, "Enough of that too or you will feel the back of my hand; that is unless you are speaking the praises of Jupiter."

"My Lord died for you as well my friend, and if you will but open your heart …"

And with that Julius began to beat Paul about the head and shoulders. Paul takes no action to protest his treatment and the beating soon stops.

Paul only smiles at Julius and quotes the scriptures quietly. "By his stripes we are healed, the Book of Isaiah."

Julius then calls Paul a mad man and walks out of the prison cell to return to his duties.

The prisoner who was yelling earlier asks Paul, "You follow a dead man?"

Paul replies, "Not really, but rather he died upon the cross but after the third day he rose from the dead and entered into heaven. It is because of this I share the good news that Jesus Christ has been crucified, died, rose from his grave and sits at the right hand of the Father in heaven," continues Paul. "Furthermore, whoever calls upon his name and believes will never perish."

"Well, my hopeful friend, comments the prisoner, my name is Amicus and I put my faith in the justice of the Senate as well as the greed of my powerful friends to achieve my freedom. This surely explains the chains you are wearing, Amicus," retorts Paul.

"Well, you may find a few desperate souls in prison that will heed your call, sir, but the most you will get out of that brute, Titus, is the back of his hand," comments Amicus.

"To what do you owe the pleasure of your chains, Amicus?" questions Paul.

"I was not a very good servant to my master," replied Amicus, "Or at least that is how it was explained to me. One day I was summoned before my master and he had me imprisoned without saying a word as to the reason why and I quickly found myself on a ship bound for a dark prison in Rome. As to why he did not just simply kill me, I do not know, but who is to question fate?" reflected Amicus. "And now here I am bound in chains next to you, Paul, bondservant of the Most High God," says Amicus laughingly. "What was that song you sang in the middle of the night, Paul?"

"Oh, the Psalm... you are referring to one of the Psalms", replies Paul. "It was written by King David a long time ago, Amicus."

"Then why does this great king, King David, not get you out of this mess?"

"He has been gone for many years, Amicus, but it is his descendant that I serve, Jesus, son of David."

"Then may you find favor with him, Paul, may you always find favor," replies Amicus.

The Roman centurion later returns to the cell with two other guards attending him and announces "On your feet dogs! We march to Rome!"

As they began to depart Puteoli for Rome, Julius spies a small contingent of Praetorian Guard approaching the prisoners from the main road. "So, who is the mystic of the desert in this foul lot?" demands the commander.

"I am, great one," chirps Amicus.

"Then you are now my prisoner," the commander continues. Deliberately the commander now turns towards Julius, (who is only now approaching him) and says, "Hail Caesar!"

Julius replies in kind and asks, "Why has the right hand of the Captain of the Praetorian Guard of Rome made his way all this distance to inquire of a worthless scribe?"

"Scribe?" replies the commander.

"I only know that I was informed by Rome that I was to bring Saul of Tarsus safely and directly to the Circus Maximus where he is to await trial before Caesar."

"Very well then, commander, not only will I release him into your custody but all of them," replies Julius.

"Those were not my orders," replies Titus.

"Well they are now," barks Julius.

Titus, not wishing to anger the centurion with his larger contingent of soldiers any further accepts the task and salutes Julius. Titus turns to the prisoners and announces that he is Titus, a commander of the Augustan Regiment, in the great Cohorts of Rome, and that they are now his prisoners. Titus then reminds the prisoners that the journey is long and treacherous, so only Jupiter knows if you will ever see Rome. Titus then turns to one of his subordinates and instructs them to take special care of Saul along the journey and to release him from his chains that anchored him to Amicus.

Paul lifts his head towards the sky and says a prayer of thanks to the Lord Most High.

Chapter Four

"Good afternoon, father" echoed from near the gate below.

As Thaddeus looks down from the almost catwalk area he often visits to pray and meditate, he observes a group of travelers entering the city. A dark-haired, olive-skinned man in his late twenties repeats himself. "Good afternoon; and it is father, isn't it?" the traveler asks with a large smile.

"Yes, yes, I am father Thaddeus, and who might you be my son?" Thaddeus is dressed in a simple monks cloak and adorns a large wooden cross strung from neck.

"I am Diego, from Catalonia to the west and being a stranger in this fair land and if it pleases you, you might assist me by directing me to a place where I might dine and rest from my long travel."

"Why yes, Diego, I will do even better than that, I will escort you there myself, replied the father."

"You are too kind to this most unworthy servant," Diego replies as he slightly bows his head to the young priest.

Diego is dressed modestly in mostly dark colors, yet upon careful observation his boots reveal that he has or at least at one time was a man of means. Thaddeus almost rushes down the stone steps in anticipation to speak someone about anything, and had often wondered why the abbot had insisted that he stay and work on a very important project which even until this day had yet to be revealed to him. Two months could be a long time to a young priest who was eager to begin his duties to God as well as his fellow man. All of the people that Thaddeus had met so far in San Gimignano were either (with a few exceptions) in the household of the Lord or were being prepared to enter God's kingdom by attending their catechism studies. Most travelers were pilgrims on their way to Rome and mostly stayed to themselves and did only what necessary as to be allowed within the protection of walls which had not been there all that long. Perhaps Diego would have news of the outside world, stories of kings and wars, of great ships and voyages, of Moors, and most of all of the crusades.

As Thaddeus reached near the outer gate he noticed that Diego had not yet entered. "Come along, my son, for I know of a good place where we shall break bread this day and talk of the many wonders of the Lord."

Diego was motionless which the guard at the gate stood in his path refusing him admission. Thaddeus realizing what was taking place, but unsure of why, looked at the guard and said, "You sir, please stand aside as this man and I have urgent business within the city."

"As you wish, father", replied the guard. He then moved away out of the way and motioned for Diego to proceed into the city while looking at the young priest in an unpleasant manner as if the priest had just cost him a small bribe.

Diego walked beneath the catwalk above, past the guards, and through archway into the small city where Father Thaddeus awaited him. "I am in your debt, father", stated Diego.

"Not at all my son, but if you regale me with news from the outside world it would be I who would be in your debt." The two men walked down the narrow street towards the square, and Diego could not help but to repeatedly look towards the heavens in marvel of the many towers which existed here. A couple of beggars, just a few of those pilgrims who came to the find work as well as safety behind these walls, start to approach the priest to seek a hand out, but suddenly stop and withdraw fearing what they think might be a sword carefully concealed under the stranger's cloak. Neither the priest nor the stranger seems to notice the beggars and continue their trek.

"I see that you have noticed the towers, my son."

"Yes father, there are so many," Diego replied.

"I count at least sixty, but there may be more, Diego. I have been told that before the walls were put in place, many of the more noble families within the city had them built for their own personal safety. These endeavors were at great expense to these families, yet it did provide work to those who needed it the most. When the wars came from time to time the owners of these towers withdrew into them with their families and simply waited war out, yet the ones who actually labored to build the towers had no such tower of their own and many were often left to the mercy of their enemies, Diego."

"Surely the city walls now provide protection for all now, father?"

"They have so far, my son, but only time will tell."

As the two men enter the main square of San Gimignano, the priest points toward a church back off to the left and then shares, this is my post, Diego, St. Mary of the Assumption. The father then carefully and deliberately makes the sign of the cross on his chest and watches carefully to see if Diego does the same, which he does not. Moreover, just outside the church is where Abbott Beauvais resides, a wise and godly man.

"I have to admit that the towers are very grand, and I think they are the most beautiful that I have seen in my travels, father, perhaps almost as grand as perhaps the great towers, Cordoba itself?"

"The towers of Cordoba, my son, what are talking about? Cordoba is a grand city in the south of Spain, and it is said that there were once several towers built there by the Moor's and that one the city was liberated, a few of the Mosques were rededicated as churches by the local priests and the towers made into bell towers. Have you seen these towers, Diego?"

"No, father, I have not, but my uncle Ricardo, a very wealthy man often visits such places and he has seen them and shared with me the greatness of the city and its towers."

"Well, seeing how neither of us have actually seen those towers, and with all due respect your uncle, Ricardo, I find I must insist that these towers here in San Gimingnano are the grandest that either of us have seen, do you not agree, my son?"

"Yes, of course, father," replies Diego in a less than enthusiastic fashion.

"Shall we?" asks Thaddeus, as he motions towards the church nearby. And the two continue their walk.

"So, my son, did you travel all this distance on foot?"

"No, father, I booked passage upon a great ship. We sailed out of Barcelona, out beyond the coast of France, into the Ligurian Sea, to Genoa, and it is from there I have made my journey upon land, father."

"I see", replies Thaddeus.

The two men proceed along the street, past the church, and downward slightly to an inn which has a few patrons present, some who are eating bread and others just drinking red wine. Thaddeus opens the door to the inn and then declares to Diego with a smile, "This inn has some of the finest food in all of Tuscany."

To which Diego replies, "The food smells enticing from out here, but how is the wine?"

"Excellent as well, yet I am biased, Diego, for the wine served here is made from the grapes grown nearby on land owned by a church parishioner and is made locally."

"Then how can it be anything but heavenly, father?" comments Musit as she greets them inside the tavern.

"Greetings to you, Musit" Thaddeus hails. "Allow me to introduce you to my guest; this is Diego," replies Thaddeus.

Musit, a dark skinned woman of African heritage who is in her middle twenties and is wearing a dark dress of modest means while carrying wine and bread to the other patrons, gives Diego a cautious and almost angry look and then asks the question, "Portuguese?"

"No, I am Catalonian."

Musit appears to almost ignore Diego and then asks,"Your regular table, father? Hugo, bring the father and his guest some bread and wine," announces Musit, and then asks the father if he will be having his usual meal.

Thaddeus looks at Diego who says nothing, and then replies, "For two please."

"And they will both be having some poultry, Hugo," Musit again blurts out as she walks to attend her other customers.

After a short delay, Hugo comes out carrying wine and bread to the father's table and smiles intensely as he looks at the father and says," I am ready to start my priestly training father."

Thaddeus looks as if he is caught a little off guard and slowly replies, "That is wonderful my son, and perhaps one day you may become a priest, Hugo. I will revisit the issue with the Abbot as soon as I think the time is right," Thaddeus continues.

"I have been studying the holy statues in the church very hard, father and always say my prayers," replies Hugo.

Musit, who was eavesdropping in on the conversation laughs out loud from across the room but says nothing. Hugo looks down at Diego sitting at the table and then comments, "Nice boots", and then he back looks at Thaddeus and says, "I must go now, father, so that your chicken does not burn," while he heads back to the kitchen area.

Hugo is a tall, muscular man in his early thirties. His hair is cut to wear he almost looks bald. His hair and eyes are dark and he speaks as if he is slow of wit and a thick accent. Hugo's clothes are of very modest means and he had no shoes. Diego ignores Hugo, looks away from him and says nothing in response to Hugo's observation and all the while thinking, "Peasant."

A fire burning in a large hearth at the far end of the east wall of the inn felt wonderful to Diego as the daylight was coming to an end on this rainy, late November day. A little bit of cedar had found its way into the fire and the room smelled better for it. Diego waits for the father to first take a piece of the bread before taking some himself. His hunger was great but he prided himself on his upbringing by an educated and wise minded ethnic Jewish family and of course his excellent manners which are a sign of his being most importantly a gentleman. As Diego ate his bread he soon tuned out the rest of the conversations going on about the room, and a room for night with a comfortable bed was what he hoped awaited him after a full stomach and a little of the wine. The bread was good, even if a little stale and the chicken was acceptable he thought to himself. One the other hand, his glass of wine was now empty and needed to be filled.

"This is excellent wine, father Thaddeus!" exclaimed Diego. Thaddeus smiles and nods in agreement. "So, father, let me tell you of Catalonia, begins Diego." But almost as soon as Diego begins his tail, he pauses as an older man in what looked like little more than a monk's robe enters through the front door.

All eyes move toward the door and one by one the people present begin to greet Father Beauvais. One by one, Beauvais goes around the room and greets individual in kind with a warm smile and a hand shake. Upon reaching Thaddeus and Diego, the abbot asks, "May I join you, gentlemen?"

"Certainly father," replies Thaddeus as he pulls out a chair for his mentor to in.

Diego immediately stands as if to offer his own chair and waits for Beauvais to sit down before returning to his chair all the while smiling a bit nervously. Musit comes to their table again and brings wine and bread for the abbot.

"Your poultry will be ready soon, father," Musit tells Beauvais with a warm smile and an almost fawning manner. Beauvais smiles kindly at her and then looks towards Diego and then at Thaddeus and says," I do not believe you have introduced me to your guest, father Thaddeus."

"Forgive me father, this is Diego who I only met today," quickly replies Thaddeus, "and he comes to us from the land of Catalonia."

"And what of the Moors? queries Beauvais.

"The Moors no longer occupy Catalonia, father," replies Diego. "A few months ago I left my island home and moved near the Pyrenees Mountains where and having lost my father I am now in the service of my uncle, the honorable Don Flugencio."

"I am told that it is only a matter of time until the Moors are pushed out of Andalusia and I have heard that Catalonia is a very beautiful country indeed," remarks Beauvais. "May I ask the name of the island you originally hail from?

"Yes, of course father, I come from the Baleric Island of Minorca, near the city of Majorca."

Beauvais stops briefly and looks towards the sky and smiles largely at what could only be God work, then looks at Diego and asks, "What brings you to San Gimignano, my son?"

Diego replies, "I am on my way to Rome to meet my uncle and assist him with bringing goods back to his estate which he acquired in his many business dealings."

"Rome?" questions Beauvais, and then looks momentarily at Thaddeus and then back at Diego and continues in a low tone. "My son, this will never do, you going to Rome now."

"Why father?" Diego asks Beauvais puzzlingly.

"Some are killing Jews along the road to Rome these days, Diego."

"I did not tell you that I am a Jew, father, nor do I dress as a Jew," Diego states while almost appearing shocked.

"You are a Jew my son, are you not, Diego? Beauvais questions softly.

"By birth I am a Jew, father, but have known of Jesus and his stories of miracles form as far back as I can remember," states Diego.

"Baptized, my son?"

"Yes, of course father, when I was but a youth in a cold river on an October morning."

Beauvais smiles as to show his approval. "You must consider staying here in San Gimignano under my protection and of course as of the monastery," replied Beauvais. "And hopefully you will tell me more of your faith in our Lord and savior Jesus Christ." (Beauvais then makes the sign of the cross and then continues.) "Do you not agree Father Thaddeus?"

"Most certainly, your Excellency," replies Thaddeus.

"But father, what of my uncle, Don Flugencio?"

"If it is allowable to you, please allow me to send someone to inquire about him and to then see to his safety as they accompany him here from Rome," Beauvais continues.

"As you see fit, father; I am a stranger in a strange land," Diego replies.

"Then it is settled, Diego, you will be a guest of the abbey and I will send inquiries in the morning," said Beauvais.

"Father Thaddeus, would you please see to our guest's comfort?"

"Yes, your eminence," replies Thaddeus. "Shall I prepare for to travel to Rome as well, eminence?" asks Thaddeus.

"No, shall send another.   I have other more pressing matters for you, father," states Beauvais. "Then please, finish your meal and allow me to make all the arrangements for tomorrow's journal," says Beauvais as he gets up from the table. Both men start to rise as Beauvais gets up but he motions for them to remain sitting.

Beauvais looks at Thaddeus and says with a smile, "I must to talk to Hugo about doing a puppet show for the children, so if you will please excuse men, gentlemen." Beauvais then goes around the room greeting parishioners, shaking hands, and then into the kitchen where he speaks briefly to Hugo. Hugo nods very intently and then returns to his cooking once the abbot leaves through the rear entrance.

Chapter Five

"Would you like some more wine, my lady?" asks the servant as he walked about the table where the two women sat in deep conversation.

"Yes," she replied, without so much of a look of acknowledgement towards her slave.

"My lady?" he asks as he tips the wine flask towards the second lady's glass, and then he heads back away from the table as to appear not to be eves dropping but not so far that he would be out of sight of his mistress.

"So, anything exciting going on with you, Apphia?" asks Antonia.

"Well, seeing how you have asked, I can tell you that there is this odd sort of man, something like a spiritualist, who is from somewhere near Tarsus. He has been raising a lot of eyebrows in Rome by some in the senate according to my husband," replies Apphia.

"Philemon said that? Tell me more", inquires Antonia with a look of interest.

"Apparently he has even the emperor bewitched with his mystical powers," continued Apphia, "or so I hear."

"The emperor?" questions Antonia?

"Yes, it appears that Claudius had nightmares concerning this man, Saul or Paul as he prefers to be called, before he even knew of his existence," Apphia said.

"What kind of dreams? About what, Apphia?"

"I do not know for certain, but a reoccurring dream where some unknown God warned Claudius not to harm this man or else," states Apphia.

"As in..." (Antonia takes her right thumbs and runs it across her throat and makes a cutting action as she makes a gurgling sound and then drops her head to one side and closes her eyes feigning death only to soon afterward break into laughter) questions Antonia.

"Careful, Antonia, the walls might have ears," cautions Apphia. "Anyway, this man has been under a type house arrest in the middle of Rome and his appearance before the emperor keeps being delayed without reason, Antonia."

"Certainly they are not afraid of this, this charlatan," snipes Antonia. "Perhaps they are, or more rightly put they are afraid of offending this unknown God and what he or she might do to Rome," pondered Apphia.

"I see," continued Antonia. "There could be crop failures, famine, pestilence, or even battles lost."

"I thought the emperor had proclaimed himself a God as well, Apphia?"

She then replies, "Perhaps it is professional courtesy that the emperors are extending by not rendering judgment," as both of the ladies quickly break into muffled laughter.

"It is also said that this Paul fellow not only has the Praetorian Guard waiting on him hand and foot, but also has them running errands for him as well delivering letters and such," comments Apphia.

"Very impressive," Apphia, says Antonia. "Oh, that is only the half of it, Antonia; they say he has even done miracles, or such, supposedly telling one of guards that his daughter who was at death's door that she would not die, but rather that she would live."

"Did she, Apphia?"

"Did she what, Antonia?"

"Did she live, asks Antonia?"

"Yes, she did, but who knows if it was a coincidence or not, but he was certainly taking the chance of being disemboweled right then and there had his words been unfulfilled."

"Quite a risk to take just to curry favor with the guards," comments Antonia.

"Or he is awfully damned sure of himself," retorts Apphia.

"Perhaps it is his God that he sure of, Apphia?"

Neither woman says anything for a few moments and then they begin to take some of the bread from the center of the table and both begin to eat lightly.

"One of the senators is concerned about the power this man and his God might over the emperor and what could all lead to, so he has also been taking note of the things this Paul is saying and seeing if any of it might lead to treason on his part," whispers Apphia.

Antonia says nothing but leans forward to listen.

"This senator has a man in the detail guarding this mystic and he periodically reports back as to the details of who comes and goes as well as what has been discussed in that state room Paul has set up in his tent," shares Apphia.

"How did this man end up in Rome in the first place, asks Apphia?"

"It is said that he is a Jew and some sort of religious teacher," replies Apphia, "and that he was traveling around the seaside speaking of this God and stirring up trouble wherever he went, so his own people wanted to kill him."

"Might have saved us all a lot of trouble," states Antonia.

"True enough, Antonia, but when he was arrested he proclaimed that he refused to be flogged proclaiming to be a citizen of Rome and then went so far as to appeal to the emperor."

"Over a lashing?" questions Antonia.

"I know, Antonia, he is now more apt to lose his head than a bit of skin from his backside."

Get over here now, you idiot and fill my glass at once!" snaps Apphia, as her servant moves with all haste to comply with his mistresses command being ever so careful not spill even a drop of the red wine.

"Shall I fill your glass as well, my lady?" the servant asks Antonia being careful not to make the least bit of eye contact with either woman.

"Oh very well," grumbles Antonia as she holds out her glass and then pulls it back towards her mouth to drink the remaining wine in her goblet only to thrust it back again at the servant. Once his duties are complete, the slave quickly steps back to his place in the corner of the room awaiting any further orders.

His name is Onesimus and is of African origin and does not speak any language well other than his own, yet knows enough of her utterances to meet his mistress' needs. Onesimus comes from a once noble warrior linage and has on more than one occasion considered choking the very life out of his mistress with his bare hands, and now waits for the perfect time to carry out his rebellion against her. Onesimus wonders if he went to this holy man, Paul, and told him of his suffering, that magic might be given to him to rid himself of this dreadful woman.

"So, where were we, Antonia...? Oh yes, the mystic of Rome," she says with a laugh. "It has even been told that the way in which he performed this miracle healing is that he took a bit of cloth from the hem of his winter cloak and said some kind of chant or something over it," continued Apphia. "And upon giving it to the solider with the daughter who was infirmed, the soldier out of desperation followed Paul's instructions. Once the cloth touched her body, the little girl was made well and woke up asking for something to eat. Fearing that the wrong people might hear of this miracle and that some in authority might not believe what happened, the guard told no one except the senator which has had been reporting too," whispers Apphia.

"So then, how did you hear about it, Apphia?"

"I am friends with this senator's wife and she told me on the promise not to reveal it to anyone, so you cannot speak a word of this to anyone," stresses Apphia. Antonia nods her head in agreement. "The senator confiscated this, this magical cloth, or whatever it is and apparently has not revealed to anyone just exactly where he has hidden it," Apphia said.

"Not even to his wife?"

"So she says. What is even worse is that Philemon seems quite taken with this mad man and has even begun going to see him," complains Apphia.

"Perhaps simply out of morbid curiosity, Apphia, and I'm sure that there is nothing more to it."

"If he comes home and decides to take up meditation or some damned strange thing, I will leave him for good this time, Antonia. I have had enough of his insane soul searching," continues Apphia. "My father helped him get his position with the senate and this could be enough to cost him that position we have worked so tirelessly to keep," says Apphia.

"I know I would not do well as the wife of a senator who had fallen out of favor with Rome, and I do not think you would fare much better, Apphia."

"Oh, I beg of you, Antonia, please stop. The mere thought of being destitute makes me shiver with fear, my sister."

Apphia quietly reflects upon her life and cannot imagine life with any fewer comforts than she has at present. She knows that her once stellar features and petite figure were on their way out as she approached middle age. Was there still enough left in her bag of tricks to attract another, influential man who would care for her? Could she still keep Philemon in line and help him not lose all by following this mystic from the east? Then she wonders if perhaps she is making too much of this in the first place.

Antonia during this time considers her chances of catching a rebounding Philemon once he had escaped the grip of this horrible excuse of a woman who sat across from her. Oh, what he could not do with her (Antonia) care and guidance, perhaps they might even aspire to the office of emperor itself? Only time could tell. Suddenly, Apphia cries out, "More wine, Onemisus!"

In a Roman Senate Council chamber sits a Praetorian Guard named Titus, when a Roman senator enters the room and motions for his assistants to depart the room. Pouring himself some wine, the senator offers some to Titus, which he declines. "So, Titus, is it, what can you tell me of this mystic from the Orient?"

"Very little, senator, as I do not supervise him that often, that is if you are referring to Saul of Tarsus?"

"Well, that is the first thing we will have to correct. Sir," asks Titus? "From now on you will personally be in charge of watching this Saul at all times, Captain."

"Forgive me, senator, but I answer on the Caesar himself."

"And I speak for Caesar in this matter, have I made myself clear?"

"I understand perfectly, senator."

"Now it is my understanding that this mystic has healed someone's daughter who was near death, here in the city?"

"Yes, it was my daughter who was healed, senator."

"Excellent, tell me how he did it and leave no detail out."

"I had prayed to Mars repeatedly to spare my daughter's life, but her health only worsened. I was in a conversation with another soldier about her condition when Paul offered to help. He tore a piece from the fringe on the hem of his cloak, prayed to his God and told me to take the cloth and lay it upon her and that she would recover. I did not take him seriously at first and had dismissed it outright, but as my daughter began to suffer more and more, I took a chance and did as Paul had instructed me and to my great joy, she sat up and asked for something to eat."

"And you are sure that the cloth healed her, Titus?"

"I am not sure of anything at this point, senator, but all I know is that my daughter is alive and well and I thank Paul's God for this miracle."

"Miracle, Titus?"

"Yes, the miracle of my daughter's life."

"So do you feel so indebted to this Paul, as you call him, that you could not spy upon him if required?"

"I am a soldier of Rome and will perform my duties as required; you can assure the Caesar of that, senator."

"I think I will meet this mystic, Paul, for myself. Bring him to me at once, Praetorian." Titus gets up from his chair immediately, salutes the senator and departs for Paul's prison tent.

Chapter Six

"You there, come here!" the men shout. An older man of small stature, wearing fine clothing and displaying a small amount of jewelry looks back at the approaching group of men and realizes that they resemble a mob more than anything else, begins to run. After him, the men now shout and pursue him with all haste. His heart pounds in his chest like a hammer which echoes deep within his ears as the men pursue him. His lungs burn and his legs ache, but he knows that if he stops, it will be certain doom for him.

As he hears the mob getting closer, he looks back to see just how close they are and to his detriment, falls down. Unshod feet, too many to count, kick him repeatedly as the angry men shout, "Jew, Christ killer, you did this to us!" Then someone kicks him in the head and it all goes black for the man of small stature.

"You two, come here," says one of the men now standing over the unconscious body. Gennero and Hugo look around to see if they could be talking to anyone else, but realize that they had not.

"How may we be of service, gentlemen?" ask Gennero?

"Helps us drag this worthless excuse for a human being over to the church so the father can interrogate him further."

"But our Abbot told us to come straight back to San Gimignano, sir," says Hugo definitely.

"I am sure that the Abbot would not mind our aiding our brothers in Christ," replies the friar quickly fearing that he too might meet a similar fate.

Upon reaching the church, Gennero turns towards the now present priest and says, respectfully, "Eminence, we will take our leave of you now."

"Who are you? I do not recognize either of you," asks the priest.

"I am Gennero, a friar and lowly monk on a personal errand for Bishop Beauvais of San Gimignano, and this is my helper, Hugo."

"Personal errand, and what personal errand are you referring to, my good man?"

"I can only discuss this with the bishop as instructed by him, Eminence."

"Yes, I suppose that is true," replies the priest with a sour loom about him. "You will though however want to stay and help me extract the truth of his crimes against the people of the great city of Sienna?"

"I humbly beg your indulgence, Eminence, but as much as I would like to see this sinner meet his fate, I must do as instructed by the bishop and depart for home at the earliest convenience," says Gennero humbly.

"Oh very well, you may go," mutters the priest. "And you'll give my regards to the bishop of course?"

"Yes, father and thank you," replies Gennero nervously as both men slowly back away from the crowd.

"Peace be with you," states the priest as the two men walk away.

"And also with you, father," says Gennero as he turns now and hurries down the lane towards the city gate.

As when they came in, the street is lined with dozens of dead, or the near dead, and most are now unable to even groan in agony. Their unwashed bodies, covered with sores and boils, some still coughing and spitting up blood, lay mostly unattended except for a couple of vagrants who pulling the shoes from one man's feet, a man too weak to resist their thievery. Hugo starts to intercede, but Gennero stops him just in time. "I suggest we leave with all haste my friend," says Gennero. Hugo cannot help but look upon the bodies and noticing an infant among them whose body looks a ghastly white and covered with sores and feel grief. Near the city gate, two men pulling an empty cart stop and begin to toss a dead body into the cart. Even with the faces mostly covered as to possibly protect them from this plague, the men look fearful of their task.

"I wanted to wait until we were out of ear shot, Hugo, but I wanted you to know that you have to be careful around mobs like that back there."

"Careful, asks Hugo?"

"Damn right, they would just as sooner beaten us to a pulp and burned us at the stake as that poor bastard back there."

"What had he done to deserve that, Gennero?"

"Probably not a thing in the world, but the priest back there most likely needed a scapegoat to cover his own ass and them finding a Jew made it all too easy for them."

"We should go back and help him then," blurts out Hugo as he starts to turn back towards the city.

"Are you crazy, Hugo?"

"We cannot let an innocent man die, Gennero!"

"He is dead already, Hugo, the moment that bunch got a hold of him; his fate was sealed." Hugo drops his head in despair. "Come on, we should get back to the monastery before they change their minds and come after us."

"What; why would they do that, Gennero?"

"Because if one scapegoat is good, they might figure that three would be even better."

"I see what you mean," says Hugo as they quicken their pace towards San Gimignano.

"Now stick with me because I am in with the bishop and I can put a good word in for you when we get back, Hugo." Hugo just smiles in reply as he has heard braggarts before. "You will be a monk before you know it, young man," says Gennero confidently.

Inside the church known as Collegiata, the Catalonian, Diego, is in the confessional and as he prepares to bare his soul with the priest he appears somewhat disheveled. The church is very ornate with frescos on the ceiling, candles burning in grand holders, and a large cross standing behind the altar. There is the smell of incense burning and the room seems to be a little on the darker side with some light coming through various points high within the sanctuary.

"I believe that I am supposed to say, bless me, father, for I have sinned," Diego utters nervously.

"As a good Catholic you should know what to say, my son," Beauvais responds calmly.

"I am not a Catholic and have never been to confession but one other time but I very much need to purge my soul before God," Diego continues. "I have been very angry with God and have not wanted to pray for a very, very long time, father." Diego begins to shake from his inner most being as his anger, rage, and hurt begin to well up within him.

Beauvais listens intensely and resists the urge to give advice and then asks, "Though not a Catholic, you do believe in our Lord and Savior, Jesus Christ?"

"I do father and have heard of him since I was a child even though I have been born and raised a Jew."

"Then you are a Messianic Jew?"

"Yes, I guess I am, father. It has been said in my village that we are descendants of some of the flowers of Jesus that accompanied our Savior to my island many, many years ago," uttered Diego.

"I have heard of such stories my son." Beauvais is barely able to resist the urge to continue down this path of theology and then remembers that he is foremost a shepherd and that this man had come to him seeking assistance.

"Now please, tell me of the pain that you carry within you and the burden it has caused you in life," the abbot requests compassionately.

Diego begins to weep softly and continues," I was to be married to a woman of a neighboring village, yet I found her to be unfaithful and I had no other choice but to end the betrothal. Her family knew of this betrayal on her part and yet chose to help her conceal it from me," Diego further complained.

"Such humiliation; please, my son, continue," says Beauvais with a sigh.

"Moreover, many of my friends and family unexpectedly died in a very short period of time from a sickness that came out of nowhere. I eventually went to a priest in the next village to seek advice, not wanting to bringing shame to my former wife to be by asking an elder in my own village about these tragedies. The priest instructed me that I should consider it all joy when the Lord disciplines us, that it would one day create character within me. The thought of God taking my friends and family in order to teach me a lesson was almost more than I could bear and for a time lost my mind, father. I was overcome with grief after the loss of family and friends and that was further compounded by people in my own village who turned their back on me," states Diego.

The abbot listens quietly.

"Men who were supposed to be Godly wanted little or nothing to do with me as if it was I was perhaps taking too long to grieve, so I ask you father, why has God forsaken me?"

Beauvais almost began to weep himself, but did not because of his office and the duties he needed to perform. "No, no, my son, God did not do these terrible things and the priest who told you that he had was terribly mistaken," Beauvais uttered with a quiver in his lip. "I have heard it said that time heals all, and I will most certainly pray that God makes it a speedy recovery," shares Beauvais. "And I will ask to penance be made by you, Diego, your step of faith which brought you here today to this sacrament of the church and confessions have restored you to the Lord presence. I strongly urge you to return to attending mass regularly and furthermore, that you spend as much time with me or Father Thaddeus while you await word of your uncle."

"If some terrible fate has befallen my uncle, Father, then..."

"Then we will face it together, my son, now go in peace. May the Lord bless you, may he make his face shine upon you," states Beauvais. "Now, in the name of the father, of the Son, and of the Holy Ghost," Beauvais prays. "Amen," both men say in unison as they make the sign of the cross across their chests.

As they depart the confessional, Beauvais hands a rosary to Diego and says with a large grin (mindful to conceal his bad teeth). "Please take this my son, and perhaps this will help you find peace."

Diego takes the rosary and puts it into his pocket and then thanks Beauvais for his kindness while departing the church. Once Diego exists the building, Beauvais almost collapses in pain but after staggering momentarily he straightens himself and soon returns to his quarters.

After resting a few hours, a more refreshed Beauvais departs his room and heads towards the piazza where he notices Thaddeus.

"Greetings father," said Thaddeus.

"Greetings to you as well, Father Thaddeus," responds Beauvais.

"Please walk with me, my son," Beauvais says softly," I wish to discuss with you the reason I detained you here. Perhaps we can talk away from prying ears," continues Beauvais?

Thaddeus nods in agreement. Both men walk together around a corner and up a deserted stair way which has a small landing which over looked a small, private vineyard, a pair of older olive trees, as well as a large persimmon tree which still bore its previous summers bounty. Looking around first to see that no one was within ear shot, Beauvais quietly tells Thaddeus that an amazing discovery has come into his possession and that he would like for Thaddeus to transcribe some of the early Roman writings that are now being kept in the abbots own private study under lock and key.

"Roman writings?" quires Thaddeus, but Beauvais only tells him that he will understand everything in time. He also reminds Thaddeus to tell no one of this conversation.

"Meet me outside of my study, Father Thaddeus, right after morning prayers. I will unlock the door for you and get you started on the work. All of the materials that you will need I already have and are at your disposal, my son."

"It shall be done father," Thaddeus says with look of bewilderment. "Father Beauvais, may I ask a question of you?" Beauvais nods in the affirmative." Why me, father, ask Thaddeus?"

"And why not you, my son?"

"I have not been out of seminary all that long and I have only been in San Gimignano a few short months, surely there are more qualified people for this task," states Thaddeus.

"I must confess that I had my reservations at first for the reasons you stated, but I have observed you and see that you love the Lord with your whole heart. You are also one who demonstrates great patience, compassion, and integrity my son. Moreover, as you know there are a great many people who have died from the great sickness that fortunately has not yet made its evil way to this city. So many priests have gone to work with the sick and to bury those who have died, and some priests have fallen victim as well to this awful plague, Thaddeus. None of the monks present can be trusted with this task. The monks are not priests and the majority of them can neither read nor write, other than perhaps their own name," complains Beauvais. "Who should I give this job to, perhaps Gennero, the abbot asks cynically? Trust him least of all, Father Thaddeus. He would be more apt to take it and sell it to the highest bidder rather than use it for the betterment of those who suffer."

Thaddeus drops his head almost in frustration and replies, "No, of course not, father. This must never fall upon the wrong ears let alone into the wrong hands, Thaddeus, and we must be willing to protect it even with our own lives should it become necessary. It will not be an easy task for you my son, but with God's help you will persevere and more awaits you here," confirms Beauvais. "But first, my son, we must take our evening meal," Beauvais utters as his once serious face turns to a nervous laughter.

"Agreed, father, and I will buy the wine," Thaddeus says with a now eager look about his face, as if needing a small bit of wine to calm his nerves.

"I must ask you about another matter, father, I am uncertain as to what to say in response to Hugo's desires of becoming a priest." The Abbot sighs but remains silent for a few moments.

"His name is not Hugo, but few people here can pronounce his name properly, father Thaddeus. His name from what I can gather is Hohlay, a refugee originally from Crimea. Apparently, Hohlay, or Hugo as Musit has named him, was taken captive by the Venetians to be more or less a slave. Upon arriving to Venice, he apparently broke free of his bonds and fled."

"I see, father."

"I have quietly given him sanctuary here in San Gimignano. He has never been any real problem since his arrival almost two years ago and do not see him being a problem in the future. I am allowing him to help around the monastery doing more laborious jobs, but I believe him too dim witted to ever be able to get through seminary successfully."

"So, then for the time being I will encourage him to help around here for now," says Thaddeus.

"A wise decision, father Thaddeus. Now may I ask of Musit, father?"

"Yes, indeed, Father Thaddeus. Musit arrived here shortly after Gennero arrived and told me that she had escaped Portuguese traders who had taken her from her home and sold her into bondage in Genoa. I do not want the town to become a haven for all runaway slaves, but God brings those people into our lives that he wants us to learn from and also watches our response to their pleas very carefully. Musit is full of spit and fire, but I believe her to be of good, moral character, Father Thaddeus. I would however like to caution you as to your being a young priest and Musit's being a vibrant young woman. Beware of temptation and flee it if you need to. Once you have gone down that path, Thaddeus, there may be no return for you short of a miracle."

Thaddeus drops his head and continues to listen.

"Remember your vow of celibacy, father, remember your vow. Let us speak no more of it, Thaddeus," says Beauvais with a reassuring smile. The two depart back down the stairs making sure that they do not slip on them as the light mist makes the steps slightly wet and appearing almost as glass.

Chapter Seven

"I present to you, gentlemen of the Sanhedrin, the facts of this case and will prove beyond a shadow of doubt that these Jews here before you are guilty of blasphemy and are deserving of death", rehearses Saul. "Deserving of death, deserving death; I wonder if that sounds bit too harsh?" he ponders briefly. "Deserving of the punishment as prescribed by our great laws, handed down by Moses and the profits, and adhered too throughout the years," Saul continues. "Yes, this is the approach I shall take once I have these rascals in chains and back in Jerusalem, the rider declares to himself in the most confident of manner. Come on, you stupid horse; get a move on!" Saul demands aloud. The horse begins to struggle against its owner's attempts to get him to move on down the road. "Confounded beast - why have you stopped?!"

The rider suddenly puts his hands over his eyes as he is now blinded by a great light, a shriek can be heard as the pain pierces his eyes as he finds himself falling to the hard ground below.

"Saul, Saul, why are you persecuting me?"

"Who are you Lord," asks Saul as he tried to find his footing?

"I am Jesus of Nazareth that you are persecuting."

As he struggles more and more to get his footing, he finally sits upright and opens his eyes to find himself in his prison tent and realizes that he has once again been dreaming. His neck is stiff and his body aches from the hardness of the pallet on which he sleeps, but Paul rises to his feet after a few seconds and wipes the sleep from his eyes and proceeds to wash his face and begins his morning prayers.

That same morning the great Senator Philemon, after departing the ship which carried him on his long journey from Colossae to Rome instructs his servant, Onesimus, that they will be making a short stop at the tent of a friend. Upon arriving there, the guard recognizes Philemon and steps aside as well as to attention and allows both the senator and his servant to approach the door of the tent.

"Is there anyone at home?" cries Philemon.

"I would recognize that voice anywhere. Please come in my brother," responds a voice from within. Philemon enters the tent and approaches the man inside and gives him a brief embrace. Onesimus follows Philemon but does not approach the other man.

"Thank the Lord you have arrived safely and just in time I might add to assist me in the doing the Lord's work," the man says with delight". And I see that you have brought a friend."

"This is my servant, Onesimus," Philemon proclaims, and then looks at Onesimus and states, "This is the Lord's own servant," Paul of Tarsus.

Paul is dressed in only a loin cloth and has another piece of cloth draped over his left shoulder. Onesimus's eyes begin to light up when he hears Paul's name and begins to bow before him, but Paul asks him not to bow and says, "I am unworthy of such high praise and am most certainly not worthy to be bowed before." Paul then asks both men to sit in comfort in one of the two Spartan-like chairs present in the tent. Philemon hands Paul a package and then sits and then motions for Onesimus to sit down as well.

"More food, Philemon", asks Paul with a smile? The senator nods in the affirmative.

"Bless you for your kindness, Philemon, and had it not been for you, as well as Titus, I might have starved to death."

"Titus?" questions Philemon.

"Yes, he has become a believer as well", Paul whispers in reply.

"Then the reports of the healing of his daughter are true?" asks Philemon.

"Yes," Paul replies as he smiles. Immediately Onesimus looks about the room and sees the cloak with a missing hem from which Paul tore the cloth and blessed it. Onesimus then knows for certain in his heart that this is truly a man of great mystical power, a man to aid him in his quest for what he cherished most, his freedom.

Both men look a bit bewildered as Paul picks up a bowl and a pitcher of water and then proceeds towards them.

Suddenly Philemon stands up and asks Paul what he is intending to do. Paul then replies, "Please set back down my friend, for I would do the Lord's work. The Lord demonstrated the example of being a servant by washing his disciple's feet, so likewise I will wash your feet, Philemon," replies Paul.

"I understand, Paul, you may proceed as you see fit", states Philemon.

"I will send Onesimus outside to wait for me," says Philemon as he turns toward Onesimus to motion for him to leave, when Paul interrupts him.

"No, I will was his feet as well," Paul responds with a smile.

Neither men seem to completely understand what Paul is doing but cautiously allow him to wash their feet. Upon finishing his task, Paul rises and walks back to a large pitcher of water and washes his hands and carefully rinses out the cloth he had been using. He then puts his robe back on and then sets down as well in front of them.

"How was your journey?" asks Paul.

"It was long and tiresome," replies Philemon. "I have to leave soon to attend to important business," and then he rises from his seat, states Philemon.

Seeing this, Philemon stands up as well. "I would like to leave my servant, Onesimus in your stead to assist you as you see fit, my brother Paul."

"I have no need of a servant, but would greatly welcome a guest, kind sir. But is it allowed?" questions Paul.

"You forget who I am, Paul, so I will instruct Titus on my way out as to what I have done."

"Very well then, great senator," Paul says with a smile. Then Paul continues, "I have not forgotten who you are, Philemon; you are God's servant as well and are continuing to grow in the Lord. May God bless and keep you, my son," says Paul as both Philemon and Onesimus briefly bow in order to show him honor.

Senator Philemon then departs Paul's tent and stopping only long enough to leave instructions with the guards outside

Paul's tent. Titus walks quickly past Philemon without so much as a word and enters Paul's tent.

"Good morning, Titus, how are you this fine day?" asks Paul.

"You will come with me, Paul, for there are questions to be asked of you this day."

Paul grabs his cloak and says, yes, of course, Titus. Both men depart the tent as Titus motions for one of the other guards to accompany them. Upon reaching a large building, the men pass through several people in the building milling about doing

Chapter Eight

"Ashes to ashes, dust to dust, oh Lord, we committee the soul of our dear departed brother into your hands," proclaims Beauvais at the graveside accompanied by Father Thaddeus and several of the monks from their monastery. Two of the sisters from the St. Francis Convent are in attendance as well as all of the mourners slowly who then in procession walk past the grave and toss a small amount of dirt onto the departed's wooden casket while lie below. A light rain adds to the solemnest of the occasion. Hugo, who was standing well back from the funeral, along with one of the monks, walks up to the grave and begin the task of filling the grave in with the dirt which is piled nearby. All of those in attendance slowly walk away from the graveside with only the sound of shovels scooping dirt to break the morning's silence. Once inside the monastery, Beauvais quietly motions for Thaddeus to follow him into the abbot's study which both men enter with Beauvais closing and locking the door behind them. Thaddeus begins to speak and is quickly motioned not to while Beauvais walks back towards the door and listens intently to see if there is anyone outside who could be in ear shot of their conversation.

"Sad that Gennero died suddenly like that in the night, father," whispers Thaddeus.

Beauvais sits down in a large cushioned chair in the corner of the room, just outside the range of the lamp which flickers upon the desk, in almost complete darkness and remains silent. After a short pause Thaddeus continues, "What is even sadder is that none of us knew he was gravely ill."

"Nothing sad about an old monk going on to his reward alone," retorts Beauvais slowly, which was soon followed by a large sigh.

"Then it most certainly was not the black-death?" asks Thaddeus before picking up the decanter of liquor present and asking the abbot if he would like to join him?

Beauvais nods in the affirmative and Thaddeus pours them both a stiff drink. Both men sip slowly on their glasses of alcohol and say nothing, when finally Beauvais speaks up and says, "I do not believe that he had any family either, at least none living."

"At least it was a quick death and he did not suffer, or at least I hope it was," says Thaddeus.

"More than some will get around here, my boy," mumbles Beauvais as he finally coughs - unable to hold it back any longer. The grayness of Beauvais' pigment is noticeable to Thaddeus even in the room's darkness.

"Are you alright, father," queries Thaddeus?

Beauvais does not acknowledge the young priest's question at first and then leaning towards him asks Thaddeus how the work of translating the documents is coming?

"Slowly but surely father," replies Thaddeus.

"I hope that you avail yourself to completing that task as soon as possible, yet not so fast as to make mistakes, my son."

"I understand, father," Thaddeus replies.

"I was going to wait to talk to you about something, but I see that now might be the appropriate time, my son," says Beauvais with raspy voice.

Thaddeus scoots closer to the abbot and gives him his undivided attention. "I will longer be able to avoid the wishes of our Holy Father, as he has made himself quite clear that I will be moving soon to Avignon and once there installed as a Cardinal."

"That is wonderful news, your Excellency; most wonderful indeed," declares Thaddeus.

"Not as wonderful as you might think, my son, as I have tried to avoid this next step in my evolution of the ministry."

"But why, father," ask the young priest?

"That is not important now, Father Thaddeus, but what is important is that you finish the task at hand and be ready to perform your new duties as abbot of this monastery, which you will begin this day with the new title of Prior.

Thaddeus looks stunned and is even speechless at first, yet is finally able to squeeze the words out; " I am not sure what to say, Eminence." Beauvais extends his glass out towards

Thaddeus seeking to have his glass refilled and Thaddeus obliges him.

"Why not try saying you accept, my son?"

"Then it is official," asks Thaddeus?

"Yes, yes, official and already documented in Avignon and signed off on by the Holy Father himself. I am to stay on as your mentor for one month and then I am to depart for Avignon. I know that this is a lot to ask of you, but the church needs you, my; God needs you."

Both men pause for a few moments and then remain silent. Eventually Beauvais breaks the deathly silence which hung in the room almost like a fog. "You know, Thaddeus, we all end up like Gennero eventually, either one way or another."

Looking pensively Beauvais continues, "He was just laying there, dead as a mackerel, pale white and his eyes wide open when they found him." Thaddeus sets back in his chair and is mute while looking a little confused. He knew it is not his time, nor place, to comment on his mentor's reflections. "Death is the one enemy that we cannot avoid, Thaddeus. It all comes down to faith, my boy, faith. You either believe or you rot, and rot is precise word for it, Thaddeus."

"We all took on responsibilities when we put on our collars and as surely as I cannot shirk mine, I will be damned if I will allow you to shirk yours, my son," says Beauvais with a smile. "Now, back to work, and do not forget that you have confessional duty later today."

"Yes, Eminence." So, no foot dragging now. Beauvais rises from his chair and pats Thaddeus on the head as if he was a small child and begins to depart the room.

"I will make the announcement as to your new position in the Lord's service before our evening meal when all of the monks will be present, Thaddeus, so do dress appropriately," says Beauvais with a slight smile.

"I will do my best not to disappoint you, Eminence."

"You shall do fine, my son, absolutely fine, so give it no more thought today. Again, my son, I urge you to return to these documents and trust no one with them, no one," says Beauvais.

One other point, father, but have you heard any word on the whereabouts of Diego's uncle?" asks Thaddeus?

"Gennero returned from Rome and told me that no one knows of this man there, which is a bit odd with him being a rich Jew and all, Thaddeus. He should have most certainly stuck out like a sore thumb, and yet no one has heard of him," states Beauvais.

"It is a large city or perhaps he tried to disguise his appearance in some way?" Thaddeus speculates.

"Or perhaps he is already dead, my son, either from the sickness that is present there or from those along the road who blame the Jews for this plague which has fallen upon us," says Beauvais.

"God forbid," prays Thaddeus aloud.

"Either way, Thaddeus, until we know something for certain we should speak none of this to Diego."

"Agreed father," says Thaddeus. "It appears that we may have a plague on our hands, not since the plagues of Moses and the Pharaohs have we seen such desolation," claims Thaddeus.

"It has been a long time since we have seen a Pharaoh and here we are still talking about them, Thaddeus."

"It is written in the holy book that God brought the plagues upon man," says Thaddeus.

"There are public disasters and private disasters, all of which can bring change of one type or another to a man, my son."

"I do not understand your meaning, your Eminence."

Beauvais looks intently at Thaddeus and states, "We all weather storms and despair, Thaddeus, whether sickness, or poverty, women and temptation, or depression, and even loss of faith." Beauvais stops making eye contact and simply looks down at his drink. Thaddeus knows not to pursue the topic any further.

"Nevertheless, Diego is under our protection, in God's house, and shall remain so, is that understood," states Beauvais with a quick smile. Thaddeus nods in agreement. "Until I move leave next month I would like for you keep your sleeping quarters as they are, and this area will be yours soon," says Beauvais. "I will also assist you in your new duties, Thaddeus, but most of all whenever you have fear and self doubt, seek the Lord and his comfort, my son. It has always been a port in the storm for me, my son," says Beauvais with a smile, or at least that is true lately. "Now back to work, there is a lot to get done, Monsignor."

Now the young abbot notices that his work has caused him to almost forget that he is to be available this evening to hear confession and hurries to put his work away. He carefully locks the door behind him on his way out and makes his way to the church next door and enters the confessional. Thaddeus no more than gets seated and he hears someone on the other side of the wall that separates priest from sinner and he slides open the confessional window and prepares to listen to his first confession as abbot. A male voice, barely audible whispers, father bless me for I have sinned. Thaddeus leans closer and says his parishioner, "Please speak up."

After a brief pause the voice begins again. "Father, bless me for I have sinned." (By now Thaddeus recognizes the voice as that of Beauvais). "It has been too long since my last confession, and in that time period I have hated my brother four times, taken the Lord's name in vein two times, and..."

"And?" asks Thaddeus?

"And the rest will have to wait."

Chapter Nine

"Brother Paul," someone approaches, announces Onesimus.

Paul looks as if he is expecting someone and replies, "Perhaps it the scribe that Philemon so graciously promised me."

After a brief delay by the guard, a man enters the prison tent and notices that one of the two men inside looks familiar to him. "I see that prison life has taken too much of a toll on you, oh mystic of the desert," laughs the man.

Paul approaches him as to great him and then says, "Welcome Amicus, welcome."

Paul then turns towards Onesimus and introduces him to the scribe, Amicus. "Greetings in the name of the Lord, Amicus," states Onesimus with a smile on his face.

"Please Amicus, make yourself at home," says Paul as he points towards one end of the tent.

"I have prepared a spot for you to sleep, and it is a bit cramped, but it should suffice for you," says Onesimus.

"So, why am I here, Saul?"

"Please, call me Paul, and you are here to help me prepare a letter to some friends of mine who need encouragement, but for now just feel at home and please have something to eat. I did not eat well in the Circus Maximus, so I will take you up on that kind offer."

Amicus walks over to a table which held loaves bread, some olive oil mixed with rosemary, and some wine as well and begins to eat and drink his fill.

"This is fantastic wine, Paul, how ever did you acquire it," asks Amicus?

"A gift from a friend," replies Paul, "and now if you will excuse us I have to speak with Onesimus."

Amicus motions with his left hand for them to leave as he continues to eat. The tent is larger than most might receive as a prison, where most would only endure a dark dungeon. Paul and Onesimus walk towards the other end of the tent and sit down and begin a discussion. "Tell me, my friend, how may I be of service to you, asks Paul?"

"I have not been in the service of the Lord that long, but would like to do more, my brother Paul."

"Have you prayed and sought the Lord in this matter," asks Paul?

"I have but the answer is unclear, and then there is of course my curse, Onesimus says which his head lowered."

"Curse?" asks Paul.

"Yes, my curse, and it seems that those in Rome do not see Nubians and therefore would not take me seriously should I preach to good news to them!" exclaims Onesimus.

"Then it is truly their loss, my brother," says Paul. Moreover, Onesimus, the Lord made your color and who is man to disregard it in such a callous way? I say that the Lord cares little about color when he pours his anointing upon someone," states Paul.

"You have become a true man of God in the short time I have known you, and Philemon has expressed as much as well. You love God and will continue to grown in the Lord, I am most sure of it, brother Onesimus. I have watched as you proclaim the gospel to the guards just outside these very walls," says Paul," and I am sure that one day you may be called upon to carry the message to the land from which you come, and it will be with your earthly master's blessing."

"I do not like being a slave, Paul, other than to the Lord." Onesimus' face takes on a look of intense sadness.

"As you know, my brother, I have spent a lot of time in chains myself for the service that I do in the name of the Lord, but consider it my gain," says Paul.

After a short pause, Paul continues, "I wish I could give you more than just words to comfort you and if it were in my power, I would free you, but I cannot even free myself as you well know. All I have is here in this tent and it does not even belong to me, but the Lord," shares Paul. "I would like to give my cloak to you, brother Onesimus, as a token of my esteem for you and your service to me these past few weeks."

"I cannot take your cloak, Brother Paul... "

"Yes you can and I hope you will, Onesimus, and although it has a small tear in it (from a time I asked for healing of the Lord for the daughter of Titus), it has served me well all these years, through many travels and I pray that it would now service you, my friend. For as the scriptures teach us, we must remember that our Lord said that the first shall be last and last shall be first," declares Paul.

Onesimus stands to his feet and graciously accepts Paul's gift. A gift that Onesimus thought at one time might be magical in nature, but now it meant even more to him than any power could have empowered him within the past. And even though he was still in servitude, he was free in his heart, a gift that no man could ever take away from him. "Yet, let us pray, Onesimus, that the Lord soften Philemon's heart and that he releases you, yet if he does not you may want to remember that you are already free in Christ and will spend eternity with him in heaven," proclaims Paul. Both men then bow their heads.

"Amicus, please see to it that letter gets on its way to Senator Philemon as soon as possible," requests Paul nervously.

Amicus leaves immediately and proceeds through the doors of the tent and past the guards. Paul says nothing for a brief time and then looks at Onesimus, who is sitting by himself in the corner of the room and then asks the question, "Have you had anything to eat?"

Onesimus replies that he has not.

"Here, please help yourself", says Paul as he gestures towards the food on the main table.

"Thank you," says Onesimus quietly and then he begins to eat.

"I am not a very good Christian," Onesimus mumbles with his head down.

"Nonsense, my brother," says Paul, "for there is no condemnation for those who are in Christ."

Onesimus says nothing in reply and continues to eat small amounts of food. "The Lord has seen me through tougher times that these and he will see us through this, Onesimus," Paul says with a reassuring smile.

"I know I should not have abandoned the service of my master the way I did, but I could not bear the thought of going back to Colossus and being under that wretched woman's thumb again," complains Onesimus.

"I wrote a letter to brother Philemon when I heard that you had fled and might be on your way back here, so turn everything over to the Lord and most of all be patient," says Paul. "For now just eat and then rest, and I will petition the Lord on your behalf, my brother Onesimus."

Shortly later Titus makes his presence known and then slowly enters Paul's prison tent as he does most days. "Greetings in the name of the Lord, my brother Titus, and do enter," says Paul.

"I am glad to see that brother Onesimus is not here, otherwise I would be forced to arrest him," says Titus.

"Well, I assure you Titus, that wherever he might be, he is under Roman guard," says Paul.

Both men laugh as Onesimus just looks over at them saying nothing. "Please do sit down, Titus, tell me what you have on your mind today," says Paul.

Both men sit down and Titus thanks Paul for the healing of his daughter. "I am not the one to thank, Titus, but the one above who has not only the power to heal the body, but the soul as well, praise God. "

"Brother Titus, have you heard any further on my appeal to the emperor," asks Paul?

"I am sorry to say that I have not," replies Titus.

How long must I sit here and rot?" asks Paul as he looks about on the ground. Paul begins to pray silently and then says, "I have to carry the message to the far reaches of the earth. I am truly blessed to be able to have the opportunity to stand before Caesar and tell him of the good news that leads to salvation, and if God see fit, then add Caesar's name among the brethren. But, I must be about allowed to return to my travels and to the care of the saints as well. Yet, I am grateful that I am allowed the honor of being able to at least send letters to these churches which God has entrusted to me. I must also remember that his grace is sufficient for me." Paul then retires to his bed pallet and rests. It would be several weeks before Paul would receive a reply from his letter to Philemon.

"It is time to awake now, Saul, and take heart and remember that the Lord is our Shepherd." Paul is awoken from his sleep by the voice of Titus announcing himself at the door of the tent. Paul looks about briefly to see if his now departed wife might still be close by, only to realize that he had been once again been dreaming. Slightly confused and disoriented, Paul sits up on the edge of his bed pallet and says to Titus, "Please enter."

As Titus enters he carries what looks like a message and hands it to Paul. "Perhaps it is good news," says Titus.

Paul takes the scroll type paper and notices a seal on it which belonged to Philemon. "Ah, hopefully a reply to my most recent letter," cries Paul. Upon carefully open the letter Paul reads the contents to himself in what might be described as an almost quiet mumble. Paul then begins to laugh with excitement and says, "This is wonderful news, I tell you, wonderful!"

"What is it, Paul?" asks Titus.

"More than I could have dreamed for, Titus." Paul continues to laugh, hands the letter to Titus and then asks the question, "Where is Onesimus?"

"I think he has gone to get bread and olive oil, Paul." Titus reads the letter and with a large smile on his face says, "Praise almighty God."

"Praise almighty God, is right indeed, brother Titus."

Within a short time, Onesimus returns carrying goods and sees both Paul and Titus standing before him smiling. With a look of puzzlement, Onesimus sets the items he was carrying upon a table and then asks, "What are you two smiling about?"

"I have the most wonderful news, Onesimus," declares Paul. "I have received a message from Philemon and to put it directly, he has given you this letter of freedom and has no further claim on you, Onesimus," states Paul.

Onesimus stands there speechless, and soon Titus says, "It is true, my brother, you are a free man indeed."

Onesimus drops to his knees immediately and begins to cry tears of joy. "Praise God, for he is great in mercy as well in compassion," voices Onesimus. Pau land Titus follow suite and begin praising God was well for this miracle.

The following weeks, Onesimus begins to go about the city of Rome and preaches the gospel to any and all who would listen. Onesimus relishes his new found freedom, yet like Paul, sees himself as a slave in the service of the Lord. Many come to believe in the Lord from hearing the words of Paul and Onesimus. What can only be described as an "anointing" would descend on Onesimus and he would preach for hours on end out in the city square and many came to believe in Jesus Christ. After about three weeks into his ministry, it was recorded that Onesimus was arrested by the Praetorian Guard and presented to the Circus Maximus to await his fate. On the flowing morning, Titus went and told Paul of the Onesimus' arrest.

"Is there anything you can do, Titus?" asks Paul. "Nothing, I am afraid," replies Titus.

"I have made inquires and apparently Onesimus offended the nephew of the Emperor and an arrest was made. Now there will little if no trial and then surely death," Titus says in an uneasy voice.

"I will petition the Lord on his behalf and ask for the Lord to intercede upon our brother's behalf. Will you join me, Titus?" Titus agrees.

"You must go to see Onesimus and minister to him, Titus, and tell him not lose heart," cries Paul. "Let him know that we are praying for him, and he must now more than ever rely on God."

"I will, my friend, I will," asserts Titus.

"So, what did they arrest you for?" asked the prisoner.

"I was accused of being disruptive," replies Onesimus.

"Did you turn over the cart of a street vendor or something, my friend?"

"No, I spoke of how I was once a slave and am now free through the power of the Lord Jesus Christ."

The other man begins to laugh out loud.

"Why do you mock me?" asks Onesimus as they both lie on the prison floor in chains.

"I saw that you had a friend who visited you, a Praetorian, and he could not get you released?" the prisoner asks.

"No, and I did not ask him to," replies Onesimus.

"Are you insane, my friend, do you want to die at the hands of these barbarians or in the jaws of wild beasts?" he asks Onesimus.

" He would have had me released if he could have, and still being in chains I know that it must be the will of God and will live contented in that, my friend," says Onesimus quietly.

"I am Horus and I come from the land that rests along the Nile. Horus means "distant" but I am sure my parents had no idea that they were sealing my fate when they bestowed that name upon me."

"I am Onesimus and was once a proud warrior, but was taken prisoner after a long battle and ended up as a slave. I then heard the message of salvation and now consider myself a slave for Christ the Lord."

"Well at least I will die next to someone from near my own home," says Horus.

"If that be God's will," says Onesimus.

"You are strong my friend and have a warrior's skills, so perhaps you can fight back when the executioner comes, or even slay a lion with your bear hands," retorts Horus?

Onesimus only laughs to himself upon hearing these words.

In the middle of the night, Onesimus is awoken to the sound of the prison door opening. Could this be the executioner coming to prepare him for his death, Onesimus wondered to himself. His heart pounded in his chest and he mostly feared that he would show himself a coward and not die a death worthy of his Lord. He remembers once seeing a lion when he was young and how much he dreaded lions. His palms began to sweat and his mouth became exceedingly dry. But upon looking up across the room, Onesimus notices a figure standing in the open doorway of what appears to be a young boy.

Shining with the glory of the Lord, the boy announces, "Fear not, Onesimus, for this day you shall be set free. I tell you that the Lord has heard your prayers and he knows that you truly trust in him. You shall not fall by the sword, nor shall you fall prey to the wild beasts," declared the angel. "Rise up and let us leave this place." Onesimus looks down and to his amazement sees that he is no longer bond by chains. Still wearing the cloak that Paul had given him, he slowly rises to his feet and stands there with great fear and trembling. Onesimus notices that all of the other prisoners were still sleeping and do not seem to be aware of what is taking place. Onesimus wonders if he is dreaming and wipes his eyes, and yet the angel of the Lord remains.

"Great one, I know that surely the Lord has done a miracle this day, and for that I am exceedingly grateful." Suddenly Onesimus' heart is filled with great compassion for the other prisoners which numbered eleven. I must tell you that I cannot leave here unless these men are set free as well.

"I only know that I have been sent for you, Onesimus," replies the angel, as he turns to leave through the door. Once seeing the angel leave, Onesimus charged towards the angel (remembering that Jacob once wrestled with an angel) and took hold of him. The angel, even though appearing as a boy, had what seemed the strength of ten men. Onesimus held on with all of the strength within him and pled for these men's vary souls. Finally the angel says to Onesimus, "The Lord has seen your heart and your compassion. The Lord has relented and it shall be done as you have asked." With that Onesimus released his grip and then begins to weep openly. The other prisoners who were awaken by the battle that was going on in their cell all heard the last words of the angel in their own native tongue and were immediately released from their chains as well. One by one they found their way to their feet, even one who had not been able to walk prior to this and made their way out of the prison behind the angel and Onesimus.

The angel lead Onesimus past the guards who did not notice any of them and then down the street into the great city of Rome. As the angel and Onesimus walked out of the city and into the countryside, the angel then spoke again to Onesimus. "You are to go now into the land of your forefathers, Onesimus, and spread the word of the Lord to all who will as much receive it, for this is the will of God." With that the angel disappeared almost as quickly as he had appeared and to his great surprise, Onesimus found himself back on a hill top overlooking the village of his ancestors. Onesimus praised God and went on to share the word of the Lord and the miracles that took place that day and it is said that many were converted.

Upon hearing of the release of Onesimus from prison, Paul gave praise to God and then said, "As it is written that 'The Spirit of the Lord is on me, because he has anointed me to proclaim good news to the poor. He has sent me to proclaim freedom for the prisoners and recovery of sight for the blind, to set the oppressed free.'"

"Did the notes say anything else about this, Father Thaddeus?"

"No, Eminence, just something about a rumor of the cloak which Onesimus had been wearing becoming an artifact and it was later enshrined."

"And all of this came from these scrolls found in Fiesole? asks Beauvais.

"Yes, father, I have translated them properly. Apparently one of the senators had a man in the circle of Paul's friends, the scribe Amicus," comments Thaddeus. Amicus regularly reported back regularly of what was said there and what had been said in the past to learn if there was even a hint of treason so he could have Paul executed. The senator, once learning of the healing of Titus' daughter, took the small piece of cloth which Paul had given Titus, and attempted to curry favor with Emperor Claudius by healing of his nightmares. He states that it did not heal Claudius and the senator left in shame and was soon told to take a political appointment in what is now Fiesole, and that his political future had come to a dead end in Rome. Apparently the senator took the new position and his servants packed his belongings and it included these writings, Eminence."

"How did these scrolls survive all this time?" asks Beauvais.

"Being sealed in the clay jars gave them some protection," replies Thaddeus.

"Are we certain that these scrolls are from the time of Paul?"

"Well, I not certain of anything at this point, Eminence."

"Angels doing jail breaks, people magically flying to other lands, outrageous, Thaddeus," while laughing.

"Perhaps, father," replies Thaddeus.

"There are several pages still to translate and some seem to be missing. I even noticed that there was an indention in the center of the scrolls as if something had been stored there at one time," says Thaddeus.

Beauvais remains silent.

After a pause, Thaddeus says, "Do you think that Gennero gave you all of the material?"

"I would not use the word gave, my son, but yes, I think that we have everything." Quickly changing the subject, Beauvais puts his arm around Thaddeus and points towards the town square. "Yet you have done well, but we must leave now and attend those who are suffering, Father Thaddeus."

Once in the city square, the two priests see what appears to be several people laying outside their doorways either dead or nearing death. The sisters from the convent were attending to those who are perishing, and Musit was no exception. Musit, noticing the priests' approach, motions for them to come closer. Mother Superior immediately walks towards the priests and before they can utter a word, she snidely congratulates them for finding the time to drop by. Thaddeus says nothing in response, while Beauvais asks, "What exactly have you done for these poor ones, sister?"

With that, the nun walks back towards the plague victims while she repeats Beauvais' question under her breath.

"Will the new bishop arrive soon, Eminence? As you know we have lost so many to this plague," asks Thaddeus.

"Several brothers and sisters are among those either dead or dying, my son, but it appears that the new bishop has heard of the troubles here and has decided not to take his new post after all."

"How can this be?" asks Thaddeus.

"We will talk this at a later time, my son, but for now you help those brothers keep those fires going and I will attend to the sick."

Upon reaching the nearest bond fire, Thaddeus notices that one of the two men tending it was Diego. "I would have thought you would have left by now, Diego," questions Thaddeus.

"Is that your way of asking me to leave, father?"

"No, my son, I am always pleased to see you," the father retorts with a forced smile due to the grimness of the situation.

"It is not a pretty sight, father," says Diego.

"No, it is not, my son."

"So, why are we building fires, father?" asks the monk standing near the fire.

"I am told that they help kill the black-death in some way, but of exactly how I am certain."

"Not very reassuring, father," says Diego.

"Well, it is the best we can do for now and of course we can pray, my sons, we can all pray for God's will and most of all his protection." Both the monk and Diego just look towards the ground and then go back to tending the fire.

"Did you ever expect anything like this, Diego, when you started your journey?" asks Thaddeus.

"I have to be honest with you, father, I did not."

"Brother, please go and tend to the animals and help see to the preparation of our evening meal, as Diego and I will tend the fire."

"Yes, father," replies the monk and he quickly departs.

As evening falls, the fires remain and burn throughout the night. Beauvais is the first to be excused from the town square, and leaves to go and lie down in his room after a quick and modest meal. Beauvais knows his health is failing and once alone pulls an old and tattered piece of cloth from beneath his clothing and lifts it towards the sky.

"Father, I am your servant and I ask that you take this infirmity away from me and make me whole so that I might serve you better," prays Beauvais quietly. After his prayer, he takes the cloth and holds it to his chest and closes his eyes and awaits the impending miracle to take place. After a few moments, Beauvais drops his hands to his side in disappointment and says, "Nothing, dash it all, nothing." He then stuffs the piece of cloth back into a pocket and lies down on his bed and falls fast asleep.

Chapter Ten

In the convent of the Order of the Sisters of St. Francis, a weary looking Musit is down on her knees and with her head covered in a nun's wimple. She labors hard with a pan of water and soap which sits near her as she scrubs the steps inside the convent with her newly acquired scrub brush.

Approaching her from atop of the steps is a figure she knows well, and he greats her with a big smile and the words, "What a beautiful day, Sister Musit, is it not?"

Musit looks up and greats him without stopping what she has been assigned to do, and then replies, "Yes, Eminence, it is a beautiful day."

Beauvais sits down just above Musit on the steps and asks her to please stop what she is doing and to join him for a moment. Musit rests for a moment, wipes her brow, and then sits on the step below Beauvais and a little to his left. "How do you like being a nun, sister?"

"I like it just fine, Eminence." She somehow manages a smile for him again.

"And how are your studies with Mother Superior Margaret proceeding?" asks Beauvais.

"The studies are alright," replies Musit with the emphasis in her voice being on the word "studies". The look of joy drains from Musit's face.

"Are you getting along well with Mother Superior?" queries Beauvais quietly.

Musit looks behind her to make sure they are both alone and then quickly grumbles in a low tone that the Mother Superior can be a "monster" at times.

"Now, now sister, you must not talk like that," shares Beauvais as he is barely able to conceal his laughter, no matter difficult one might be. I do not mind telling you that it took a great deal of convincing on my part with Mother Superior to get you admitted in this Order, and I spoke highly of you and said that you would most certainly complete what you have started, sister."

Musit begins to weep lightly. The Cardinal takes the end of his robe and gently wipes her tears and reassures her that all will be well. Musit then reminds Beauvais that she must return to her work and then rises and thanks him for checking in on her. Beauvais slowly rises and his poor health is more noticeable as he does so.

"Shall we have a word of prayer before I go, sister?"

Musit begins to ask him if he is feeling well, but refrains when she hears the Mother Superior approaching from the distance. "Most certainly, father," replies Musit as she then bows her head.

Beauvais blesses her and prays for God to strengthen her, and then he prays silently for Musit and her grief of recently becoming a widow.

Her husband was very old when Musit married him and the marriage had been arranged by Beauvais in an attempt to make Musit more acceptable in this small city. Now he had passed away and left Musit with nothing more than a ran down shack of a dwelling and a fair amount of debt. Feeling somewhat responsible for her situation, Beauvais could not refuse Musit when she approached him in the sanctuary and asked his help to gain admittance to the convent as a nun. The Mother Superior had not been receptive to Musit's joining, but when push came to shove, Mother Superior had no choice but to knuckle under to the request of the newly appointed Cardinal.

Once Musit was permitted to join this great order, Beauvais would do his best to see her succeed. Yet, he felt that the young nun should not be seen as receiving favoritism as it might keep her from doing her very best as well as cause the other nuns to resent her. Beauvais knew that if Musit was going to make it, she would most certainly have to be helped and accepted by her sisters within the order. The prayer was now over and Beauvais quickly turns to meet Sister Margaret, who he addresses as Mother Superior, not wanting to agitate her any more than he already had.

"Those steps are not going to clean themselves, Sister," scolds the Mother Superior.

"Yes, Mother Superior," replies Musit as she returns to her scrubbing. "And furthermore, you must remember that cleanliness is next to Godliness, Sister Musit."

"Yes, Mother Superior," again Musit responds with a low sigh.

"I will leave you all to your work now," says Beauvais and he immediately departs the convent. Margaret almost stands over Musit as if doing that would make the cleaning more efficient and then she looks around at the departing Cardinal with a touch of distain in her face at what she believed was most certainly his dislike for anything that required actual work.

Beauvais leaves the convent grounds quickly and makes his way through the crowds of people on the street, stopping only briefly to say hello to all he passes on his walk. Entering a butcher shop, Beauvais is greeted by and older man working behind the counter.

"Congratulations, Eminence, on your promotion," says the man.

"Nonsense, Francesco, I am but a simple man of the cloth and I hope that you will see me as such."

"As you say, man of the cloth," Francesco replies with a big smile. "Are you going to see your mother today, father?"

"Yes I am and would like to pick up some bread, cheese, and salami for her if I might."

"Of course father, I will as always wrap up my best for you and your wonderful mother," Francesco says excitedly. I made this salami from wild boar and have to say that it is some of the finest I have ever produced, father. Please try a slice and tell me if it is worthy of a Cardinal?"

Beauvais takes the slice and eats it immediately and then claps his hands together and says, "Bravo! My compliments, Francesco, a culinary masterpiece fit for a king, let alone a Cardinal." The butcher beams with pride at Beauvais compliment.

"I must say father, that I always enjoy visiting with your mother when she comes in for conversation on her way to the wine cellar, father."

"I see," replies Beauvais, as the smile drains from his face.

"Well, I must be going now, Francesco." With that Beauvais takes his food and hands Francesco some coins before thanking him and departing the shop.

Upon exiting, Beauvais walks a few paces and then takes a turn down a narrow lane pulling a key from his pocket which is made of iron. The Cardinal stands for a moment outside an almost hidden doorway along the lane and then unlocks the door and makes his way into a long breezeway to another door only a few feet in front of him. Upon reaching the inner door, several underfed cats scatter in the small courtyard at sound of his approach. Beauvais opens the wooden door and slowly walks up the steps of the narrow tower and only knocks briefly before letting himself into the main living area. The room is dark except for one end of it and it is there that he can make out the figure of an older, unkempt woman dressed in dirty clothes and carrying a half empty bottle of wine.

"Oh, it's you, grumbles the woman, and of course empty handed as usual."

"What, empty handed?" asks Beauvais? "I have brought you some more salami, bread, and cheese, mother."

"I need more wine, damn you, more wine," his mother demands of him.

"I think that wine is the last thing you need right now, mother, come let me prepare something for you to eat."

"I want wine, did you hear me, wine, Ambrose."

"Why do you insist on calling me by my middle Christian name, mother? And no more wine for now, at least not until you eat something."

"So, if I eat something then you will bring me more wine, Ambrose?"

"Yes, yes, but first you must eat something."

After looking around the room, Beauvais looks at Isabella and then asks her, "Where is all of the cheese and bread I left here the first of the week?"

"What, bread and cheese...? Oh, I gave some of it to my cats outside, and they loved it."

"You cannot keep feeding them your food, mother, you have to keep up your strength," says Beauvais in a soft yet scolding tone as if someone outside might be listening in on their conversation. "I should run all of them off; I mean really, mother."

"You do and I will do more than that to you," she replies. "Now please sit down and wait until I have finished with your food." His mother eventually sits down and in the dim light you can see that she was once a very beautiful woman whose looks and poise had long left her through age and most of all by way of the wine bottle.

"Just going to take that, Ambrose," she asks?

"Take what?" he asks.

"You are not a real man, nor have you ever been a real man, Ambrose. You were always a disappointment, Ambrose."

Beauvais acts like he does not hear her and continues preparing her meal. All those years ago, how beautiful I was and then you came along and ruined my life, giving birth to the great bishop of the church.

"I am a Cardinal now, mother, appointed by the Pope himself only recently. I was going to announce it over our dinner tonight, mother."

"Does it pay any more?" she asks cynically. Beauvais makes no reply.

"Your pasta and fresh tomatoes are almost ready."

"Why did you not have the guts to marry her after you had defiled her, you pathetic weakling?!"

"Your food is ready now, so please eat, mother." His mother pretends not to hear him.

"The food is exactly how you like it, mother!"

She takes a small bite and then spits it almost across the room and says, "What are you trying to do? Poison me?" She then hands him back the plate of food almost dropping it and then tells him that she needs more wine.

Beauvais looks at her with discuss and lets the plate sit on her table for awhile hoping that she will eventually eat some of it. Both sit quietly for what seemed like an eternity to both of them until Beauvais finally breaks his silence. "I have always loved you, mother, and always will."

"Liar," she then retorts sharply.

"I was wrong I know I was breaking my vow of celibacy all those many years ago and perhaps I should have married her, but instead I fell to my knees and begged God's forgiveness for my sins. It took almost a year of self-imposed hell to finally be able to look at myself in the mirror again after our one night together. My sins against God as well as against Isabella were great.

"For whatever good that did me, Ambrose, complains Isabella, I still do not have any grandchildren."

After a brief pause he continues, "Have I not cared for you all of these years, mother? As well as for father until God punished me for my wicked ways by taking him from us far too early?"

His mother softly weeps as if the wound was still fresh in her memory.

"I have made my penance all this time and then some."

Both sit silently and avoid any eye contact between them. "Please eat something, my dear." She refuses eat and just sits almost motionless. "I have to tell you that I will be leaving soon to join the Pope in Avignon and I can no longer avoid it."

"So, you are going to go off and enjoy yourself and leave me to rot in this prison you have made for me, Ambrose?"

"Oh, hardly a prison, and you know the way out any time you choose to leave. And what do you really know of prisons anyway, mother? What, no quick reply to that?" asks Beauvais.

"Soon I will find a place for you near Avignon and will send for you."

"No, I will not leave my home I tell you, it is simply out of the question."

"Well, we can talk about it in more detail later, mother."

"I have managed to appoint a young priest to the position of Pryor while I was still the bishop and he seems like a good man to me." Isabella says nothing and crossing her arms she then glares at Beauvais with distain. It is only then that even in her half drunken state she notices the grayness of Beauvais's face and she becomes inwardly concerned, yet she says nothing. "I have not been able to persuade the Pope to appoint this new man to the position of Abbot so he can be more or less autonomous. The Pope is insistent on promoting another man to the position of Abbot, a man that I neither like nor trust. He is an opportunist in the worse way and has only held on to his flock by flattering anyone he could above him. I shudder to think what he will do to this parish," says Beauvais reflectively.

"I will have more influence as a Cardinal yet less in this parish, or at least for awhile, my dear. In time all will be well again, you can trust me on that, mother. Trust me indeed," he repeats himself quietly.

She briefly looks at him as if she puzzled by his words. "Let us just say that I may have stumbled on to something that should allow me to write my own ticket as far as the church is concerned, mother, but of course it must be handled carefully and most of all quietly. Very, very quietly," comments Beauvais quietly with a look of confidence in his face.

"Whatever are you rambling on about, Ambrose?"

"It is not important now, but what is important for you to know that I will always take care of you. Now please, eat something," says Beauvais as he coaxes her take the plate of food he has prepared and finally gets her to take another bite. "Now I will leave you to your mid-day meal and promise return in a couple of hours."

His mother ignores him as he picks up his hat and walks over to kiss her upon her forehead before he departs. Once he makes his way back down to the court yard, he finds a seat, sits down, and then weeps. Eventually Beauvais collects himself and makes his way back through the outer gate and into the narrow lane he suddenly notices the strong smell of smoke coming from the town square and hastens his step towards the piazza. Upon arriving he notices a large fire burning out in the middle of the piazza with two city officials, (the mayor hastily giving orders sergeant of the city guard), standing nearby. It is at this point Beauvais realizes that this most assuredly meant a turn for the worst and the apparent arrival of the black-death in San Gimignano.

Chapter Eleven

"Hugo, please come here quickly," cries Beauvais.

Hugo runs up to the Cardinal who is standing next to a covered wagon attended by two monks. Father Thaddeus stands on the far said of the wagon and has a look of almost terror on his face.

"How may I assist you, father?" asks Hugo as he looks at Beauvais.

With a great deal of effort, Beauvais manages a quick smile and says, "Hugo I have a very important task for you this day."

"Yes father, anything," replies Hugo.

"I would like you to accompany these brothers and take my staff as well." Beauvais hands the rather large staff to Hugo which now looks somewhat smaller now being in Hugo's hands. "These brothers are taking my mother, my precious mother to stay with family, and I would feel at ease if I knew I could count on you to help in her protection along this journey."

"It shall be done, father," says Hugo with a very proud look on his face. Hugo then gets into the back of the wagon and the Beauvais thanks Hugo and walks around to the front of the wagon to give the monks any last instructions.

"If anyone attempts to impede you along the way, tell them that you are one urgent business for the Vatican itself and in the service of Cardinal Beauvais."

While sitting on the back of the wagon, Hugo notices Father Thaddeus walking closer to him. Then in a quiet voice father Thaddeus says to Hugo, "Please my son, bow your head in prayer." Hugo does so and then hears Thaddeus say in a louder voice, "As Prior of this monastery and by the power invested in me by the Holy Roman Church, I do hereby raise you to be listed among the names of those who have entered this holy order and impart upon you all rights and benefits befitting your title. I now declare you to be henceforth, Brother Hugo. Now, may God bless you and keep you this day," the abbot states.

Hugo is almost brought to tears and then with a wave of a Beauvais hand, the wagon departs with the mother of

Beauvais safely inside. Beauvais looks at Thaddeus and does not seemed pleased but then after a moment of reflection says quietly to Thaddeus with a slight smile, "I guess it was going to happen eventually."

"What do you have against him anyway, Eminence?"

"Nothing of importance, but in all actuality it was your call, Thaddeus. And how did it make you feel making your first big decision as Prior?"

"It felt great, Eminence, it felt great," replies Thaddeus with a smile.

"I must go to visit a parishioner now and I will leave you to go to the square and see to things there, father", says Beauvais as he departs toward the far end of town.

After he makes his way down a narrow lane, he comes to the home of a very poor parishioner and small daughter. Upon arriving they both greet him and welcome him into their home. "How may I be of assistance, ask the Cardinal?"

"I am greatly troubled, father, by all of the deaths inside these city walls," the woman complains. "The mayor and all of the city officials have fled for God knows where and we are left here to fend for ourselves, father."

"I see," replies, Beauvais.

"I have a favor to ask of you, father."

"Yes, if I can."

"My daughter is very young and my husband has gone to be with God, so if anything was to happen to me, I would like your promise that you will see to the care of my child, father."

"Nonsense, Teresa, I am sure that both you and Zita will be fine."

"Promise me, father, please promise me." Beauvais says nothing and then looks at the girl wondering how he could ever take care of her.

"As you can see father, she has a withered arm, a burden she has endured from birth, and I fear that no man worth his salt will want to marry her and she end up barren and alone."

"I will speak to the sisters about her care should she require it, it is the best I can do for now, Teresa."

"Thank you father, thank you."

"Now, shall we have a word of prayer before I must be on my way," says Beauvais. And before they can begin their prayer, Zita hugs Beauvais around his waist and her withered arm is instantaneously made whole before their vary eyes.

"My God, it is a miracle, father, a miracle," Teresa extols!

With that Beauvais exits the house and heads back to his study without saying a word. Once there he locks himself in and remains there all day. As evening falls, he hears a knock at the door which he ignores. Soon a voice follows, "Eminence, are you alright?" asks Thaddeus.

"Go away, I am in prayer," snaps Beauvais.

"But I must speak with you at your earliest convenience of a matter of the utmost importance," replies Thaddeus.

"Good God, did you not hear me, man, I told you I am in prayer!"

"As you wish, Eminence." With that Thaddeus departs for evening prayers.

Beauvais lies on his bed and looks at his ceiling and quietly asks the question, "Why her, God, and why not me? Have I not served you for many years? Did I not give up the love of my life in order to serve you? Have I not endured richer but less deserving men being promoted over me within the church? Have I not refrained from taking a mistress while others did and nothing was ever said, Father? And now, this…. this miracle," snaps Beauvais bitterly?

"Everyone will want to be healed now, or a family member healed. The people will expect me to provide more and more miracles, father. How will I ever cope with this situation? I fear a calamity has befallen me and that men once disappointed will tear me to shreds, or worse. Why did this have to happen now?"

After a about an hour, Beauvais goes out of his room and finds a brother down the hallway. Brother, will you please find Father Thaddeus and have him report to me as soon as possible. The monk nods his head and departs to find the Prior.

"Yes, come in Thaddeus," says Beauvais now more collected.

"Father, there is a woman outside the church with a young girl and the woman is claiming that you healed her," says Thaddeus.

"These crazies are a dime a dozen, my son, and the times we are in bring them out of the wood work."

"I see, Eminence," replies Thaddeus. And this is the Church's official opinion?"

"Sit down Thaddeus, and let me clue you in on a thing or two." The Prior takes a seat in front of the half drunken Cardinal.

"Would you first like a drink, my boy?"

"No thank you father," replies Thaddeus.

"Have it your way then," retorts Beauvais. "In this town I have always spoken for the church, and now as Cardinal, it is even more so. I tell you now that this was no miracle and you will do your best to reassure the people of as much."

"But there are people who are proclaiming that they have known this child and until today, was always afflicted," Thaddeus says timidly.

"Rubbish!" responds Beauvais. "She simply had not grown up yet, and it just took a little longer with her is all. Do I make myself clear, father?"

"Crystal, Eminence." Beauvais sits back in his chair in a less aggressive manner and sips on his drink. After a long pause, "So, you have the piece of cloak after all," questions Thaddeus quietly.

"What on earth are you ever talking about, you fool?"

"There is no one else here but us, and I would like to know what you have gotten me into, Eminence, I think I have earned that."

After a few minutes of quiet reflection, Beauvais decides that he is tired of carrying his burden alone and to clear the air one and for all. "What I am about to tell you does not leave this room, not even for an instant," whispers Beauvais.

"As always, father," replies Thaddeus.

"Gennero came to me with these scrolls but he had no idea what he truly had in his possession. He was getting on in life and I gathered he had pretty much been viewed as a misfit most of his life and sort of saw this as a possible way of getting a soft spot to land for his remaining days, but only after he had offered them to God knows how many others. Well, no one took him seriously and neither did I at first, but once I viewed the scrolls I knew that they must be of some importance, so I granted him admission into the monastery as a brother, which he all too eagerly accepted. Within a few weeks I caught wind of men inquiring of the whereabouts of both Gennero as well as any items he might be peddling. Fortunately I had the sense to send him out to a distant part of the parish to attend the goats and most importantly out of sight when he first arrived. I kept him hidden for over a year before the inquiries stopped. I did find a piece of cloth hidden inside one of the scrolls and yes, I assumed it too possibly have been the same cloth once given to Titus."

"If you already knew this, Eminence, then why keep me here to translate the scrolls? asks Thaddeus.

"Because I am getting older and my eyes are not what they once were. Once I had the cloth in my possession I tried to use it to heal myself many times over, but to no avail. I figured that possibly I had missed something and wanted younger eyes to view the scrolls, and then you came along. It was an answer to a prayer.

"The problem is the cloth just did not work, no matter what I tried or how hard I prayed, that until today, my son. I admit that I wanted to heal myself for selfish reasons, but who would not in my situation? I thought I might have some sort of quiet miracle and perhaps get more recognition by Avignon, but doing my best to keep them in the dark as to the source of any miracles that might happen."

"Why keep them in the dark?" asks Thaddeus.

"Because if there were actual miracles being performed here in San Gimignano, the Pope once learning of the cloth and the scrolls which accompanied it would be as good as gone."

"How can this be, father?"

"Well, simple, Thaddeus, the Pope would order it brought to Avignon, build a shrine to it, and then claim any credit as well as any gold profited from pilgrims in search of a healing."

"But is not the Holy Father your friend, Eminence?"

"Friend, hardly," retorts Beauvais. "We grew up in the same town as boys and I once punched him the nose for being wealthy when I was not. He feared me so he made me his friend," grumbles Beauvais. "Over the years our ties grew, and he always viewed me as someone he could trust, but I have never trusted him, not even for an instant. I have used that trust to my advantage on occasion, and did so to get you promoted to your situation now."

"I am too young to be Prior, let alone Abbot."

"An Abbot, hell you will soon be the auxiliary bishop of this fair town if you do as you are told."

"Forgive me, but that is insane, father," Thaddeus replies.

"Well, in most instances I would agree with you, but these are extraordinary times and calls for extreme measures," says Beauvais calmly. "And I have no doubt that that you will be up to the task, Thaddeus, no doubt at all."

After a few moments of deathly silence, Thaddeus speaks out. "This is your way of keeping me in line, is it not, Eminence?"

"I knew that you were a very bright young man when I first met you," replies Beauvais.

"And with this cloth you could heal all of those poor souls who lie languishing down in the city square, and yet you do not," protests Thaddeus.

"It is not a simple as that, my young friend."

"No, then please explain, Father?"

The cloth does not work on command, and I am not even sure how or if it worked on the young girl today. All I know is that she hugged me and her arm was restored. Hell, I had even forgotten that I had it in my pocket."

"Well we must try father, or many will parish needlessly."

"Alright, fine, we will just march out of here, tell the whole world of Paul's cloak and begin the miracles," decries Beauvais. "And then what after all that the miracles do not happen, my boy, what then?"

Thaddeus remains silent.

"I will tell you exactly what will happen, those nice, kind people who are just outside the church will turn into a mob once they their expected miracles do not happen they will tear us limb from limb. Moreover, they might desecrate the church as well in their fury."

"Perhaps the miracles will happen, father, have you ever thought of that?" asks Thaddeus.

"That would be a catastrophe, for can you imagine with all of the people who are now dying all over the continent, how many people would flock here in search of healing," cries Beauvais? "Do you know how many would die along the way and how many would die being crushed in the crowds? And what of those who would seek to profit from the misery of others and how they might like to take it away from us? No, Thaddeus, we will not do this openly.

"We have to try father, and if you will not, then for the greater good, perhaps I will."

"If you do that then you will suffer the worse consequences, sir," retorts Beauvais. "I remind you that the people are afraid and looking for anyone to blame, and if you cross me I will destroy you, my boy. I will defrock you and cast you out, my little friend. And it gets better, for I tell these nice people that you are in league with the devil and that only recently saw you poisoning wells, the vary wells which lead to this black-death."

"They will not believe you," says Thaddeus.

"Are you most certain, because I am the only priest that most of them have ever known and you are little more than a stranger? Furthermore, I will tell them that your little friend, Diego, is an anti-Christ and behind all of this and that you are in league with him to spread disease and sickness among them."

"Not even you would resort to that," questions Thaddeus.

"No," replies Beauvais. "I will sit by quietly while the people put both you to the stake. The fires will burn hot and the stench of your flesh roasting will travel for miles, so you just think about that my young friend."

Thaddeus' face becomes pale as is he has seen a ghost.

"Just see how long you and your Hebrew friend last with that angry mob," chides Beauvais. Then the just as quickly, Beauvais relaxes back into his chair and says snidely, "Or you can keep your mouth shut and trust me to handle this, and there is no reason why life cannot on for the both of us, Thaddeus. What shall it be, boy?"

"I need time to think, Beauvais."

"Address me by my proper title, sir, and I must have your answer now," barks Beauvais with his rotting teeth clinched.

Thaddeus looks around the room and then up to the ceiling as if seeking an answer. "You hold all of the cards, and so we must do it your way, Eminence."

"Yes, and never forget that my boy. Now as a sign of your faith and obedience, Father Thaddeus, I extend my hand to you and request that you kiss my ring."

"Yes, Eminence," replies the priest and he does so begrudgingly.

"Smart boy," arrogantly remarks Beauvais, "and I remind you to never speak a word of this to anyone. These are trying times and we could even fall back into the dark ages, my son. The people need their symbols, the churches, their God to lean upon in times like these, Thaddeus. Please leave this to me," cautions Beauvais.

Chapter Twelve

The sun hid itself behind the clouds that mid-day as the priest, Thaddeus, struggles to find some sort of original prayer to express to God on behalf of those suffering. So many had he prayed for and still they died. He finishes his prayer only to look down in time to notice the last glimpse of life left Teresa's no still body. To his left side stood a small child, Zita, as well as Sister Musit. Thaddeus looks heartbroken and eventually is able to turn to Zita and says, "I am sorry, little one, but your mother will not recover."

"I know, father, she has gone to be with God."

"That is right, Zita, your mother has gone to be with Jesus." Thaddeus struggles to get to his feet and says, "Go with Musit now, Zita, and she will get you something to eat."

"Where is Father, Beauvais? asks the little girl. "I want Father Beauvais!"

Musit says, "He has gone to see the Pope and will most certainly be back soon. Let us go and eat something now, Zita."

"It will be alright; I will not let anyone harm your mother, now please go with Musit."

The two depart for the convent and Thaddeus manages a smile for the child as long as he can, yet his smile is interrupted by the sound Sister Margaret calling to him.

"Father Thaddeus, come quickly," cries the Mother Superior. The young abbot hurries over to her to find an older man lying on the ground, his face is ashen, and death seems to be close at hand. "Hurry father, the last rites," demands the nun, and Thaddeus gets back down on his knees and prays that prayer as he has done too many times to count as of late.

"And where is his Eminence today?" snidely asks the Mother Superior.

"He has gone to Avignon on Vatican business of what I am assured is of the utmost importance," replies Thaddeus.

"Important business, my foot," scolds the nun.

Thaddeus does not respond to her comment and continues to pray. "If you ask me we are better off without his prancing around, all high and mighty," the Mother Superior continues.

"That is enough, Margaret," snaps Thaddeus. The nun looks at him in shock and almost cannot believe her ears. "We just do not have time for this pettiness right now, sister."

"I am sorry father, but these are trying times. We have no physician, no herbs or medicines of any count, and no leeches either to cleanse the blood, father."

"These are trying times for all of us and test our faith, but we must be faithful and diligent," replies the young abbot. "And most of all stay strong for these most unfortunate ones, sister."

"Forgive me father, please, I spoke without thinking."

"There is nothing to forgive, Mother Superior, and I do wish to thank you and all of the sisters for your tireless efforts at this tragic time. If not for you, sister, I am not sure where we would be at this point." Thaddeus smiles at Sister Margaret and she finally smiles as she wipes away her tears.

"Father, do you want me to take Teresa's body down with the others and bury her," asks Hugo.

"Yes, Brother Hugo, and please handle her with the greatest reverence."

"I always do, father," says Hugo with a slight but forced smile.

"Diego, Diego, can I impose upon you to assist Brother Hugo with the task of removing the dead?" asks Thaddeus.

"Of course, father, anything," replies Diego. "I am not ready to turn my boots and cloak in for a monk's robe and sandals, father, but I offer my services to you as always."

"At this point, my son, I gladly accept your humble offer, says the abbot with a smile." As the two men depart carrying the now lifeless body, Thaddeus can hear Hugo in the distance say, "Nice boots."

Thaddeus looks around the square to notice that none of the city officials are present other than two soldiers and they did not seem all that enthusiastic about being there. How would he ever cope he asked himself, and as much as he disliked Beauvais, his return would be a welcomed site.

"Eminence, there are armed Papal Guards at the gate," says the carriage driver to Beauvais.

"Stop when you get to them if they ask you to, otherwise pay them no mind."

"They are walking out and motioning for us to stop, Eminence, what do you want me to do?"

"Do as they say and I will talk to them, driver."

"Stop, commands the captain of the guard. You must turn around immediately, no one is allowed into the city.

"I have business in Avignon with the Holy Father himself, now step aside," barks Beauvais from within the carriage.

"And just who might you be? the King of France?" ask the guard rudely.

Now that the carriage is at a complete stop, Beauvais makes his way out to the ground below and stands before them in his Cardinals robes and adornments. "I am Cardinal Beauvais, personal assistant to the Pope, who may I ask is inquiring?"

The guard, realizing that Beauvais is a man of great importance says, "Forgive me Eminence, of course you may enter."

The guard then motions for the carriage to be admitted as Beauvais returns to his previous seat. The guard bows his head in a salute as the carriage moves forward and Beauvais motions in with his hand at him as the move forward without ever looking at the man.

"Straight in driver, stop for no one, and do not spare the whip," orders Beauvais.

Upon entering Avignon, Beauvais notices a large number of dead or dying people along the streets and in the square. The bonfires were still burning, but there were few to tend them. An occasional priest offered prayers, but they seemed few and far in between. A physician attempts to use leaches on one dying man in hopes of curing him. The stench grows as the go farther into the city. Upon reaching the Papal Palace, Beauvais enters to find the place in total chaos. People and priests scrambling to take their leave of the city walk by him as if he is not there. Beauvais asked if anyone knew who was in charge, but he got no real reply from any of them.

Suddenly Beauvais notices someone he knows. It was Bishop Jacinto from all those years ago, surely he would know what was going on, thought the Cardinal? Beauvais called out to the bishop and to his surprise, the bishop stopped to see who was calling to him. "It is your old friend, Beauvais."

After a few moments, the bishop recognized him and asks, "What are you doing here, Eminence?"

"I am here to see the Holy Father," replies Beauvais.

"The Holy Father, the bishop asks with a surprised look on his face? The Holy Father fled days ago and left this mess for us to deal with alone," complained Jacinto.

"Fled," questions Beauvais?

"Yes, and it would be wise of you to follow suit, Eminence."

"And the whereabouts of my mother," asks Beauvais?

"I heard that she died almost two weeks ago, my friend, did no one notify you?" Beauvais looks downcast at the news of his mother's death. The bishop starts to make his way towards the door when Beauvais asks, "So, who is in charge here?"

"No one is at the moment."

"The physician, Guy de Chauliac, stayed behind to minister to those he could, but now even he has fallen to this plague and is near death as we speak."

"Where is Guy?" demands Beauvais.

"He is back there," says the bishop as he points towards the back of the palace before departing.

Beauvais makes his way through the crowd and finally finds Guy lying in a bed originally built for the Pontiff himself. The look of death was upon Guy, he ever so slightly groaned with pain, and worst of all he was alone.

"Guy, Guy de Chauliac, is that you?" asks Beauvais.

"Who is there?" Guy replied?

"It is Beauvais from San Gimignano."

"What are you doing here, Eminence? For death is everywhere."

"I am here to tend to you my friend," replies Beauvais. The Cardinal kneels beside the bed and begins to pray for his friend, but after awhile notices no apparent improvement. "How long has it been old friend?" ask Beauvais.

"I am not sure, Eminence," replies Guy as he struggles to speak.

"Rest now and save your strength," advises Beauvais. As he observes his friend he notices that Guy is burning up with fever. Beauvais looked about the room and then says, "Let me find something to wipe your face and brow with, my brother, yet he sees nothing that will suffice."

Not wanting to leave his friend, Beauvais remembers the cloth in his pocket, a very old and special cloth. He had not dared to use it in any meaningful way since the healing of Zita and her withered arm. What if it did not work, how could he get his friend's hopes up only to have them dashed again? And how would his own faith survive if it failed to deliver another miracle in such a time of great need, Beauvais pondered. Yet, no time like the present and with that, he pulled the cloth from his pocket and begins wiping the forehead and face of Guy de Chauliac.

Beauvais looked for any signs of a miracle, but none were present. With this his heart sank and he put the cloth back into his pocket while Guy fell into a deep sleep. Beauvais found a comfortable spot in another bedroom and decided to stay the night. Upon awaking, Beauvais was shocked to find his friend, Guy, sitting up in a chair, the sun shining upon his face and eating some bread.

"Guy, are you feeling better?" asks Beauvais.

"I am my brother, and it is surely a miracle from God above!" declared de Chauliac.

"A miracle indeed," replied Beauvais. After a light breakfast, Beauvais attempted to find his mother's grave, yet they were unmarked as of yet and there were so many. Finally Beauvais sat next to the cemetery and grieved openly for the mother he had lost.

Chapter Thirteen

Beauvais felt his heart pound within his chest as he ran towards the hill in front of him. His breathing labored as the hill seemed to get steeper until he could finally run no more and fell hard upon the ground below him. He struggled to roll over onto his back and listened for the sound of approaching footsteps when he was noticed a pair of boots standing just above him next to a large olive tree. "I know those boots;" he laughed, "Diego, my son, it is you!"

"Lie still father and let us keep them in the dark as to my presence," whispered Diego.

The band of angry men who had just killed the Cardinal's driver and taken the carriage had now turned toward their angry gaze upon the Cardinal himself and began towards him. The men slowed their approach as they assumed that their prey was now most surely helpless.

"Deceive us will you with your piety and your statues," shouted the men in an almost uncontrollable rage!

"Get his cross of gold and his boots first, lads," said one of the men. Beauvais manages to somehow sit up and then sees his pursuers and quickly asks for mercy from them, but his pleas seem to fall upon deaf ears as the men move to encircle him.

"Those rings will fetch a fine price," declares one man as he begins to bend over Beauvais.

As he reaches out towards the rings he suddenly notices the point of a sword in his face. "Whether you live today to make amends for you sins depends greatly upon what you do next, my friends," says Diego with a since of calmness in his voice. The man withdraws his hands and steps back to appraise the situation as do the others.

"Father, let me help you up," says Diego as he uses his free hand to assist the priest yet never taking his eyes off of the other men. Beauvais struggles to his feet and thanks Diego and then directs his comments towards the gang of bandits.

"You have the carriage and your lives, but if you value them then I suggest that you leave now," says Beauvais calmly now that he has somewhat collected himself.

"We found him and he is ours;" complain the men, "Go find your own plunder and leave ours be!"

"You heard the father; it is time for you to leave now as he suggested," says Diego as he points his sword toward them.

The men wonder if they can disarm Diego without losing their lives and finally speak out, "There are six of us and only two of you. Leave the cross and the rings and we will let you leave with your lives," declares one of the men confidently.

"I am afraid that I cannot allow that gentlemen, as I am this man's guest and could not repay his hospitality with such an insult," retorts Diego.

"Why do you protect this vermin? one man says.

"They take our livelihoods, eat our food, live in luxury while our people die and we live in squallier."

"They promise us God's favor, and then this curse befalls us," another man states.

"Or do you protect him because you are a Jew and in league with him, Christ killer?" they declare.

One of the men begins to move towards Diego but just as quickly stops not wanting to risk being harmed. "This is your lucky day, priest, but there will be other days, other opportunities for us to meet again," says one of man as he points his finger and moves back towards the carriage.

The sight of Hugo and two other monks coming over the hill towards them was more than the thieves cared to tackle. Once Diego realizes that he has some assistance, he walks down towards the carriage, sword still in hand, and orders the men to leave immediately. The highwaymen take the carriage while pushing the driver's body to the ground as they flee. The body bounces with a thud and soon the sound of hooves begins to fade. Hugo shouts insults as he runs part way down the road in pursuit before finally giving up the chase.

"Come Hugo, and please help me up the hill now and onto the cart," asks Beauvais.

"Have the other monks bring my drivers body up for burial as well, and I will instruct Father Thaddeus to perform the burial himself, but now please get me back to my room," strains Beauvais, his face now gray in color.

"How did you ever find me, Diego?"

"I was assisting in burying the bodies and left momentarily to relieve myself when I heard a commotion coming from down below. Upon investigation saw your hasty approach, and the rest you know is history," responds Diego.

"Well, I want you to know that I am in your debt, sir, as am I to you all," says Beauvais.

After finally reaching the town square, Diego informs Thaddeus of what has taken place and both men watch Beauvais make his way back towards his quarters. The Cardinal stops only momentarily to address the crowd by saying, "It has been a long day for all of us and I suggest we all get some rest and meet back here in the morning."

"Well, until tomorrow then father," says Diego as he decides to go and get something to eat.

"Yes," replies Thaddeus, "and thank you again for your service to us."

Diego nods his head and makes his way towards the café but finds it to be closed. Thaddeus is exhausted and begins the long trek back to the bell tower, above the gate, which he calls home. Diego remembers that there is a persimmon tree which is still heavy laden with fruit out beyond on the westward wall and decided to help himself to something to eat.

Now that his stomach is full, Diego notices the day is drawing to an end and makes his way back towards the monastery before it is too dark to navigate. Along his way he cannot help but hear a woman inside her home wailing for her lost husband and asks aloud, "Why God, why?"

A little further along, Diego notices a man lying in the piazza near the well calling out to him, "Help me kind sir, if you will?"

"I have given you silver in the past and you should have saved some of it back," replies Diego.

"Silver will not save me this time, kind sir, only God can," says the beggar as he reveals signs of the black-death on his withered legs and hands. Diego steps back not wanting to possibly contact this illness and offers to go and get the priest.

"I am sure that I will be dead before your return, kind sir, if only you would pray with me before I go to meet my maker," the beggar pleads.

"I do not know the words because I am not a priest," mumbles Diego in fear.

"I have lost my vision and know that death is close at hand, kind sir. Please, please pray with me." After a moment's hesitation, Diego overcomes his fear and grants the beggar's last request. As Diego kneels beside the beggar, he notices a stench upon the man, and surely this was the smell of death.

As Diego attempts to pray, the beggar asks him, "What is it that you seek, kind sir?"

"Nothing, just lie still now and save your strength."

"I sense that you have traveled a great distance in search of something, please, kind sir, tell me what that is?"

Diego stops praying and sits down in the piazza and just reflects if for only a second. "I seek an end to my pain," replies with tears he can no longer hold back.

"That which will make you whole?" asks the beggar.

"And how is it that you know so much about this, beggar? demands Diego.

"All I know is that it is not the hem of one's garment that can restore a people, but God alone for those who as much believe in him," replies the beggar.

Diego pulls himself away from the beggar while stumbling over himself getting to his feet.

"Remember as the scripture says, you do not have because you do not ask," says the beggar. Suddenly the beggar becomes whole, takes on the glow of angelic light and stands before Diego as a very large man with huge, bird like wings upon his back. For a reason unknown to Diego, more sadness wells up inside him and he begins to weep openly and for the first time in two years he now feels a sense of relief from his all the hurts he had buried deep within him. The angel reaches with his right hand and touches Diego with his finger in the center of Diego's chest.

"It is your faith that has healed you," says the angel, "and this is where you shall serve the Lord Most High." At this point Diego's sadness turns to joy as he watches the angel ascends into heaven.

"Who would ever believe such a story," thinks Diego, "Who in their right mind?"

The next two years come and go and those have survived the black-death thus far figure that they will most likely be spared and most thank God for their lives, yet some do not.

As the morning's sun had at last begun to break through a small window in Beauvais' small monastery room, the Cardinal struggles to roll over in his bed and knows he has not had a good night sleep. He lies there listening to the sounds of birds beginning to sing from just outside his window. It was now early and the black-death had come and gone and as the season changed the city hoped for a renewal of life as well. Beauvais was no different in his hopes for a life renewed, but his face remained gray and even in the early morning light seemed quite pale in color. Beauvais knew his end was near and he did not relish the thought of what might await him in the hereafter. Morning prayers would soon be called for, but he had made up his mind that he would miss them. Clinching an old cloth rage in his hand, Beauvais hold it with to his bosom, closes his eyes, and quietly prays in earnest. "Spare me this day, Father, spare me. I beseech you, Lord, spare me." Beauvais pulls the cloth ever closer to himself after closing his eyes and nervously he waits the Lord's presence and most of all his healing touch.

"Nothing again, Lord," he whispers out into the air towards God above. "Why do you heal the others, Lord, and not me?" Beauvais questions to himself. His intermittent cough that he hampered him for so long makes a brief appears and then subsides as it always has. With a hoarse utterance, the Cardinal mumbles out, "A bastard, I am mostly surely a bastard, with no father here on earth nor apparently above. It seems that I am totally alone, God. Why, God, why? I have rarely asked for anything for myself, but to die like this, Lord?? He begins to groan aloud, yet softly, his inner anguish can no longer be contained and yet his tears only briefly flow. "I am alone and otherwise surrounded by strangers." Wiping his eyes with his sleeve, he attempts to at last sleep before he is forced to start another day. "It is unfair, unfair, unfair," he groans to himself as he turns his head towards his pillow. "Forgive me of my sins, father, as I do not wish to be damned in hell for eternity. Forgive me, father," begs Beauvais before finally falling back to sleep.

After a short period of time passes, the Lord comes to the Cardinal in a dream and says to him, "Your sins are forgiven and this very day you shall be with me in paradise." Ambrose opens his eyes briefly, closes them again and takes his final breath.

"Father, father, come quickly!" exclaims Brother Hugo as he comes running down the street towards the tower above the city gate. Thaddeus looks to see what the trouble is and sees Hugo's fast approach.

"What is the matter? Hugo, you will wake what is left of the city," scolds Thaddeus.

"It is the Cardinal, and I think that he has perished in the night."

After a brief pause, Thaddeus looks at Hugo and says quietly, "Go to his room immediately and allow no one to enter. I will be there directly, Hugo, go now and hurry."

"Yes, father," replies Hugo and makes his way back toward the monastery.

Thaddeus goes back into his room and sits back down. "I knew this day was coming and I have to admit that I thought it might actually be a relief to me, but I must confess, Lord, that I find no pleasure in his death. Forgive me father," he utters under his breath, "for I have sinned." With that Thaddeus bends his head down and quietly begins to weep.

"He has not been disturbed, father," says Hugo upon the priest's approach.

Thaddeus now enters the room where the Cardinal had passed in the night. "Shall I contact the magistrate, father?"

"No Hugo, but go to the sisters and inform them of what has occurred."

As Hugo leaves for the convent, Thaddeus slowly walks toward Beauvais now lifeless body and simply stands there for a moment wondering what he had to do next to prepare him for burial. He was after all a Cardinal and great care must be taken in the preparations of such a solemn, yet important church function.

As Thaddeus stood there, he notices the cloth rag gripped in the right hand of Beauvais. Hearing the voices of monks approaching in the hallway, he quickly pries the rag from Beauvais' hand sticks it in his own pocket. As the monks enter the room, Thaddeus announces that their brother has now gone to be with the Lord and that they should carefully prepare his body for burial. Thaddeus prays the last rite over his mentor and then departs the room.

Upon reaching the small piazza next to the church, Thaddeus notices Mother Superior walking towards him and hailing him. "Is it true, father that the Cardinal is dead?"

"Yes, it is, sadly. I would like for the Sisters to attend his funeral and I will send a message to the Pope immediately as he may want to attend as well as I hear they were very close."

Margaret moves in close to the priest and begins to whisper. "It is well and good that you inform his Holiness of the death of our brother, but I do not believe that the he will be attending the funeral."

"Of course that is a possibility, Sister, but he is a very busy man."

"Apparently not so close as to visit poor Beauvais when the sickness took hold of him all those months ago, and still not so close as to visit him once the plague gripped him," says Margaret bitterly.

"The Pope cannot be everywhere at once, Sister."

"Yes, father, I know, but with all due respect you would think he would make time for his own brother?"

"His own brother, ask Thaddeus? Whatever are you talking about, woman?"

"Half-brothers to be more precise, father."

"How do you know this, Sister, how can this be?"

"A few years ago I went to a function with and met the Pope at his installation. While there I overheard some of the Cardinals talking about his Holiness and his bastard half-brother."

"Beauvais?" utters Thaddeus.

"No wonder he got things pushed through so quickly with the Vatican, Margaret. I had no idea, as father Beauvais never spoke of this to me except to say that they were childhood friends."

"From what I have learned Beauvais' mother was a poor woman from the wrong side of some French village, and his father was a man of great means, young and foolish. He never acknowledged Beauvais publically and soon afterward married, father, and produced an heir. And that heir grew up to be Pope."

"How many others know about this?"

"As far as I know, only you and I now, father."

"Then out of respect for the dead, let us keep it that way, Margaret."

"Yes, father, I agree."

"And if you and your order could help with the funeral, we would be grateful."

"Of course, father."

"And let us assume for the time being that the Holy Father might decide to attend and make this go as smoothly as possible."

"Agreed," says Margaret as she departs.

Chapter Fourteen

"Good morning father", says Musit as she greets Thaddeus in the garden outside of the convent.

"Good morning, sister, how are you today?"

"Wonderful, father, just wonderful," she replies with a smile. Thaddeus stands up quickly and excuses himself and begins to walk away quickly. "Where are you off to today, father?"

"I must visit a parishioner, so I must be on my way," he replies quickly without looking at her.

"Bye, father."

Thaddeus begins quietly repeating the rosary quietly as he walks down the city lane towards the gate and then seeing a city guard at the entrance he pauses only briefly to give him a greeting. "Well, it is nice to see the city finally putting a guard at the gate again," the priest thinks to himself. "This plague took so much from us, Lord," he reflects as he walks down the trail towards the countryside. The sun is shining on his back and the air has a hint of spring time in the air. "Heavenly Father, I know a man in my position is not supposed to take a wife, and I do try to live a pure life, but still I am tempted by her (Musit). Help me, Lord, for I have refrained from ministering to Musit and I have even burned my finger in the candle to punish myself for looking at her, still Lord, I do desire her. I ask, I beg for your assistance, Father." Then Thaddeus becomes almost pensive and begins to doubt himself. "I am not a worthy servant for I have fallen in respect as to my purity. I have not had carnal knowledge of this woman, yet have in my heart. I am such a fraud I fear. How can I minister to others when I am not master of my own body? I just cannot seem to shake off these sinful desires, this lust. How many times have I secretly dropped to my knees and prayed for this temptation to be taken from me and once it seems to be gone; I only fall prey to it again at a later time. I am most assuredly like a dog who returns to his vomit. Is there no hope for me?" he asks aloud. Thaddeus then attempts to concentrate on the beauty of the countryside in attempt to find some relief from his tortured soul and mind as he walks along the trail.

After a long walk down the trail, Thaddeus notices the sound of a dog barking at him in the distance. He strains to see whose dog it might be and then sees a large figure come out of a small, one room house and he knows it to be his friend, Hugo. "Greetings father!" shouts Hugo from down the lane with the wave of his hand and a smile on his face.

"Greetings my son," Thaddeus replies as he approaches the home slowly allowing the dog to approach and briefly smell his leg.

"Stop that, Ambrose, leave the father alone," says Hugo as he motions for the dog to make way.

"You named your dog, Ambrose, Hugo?"

"Yes father, after Cardinal Beauvais," replies Hugo.

"I see, my son."

"Yes, father, I only learned that his first name was Ambrose at his funeral, and named my dog after him."

"I am sure he would feel honored, my son," says the priest with a bit of a chuckle. "I see that you have broken ground for a garden, Hugo, and your chickens seem to be doing well."

"Yes, father, I have been very busy here, but the place is coming along nicely. Come and sit down, father," says Hugo as he motions towards a couple of large, recently cut trees stumps, "and I will fetch a cold drink of water for you."

"Thank you, my son, I do not mind if I do. I have brought some bread and cheese and hope they are to your liking, my son."

"Yes father, I am sure they are and thank you." Hugo takes a jar and heads towards a small spring just at the edge of the clearing and soon returns to find Thaddeus sitting and wiping his brow of perspiration.

"Here, father, some good, cold water for you," says Hugo as he passed the priest the whole jar.

"I do not have a cup to offer you, so I hope that you will not mind, father?"

"This will be fine, my son, and thank you." Thaddeus takes the jar and sips from it briefly and then sits it beside the stump out of the way of his feet. Hugo sits and both men endure an almost deathly silence. "It looks like it might warm up soon, says Hugo."

"Yes, father, soon I think."

"And things are going well here then, my son?"

"Yes, father, well indeed."

"So, you are happy?"

"Yes father, I would say that I am more at peace here." The dog now runs up and sits beside Thaddeus and allows the priest to pet him.

"He is a nice dog, Hugo, where ever did you find him?"

"He came with the house I believe, father. When I discovered this place, unattended and in disrepair, I looked inside for any signs of life only to find no one residing here accept this dog. He looked hungry and after cowering for awhile, he made his way up to me and after feeding him some bread he has been my friend ever since."

"Amazing what a small amount of food can do in some situations, Hugo."

"Yes, father, that is very true."

"So, the people here must have perished in the plague?" says Thaddeus.

"Most likely, father, and I know it is a sin to steal, but I found no one who laid claim to this place, so here I will stay."

" I see, Hugo, and you are most certain that you will not return to the monastery and rejoin the few remaining brothers there?"

"Yes, father, I am most certain. I hope that you and I can still be friends, father, and that you will remain my priest as well?"

"Of course, Hugo, of course I will. Nothing would please me more than to consider you and Ambrose as a part of my flock here in the Tuscany."

"Thank you, father, that means a lot to me and Ambrose, I know," replies Hugo with a smile.

"Yes, you have a wonderful spot for a garden, my son."

Hugo turns to looks towards the newly tilled soil and says, "And you will come and help me pick some of once it is ready to harvest, father."

"Yes, my son, fresh vegetables are always a welcomed sight." The two remain silent for awhile longer and just sit on the stumps looking at the trees and skies, but most of all avoiding any eye contact. "I certainly hope that it was nothing I did to persuade you to leave the order, my son," Thaddeus asks in a sincere voice.

"No, no, father, that was not the cause of it."

"Then what was it, if you do not mind me inquiring?"

"It was for a lot of different reasons and a very long story, father."

"I enjoy long stories, my son."

Hugo looks a little perplexed and then finally says, "I know that we are not in a church father, but may I make confession to you here and now?"

"I am God's servant, Hugo, no matter where I am."

Hugo bows his head and begins to pray silently. Thaddeus blesses him and them makes the sign of the cross with his hand. After another long pause, Hugo utters shakily, "Father, bless me for I have sinned. It has been two weeks since my last confession. I have to confess that I did lie to Father Beauvais out of fear about being captured by slave traders, because I actually left the Crimea and journeyed to Venice where I joined the merchant fleet to find my fortune, but soon tired of it all. Once in port, I fled ship under the cover of darkness. I have hidden my past all this out of fear of being taken back to serve in aboard ship again, but I believe that after all of this time no one would be searching for me."

"Why did you become a sailor in the first place, my son?"

"I guess I was looking for a home, father. A home; how so?"

"I have never truly felt at home anywhere sine I was a small child and had an inner desire to find this place, where ever it might be. I thought that by going to see I might see many places I would not have otherwise and took the chance that one of them might be that place... home."

"Yet, you did not find it, Hugo?"

"No father, and made the decision one day that once back in port I would leave the ship and head back to the land from whence I came. After I left the ship I started back down the road I had arrived on, but felt too much shame to return as what I thought might be seen as a failure and instead headed west and eventually landed in San Gimgnano."

"I see, my son."

"That is when I met Father Beauvais, who talked me into staying and eating a meal and then staying a little longer until I am where I am now. I owe him a great deal, father."

"I am sure he would be proud of you knowing that trusted enough to stay and make this peaceful spot your home, Hugo," says Thaddeus with a sincere smile.

"But for how long, father; how long until I feel the urge to depart and seek safety?"

"Only God knows those things, my son, only God."

"If I may make an observation, Hugo, it appears that you may have be running, and with God's help you will no longer have to?"

"Or perhaps just seeking solitude, father?"

"Why could you not find solitude in the monastery, my son?"

"Not really sure why, father."

"I know there was a lot going on at the time, but I thought that you were happy with us, Hugo."

"I must admit that I was happy for awhile, but I never truly felt like I belonged there either."

"Did something happen in town, Hugo?"

"No one thing to speak of, perhaps many things, father."

"Please tell me, my son."

"I do not speak the native language and the other monks seemed to think I was not very bright by my speech. Also, San Gimignano is very small and the people in the town seemed to resent the fact that I was no from here and I just got tired of being an outsider, father."

"Things take time, my son, acceptance takes time."

"I just think that no matter of time will change things, father. I have spent the major of my life as a sort of outcast," says Hugo.

"Outcast?" asks Thaddeus.

"Yes, father, an outcast."

"But why, Hugo, please explain?"

"I lived in many places as a child. My father had to go from place to place to find work and once he got settle somewhere he would send for my mother and me and once there, we would soon have to move again. Eventually I just stopped trying to make friends and just waited to once again be uprooted, and now have grown too accustom to it, father, to ever do anything else.

Thaddeus just sighs and says nothing.

"I do believe in Christ and seek to serve the church, but I am not comfortable living in the monastery, father. I am not comfortable living around people in general to be more precise, father. I saw so many people die during that black-death and buried far too many as well, that now sometimes when I close my eyes I can see them calling to me from the grave, father."

"I had no idea Hugo that you were suffering such things, yet those days were hard on all of us. I should have been more aware, my son, and for that I do apologize."

"I managed to do my duties up until Father Beauvais died, and it was at his funeral that something inside of me said, enough."

"I had wondered why you left when you did, my son, and now I understand why." Both men sit quietly and say nothing when suddenly Thaddeus bumps the water jar with his leg and knocks it over. The dog is quick to lap up its contents. Hugo begins to pick up the jar, but Thaddeus motions for him not to. "I guess our friend was thirsty too," says Thaddeus laughingly.

"Yes, he was, father," says Hugo with a smile.

"This really is a beautiful spot, my son, simply beautiful."

"Yes father, it is very tranquil too and my dog you will be pleased to know earns his keep."

"Is that right?" asks Thaddeus?

"Yes, Ambrose can smell out a truffle quicker that a wild boar."

"Well, that is good news, Hugo. Do you find many truffles here?"

"Yes, father, quite few."

"I love truffles, Hugo, and I would be willing to purchase some from you from time to time should you have any extra."

"May I ask a question of you father?"

"Yes, of course, my son."

"Do you believe that a person can be cursed?"

"Cursed?"

"Yes, cursed."

"Cursed in what way, Hugo?"

"Well, since I was a child I have more or less been an outcast. I like people, but they rarely like me."

"That is nonsense, Hugo, everyone likes you."

"With all due respect, father, I can be around any group of people for only a short time and soon begin to alienate them one by one, or all at once it seems. I have mostly stayed to myself and I am often loved in a crisis because I am will to do jobs that most others will not do, but this just to find acceptance and that rarely lasts if at all."

"I did not know this, Hugo."

"I have at times made fun of someone less fortunate so that the people around me will take focus off of me and instead brutalize them, and when I do, I feel bad."

"That is an amazing insight, Hugo," says Thaddeus.

"So, I see myself as cursed, father."

"Perhaps it says more about the state of the world, than it does about you, Hugo?"

"What, father?"

"Well, we think that we have progressed so far in life, but perhaps we have not."

"I am not sure I understand, father?"

"Let us look at chickens, Hugo."

""Chickens? questions Hugo.

"Chickens have a pecking order and they will peck a chicken until it either fights back or yields to the will of the flock."

"I see, father."

"But sometimes, Hugo, they will peck another chicken to death just for being a little different from what they are used to seeing?"

"That is sad, father."

"But we are more that chickens, and with God's help, we, as a people will continue to grow in his likeness and grace."

"Amen, father," says Hugo with a melancholy voice.

"Amen is correct," Hugo, "Amen."

"The world was always more or less than I expected, father, and now it has become a very ugly place to me and to be honest I want nothing to do with it for the most. In this place, this place of solitude, I can feel safe and have so few visitors that I can manage to welcome them, yet I fear I will somehow lose myself should I go back to town. How would I ever see people there and not think of the horrible things that they had done to one another during that ugly, ugly sickness that killed so many, father?"

"Time heals all, Hugo, along with forgiveness and a lot of God's grace." Hugo drops his head to hide the despair that is resident on his long face. Thaddeus sits and says nothing and then begins to pray quietly. After awhile Hugo sighs loudly.

"Since you asked a question of me, may I ask a question of you, Hugo?" Hugo nods his head in the affirmative.

"If you could you would choose to stay in the church, moreover in this order of monks as well?"

"Yes, father, I think I would if I could."

"I see," replies Thaddeus. Hugo turns his head to the distant tree line and seems to tune everything else out for a few moments.

"I am always restless, father, it is just who I am. Let me get you some more water, father." Before Thaddeus can say a word in response, Hugo lifts the water jar from the ground and heads towards the spring, all in one motion. Hugo comes back from the spring with the jar in hand and finds Father Thaddeus standing next to where they had just been sitting.

"Brother Hugo," says Thaddeus, as he puts his right hand on Hugo's shoulder, "I speak here, today, as Prior, that I do hereby bless you and commission you to be the Church's representative of the spring which you just now drew water from. I also bless this spring and entrust you with its care and that you would make yourself available to any weary traveler who might happen by this way to help quench their thirst upon their travels. If you accept this charge then I do also declare that you are still a member of our order and a member in good standing. Furthermore, upon acceptance that you, as well as this spring are now and always will be under the protection of the church. Will you accept this charge, Friar Hugo?"

"I shall, father," replies Hugo as he struggles to hold back his tears.

"From this day forward you shall be known to us as Friar Hugo, Keeper of the Blessed Well Spring of Tuscany. Take heart, now, Friar Hugo, for you will always welcome at our table and are encouraged to pray for us often as we shall for you."

"May God bless you and keep you."

"And may God's peace be with you, my son."

"And also with you, father. In Christ's Holy name, we pray, amen."

Chapter Fifteen

"Good morning, my son!"

Diego strains as he looks partially into the sunlight at the approaching figure walking towards him. "Good morning, father, how are you today?" replies Diego.

"I am well my son," says Thaddeus. Your wife said I might find you here pruning and training vines." A small fire burns nearby in which Diego deposits any unwanted vine leaves and clippings.

"Yes, the work required in a vineyard seems to be never ending, but it is good work," said Diego with a serene look on his face. "The vines are young and need to be trained, but they should come along nicely. The olive trees have sprouted up nicely and a few of them are from the seed of olives I carried with me from my home village. I did not think they would still be any good, but six of them did prove to be alive, yet the seeds from the oranges did not survive. These vines are not from Catalonia, but they will have to do. They are all I have to work with, father," says Diego laughingly.

"I had no idea that you knew of such things, Diego."

"The best wine in the world comes from Catalonia and soon you shall see."

"I will take you up on that offer, my son," says Thaddeus with a large smile.

"Pity none of the orange seeds sprouted as they are from Catalonia as well, a place called Valencia."

"I have never heard of them," replies Thaddeus.

"They are famous the world around, and all the men in my family have relished them going back as far as our family history can be remembered," says Diego with a big smile. "What I would not give now for just one Valencia orange," comments Diego with his eyes now closed.

Thaddeus decides not to interrupt Diego's moment of remembrance and waits patiently for the moment to pass all the while wanting to laugh, but not daring to.

"I like your beard, father."

"Well, I think it makes me look a little more mature, and the last thing the people want is an immature Prior, Diego. It seems like only yesterday that you arrived in San Gimignano asking for directions, my son, and God has most certainly blessed you, a wife, a child upon the way, and a wonderful estate."

"He truly has, father."

"I wanted to meet with you to let you know that it is rumored I am being reassigned sometime in the near future, my son."

"To where is the Church sending you, father?"

"I may be reassigned to France."

"France, father?"

"Yes, to St. Julian the Poor, in Paris, actually."

"But I thought that they were happy with us, father?"

"And so I am and I sent word to the Vatican that my work here was too important to leave and eventually they may see it my way, so we shall see."

"Still staying in the bell tower, father?"

"No, it seems that I will be staying in my new home, a tower left to me apparently by Cardinal Beauvais."

"I did not know that he owned a tower, father?"

"Neither did I, but it is the one where his mother had lived, and I have accepted it with some reluctance."

"Why reluctance, father?"

"I have never owned any land, as my older brother will inherit our father's land and I thought that the oath of poverty I took last year had sealed my fate as far as owning property went, but apparently it did not."

"I believe that it is God's good blessing on your life for surviving that hell we all just went through in San Gimignano, father."

"And look at me, father, as I never dreamed in my wildest dreams that I would have my own vineyard, and now look around you."

"Perhaps," says Thaddeus pensively, "Perhaps."

"I was under the impression that you wanted to visit with me on some important business, Diego?"

"Yes, father, I do."

"So how may I be of service to you?"

"If you will forgive my continuing to work while we chat, father, I would like to speak with you of something of great importance to me."

"Of course my son, listening seems to be what I do best."

"I have decided that I would like to join the church and become a member of this parish, if you will have me?"

"Yes, of course, my son, and I can teach you the catechisms in order for you to convert to Catholicism."

"I am so happy that you have made this decision, Diego, happy indeed."

"Well father, I know that I am not yet a Catholic, but I feel that I must bare my soul before someone and have not done so in some time." Thaddeus says nothing and just listens intently.

"As you know, I came to San Gimignano those two plus years ago, but have to confess that I did not do so by accident, father. I am not from here and a Jew by heritage, but that is only part of the story."

"Yes, my son."

"As you might know there are stories of Jesus visiting my island many years ago to preach the gospel to the Jews who were living there, but what is not so widely known is that the Apostle Paul also visited there many years later. It is said that he even took a wife there before he returned to Rome and met his end."

"And you know of this how, my son?

"I can tell you, father, I was a very unhappy, young man who felt he had something to prove to the world and made my way here to do so. I had heard stories of a man who had worked for the church had discovered some very old scrolls that had come from Rome. That these scrolls were once the property of a Roman senator who had long ago fallen out of favor and had been banished to Fiesole to live out his days. I had also heard that the man who had possession of these scrolls had secretly sought to make a fortune from them, and his trail ended here."

"Gennero," says Thaddeus quietly.

"Or so I thought too, father. Yes, it was Gennero who came upon these scrolls, and I have to speak evil of the dead, but it was Cardinal Beauvais who attempted to profit from the scrolls, or should I say what the scrolls held."

"Are you sure of this, my son?"

"I am father," replies Diego.

"Do you remember the time when the good Cardinal was coming back from Rome and was ambushed by the highwaymen?"

"Yes,"

"... and you rescued him, Diego..."

"I remember."

"Well, one night last year I came across one of these men, drunk, and once alone, in fear of my sword. He confessed to his crimes to me, yet learned even more than I ever dreamed possible. He admitted that they had been in Avignon and had overheard two priests talking about a Cardinal who was coming there soon to attempt to sell something of great importance to the Pope himself. But learning that the Pope was not in Avignon, they wondered how could this be?"

"Beauvais," whispers Thaddeus to himself.

"They thought this was their chance to finally escape poverty when they saw the Cardinal (Beauvais) leave Avignon in all of his glory, and they decided that he might be the one. So, these men set out to rob him of this great treasure, but knew not what it might be. It was only by pure luck that the ambush took place where it did, or who knows what might have happened?"

"And what did you do with this admitted thief," the priest asks with a concerned look upon his face?

"I considered punishing him for his misdeeds, but decided to release him and told him that the Lord had been good to him this day.

"As indeed he had, my son," said Thaddeus with a slight smile.

"At this point I decided that Cardinal Beauvais must have the artifact that I sought and he would give it to me eventually, but most likely at the end of my sword, but the plague took his life without his revealing where he had hidden it. At this point, father, I no longer cared about acquiring the object as my heart had changed. God had worked a miracle in my life, father, and I now felt at home here in San Gimignano, in a land that I was not from.

"I have never told this to anyone, not even my new bride, but I must tell you," shares Diego quietly. "The same night after I rescued Father Beauvais, I had gone out to the persimmon trees to find something to eat and upon my return found a dying beggar lying next to the well in the piazza. This poor man begged for someone to pray with him before his imminent demise, and with no one seeming available, I decided to assist him in any way I could. While we were praying he asked me what it was that I was seeking. At first I did not understand the meaning of his words, but they pierced me like a sword into my most inner being. Again he asked me what it was that I sought, and with his he changed form and stood before me and glowed like the sun and reached out with his finger and touched my heart and with that, I was healed. He went on to tell me that God wanted to use me here in San Gimignano, and so here I have stayed and even took a wife as well from among the people. Thaddeus only looks at Diego with his eyes now wide open."

"I know, father, you must certainly find me as one who has lost his mind, but I tell you father, it did happen just as I have described." A short period of silence hangs heavy in the air while Diego trains his vines and the priest looks pensively about the vineyard.

"So, what had you been seeking when you came here, my son," asks Thaddeus nervously?
"I sought that which belonged to me and now must be gone, and its whereabouts buried with him who concealed it, father."

"Why do you say this item belongs to you, Diego?"

" As you may not know, many years ago, Paul, a servant of Jesus Christ, tore a piece of his cloak and gave it to a Roman soldier, a Praetorian of great importance, and instructed this soldier to place it on his daughter and that she would be healed. The soldier, whose name was Titus, did not take this man, Paul, seriously, but as he watched his daughter languishing and nearing death, he decided that he nothing to lose, and did as Paul had instructed him. To his great surprise, she sat up and asked for something to eat." Thaddeus says nothing and his eyes grow larger and more fixated as Diego tells his story. "Soon Titus becomes a believer in the Lord, Jesus Christ, and not longer after so did his daughter. Once restored, she began, under her father's supervision, to visit this man who had displayed God's greatness and she grew in the Lord daily. Titus changed her name to Raffaella, which she agreed because loosely translated means "God heals"."

"But how could these things be possible and how could you know about this, my son?"

"I know this, father, because that woman was my great grandmother, several times over."

"But you are a Jew, and Titus was a Roman?"

"Her husband was a Jew, father. Her husband; who was her husband, Diego?"

It suddenly dawns on the priest what the answer had to be, and then says, "It was Paul himself. He was her husband? But she was a child, was she not, Diego?"

"She was not a child and she married Paul shortly before they left Rome and together they traveled to the island that I would eventually call home, Minorca".

"But why travel to Minorca?"

"There was a Jewish settlement there, father, and even rumors that the Lord himself had once visited Minorca. It is also said that some of the earliest disciples had settled in Minorca after our Savior descended into heaven and Paul thought it would be a good place from which to spread the gospel from as well as to raise a family. Paul settled down for a brief time and was a good father, but grew restless for Rome, and his mission there which he saw up to this point as a failure. Paul learned that there was a new Emperor in Rome and saw this as a sign from God and sailed for Rome shortly after. Raffaella begged Paul not to go and reminded him that they had a home together as she was now with child. His calling was too much for him and Paul departed anyway and promised to soon return. Not long after Paul reached Rome, he was arrested and put to death by the new Emperor who saw himself as a god. I was told that Paul believed that the Emperor might become a believer and then eventually the whole of Rome, or possibly once converted, the Emperor might possibly turn the reins of power over to Paul himself."

"I have never heard of his, my son."

"Well, Paul was a citizen of Rome, so I guess it was possible, but would have had been truly God's will for it to have taken place at all."

"Agreed," replies Thaddeus. "Can you imagine what might have happened had Paul succeeded, Diego?"

"Well, he apparently talked about perhaps setting up a second capital in Jerusalem itself and his ruling Rome from there."

"Can you imagine Peter and James having to come to Emperor Paul for permission to run the church's affairs," says the priest laughingly.

Diego chuckles and continues. "It seems that Paul thought this would all take place when he went to Rome, yet when it did not happen, he even questioned his own calling for a time. Once a new Emperor was installed, Paul saw this as possibly God's hand and made the decision to then go to Rome."

"And it cost him his life," retorts Thaddeus solomnly.

"Eventually Raffaella gave birth to a daughter, who she named Paula, in honor of her father. She and her Paula lived the remainder of their live on that island and always talked about the cloth given to Titus by Paul all those years ago and the healing which it brought that day. The legion of the "sacred cloth" was passed down from generation to generation until it reached me. It was always believed that a Roman senator had taken it, but the exact location remained a mystery until recently. And so my journey began for Tuscany, not knowing what I might find once I arrived, little did I know I would discover my home here."

"What of the cloth, Diego?"

"It seems that its whereabouts died with the Cardinal and I am fine with that as I no longer need it to make me whole."

"I see, my son."

Thaddeus starts to tell Diego that he has the cloth in his possession, but at the last minute does not.

"I just wanted to confess my sin of deceit and ask your forgiveness, father." After a short pause, Thaddeus tells Diego that he forgives him and that his confession is safe with him. "You will stay for our midday meal, father?"

"I do have a few things to do today, my son."

"My wife would never forgive me if I let you leave without tasting her cooking, father."

"We are having some excellent lamb, father."

"How could I resist then? I accept your gracious invitation to dine."

"Excellent; Salice will be so excited to have company. Come now, father, let us go to the house and prepare for our meal." Both men walk up the hill to a beautiful rock house which overlooks the newly planted vineyard and orchards.

Chapter Sixteen

"If you wish for your future children to be accepted here, they must be raised as Jews, and the males must be circumcised in accordance with our laws, Saul."

"Again, gentlemen, I tell you that you must be born again. It is the heart that Christ circumcises, not the body. For the flesh withers and passes away, but the word of God remains forever."

"So you will not consent to your heirs being circumcised, Saul?"

"It is true that I was born Saul, a Pharisee and the son of a Pharisee. Was brought up in the proper ways of honoring our laws and eventually became a servant of the Temple. But I do remind you that my name is now Paul, a name that the very God in which you claim to serve gave to me when he changed me from serving the Sanhedrin with great zeal and remade me into the man you see before you. I am Paul, a servant of Jesus Christ, and now stand boldly in front of you here today, you keepers of the law. Yet, if you truly knew the Lord, then you would know this to be so," says Paul, "for Christ fulfilled the law when he died on the cross and on the third day, God raised him from the grave."

The Jewish began to mutter and argue among themselves over Paul's words.

"Moreover, when Jesus healed a man and was rebuffed for healing on the Sabbath, did he not call those present hypocrites? So do I declare you a hypocrites; a den of vipers, you so called men of God now living here in Minorca. It is not I who serve Satan, but rather you deceivers of men requiring them to bear burdens that you are not willing to carry yourself."

At hearing this, the Jewish elders immediately stood up and began to leave the synagogue. One man stopped in front of Paul and said, "You are no Jew and you are unclean as well as your heirs, and then he spat upon the ground."

"On the contrary, I and any who believe upon the Lord Jesus Christ are completed Jews for having believed upon his death and resurrection," declares Paul.

"Again with this Jesus, Saul, and your blasphemy!"

At that point Paul leaves the synagogue along with two other followers of Jesus and head for Paul's home where they are greeted by his wife, a noticeably pregnant, Raffella.

As she greets Paul and his friends, Raffella asks, "Please tell me that you have not been squabbling with the Rabbis' down in village again, Paul."

"Only setting them straight on issues of the law and the will God, my dear," replies Paul.

Raffella just rolls her eyes and smiles at her husband and then says, "You know that it only antagonizes them and gets you upset."

"As iron sharpens iron, so one man sharpens another," states Paul quickly.

"Proverbs," quips Raffella with a large smile.

"You learn very fast, my love," says Paul with delight as he kisses his wife on the cheek.

"The evening meal will be ready soon, so will our guests be joining us this evening, my husband?" asks Raffella with a blush in her cheek. Both men politely excuse themselves and with a Christian embrace do the men leave and depart the pleasant, but modest home.

The smell of soup cooking as well as the aroma of fresh bread fill the air and Paul reclines on a large pillow on the floor and loosens his sandals. "Do I have time for a quick nap before dinner, my love?"

"Yes, a short nap, but do not get too comfortable there, we have plans for tonight," she replies.

"Oh, right, I will not sleep long." As Paul settles in and gets comfortable on the pallet, he goes over the details of the day in his mind and then asks quietly in prayer for God's further guidance and wisdom. "I think today went better than it had before, Raffella."

She does not reply and continues tending to her meal preparations. The sound of a guitar making melodic music can be heard faintly coming from a distant neighbor's house. After awhile, Paul breaks the silence and says, "I think that they are getting closer to seeing things more to our point of view, my dear."

Raffella enters the room carrying bread to the dining table, and replies, "You know very well that they will never accept me as being a Jew, converted or otherwise, and my being Christian complicates things for them even more, Paul."

"The Lord will make a way, and in time you will see, that the Lord will make a way," says Paul, as he takes an orange from a bowl on the table and begins to peel it.

"They will never truly accept me as one of them nor will they ever accept our children as anything other than unclean," says Raffella sadly and quietly.

"But our brothers and sisters in Christ all accept you and love you, my wife, and we will always have a place here with them." Raffella says nothing and goes back into the cooking area of their home and after consuming the orange as he always does, Paul then falls into a deep, deep sleep.

"Paul, your journey is not over and soon you shall see where it is that I will send you. Fear not, for greater is he who is within you that he who is in the world," continues the voice in Paul's dream. Paul awakes and quickly sits up and looks around to see who had been speaking to him when he realizes that he has been dreaming. The night goes into morning and Paul goes into the village to learn that there is a new ruler in Rome, a new Caesar named Nero.

"When were you going to tell me, Paul, that you are leaving," asks Raffella?

"It will only be for a little while and I will not be leaving for a few more days, my dear, and do not be concerned about these matters as the Lord will most surely go with me along the way."

"But why does it have to be now, before our baby is born?"

"Who knows God's timing, but as scripture says, He desires obedience over sacrifice," replies Paul. Raffella sits quietly in her room and says nothing as Paul attempts to comfort her, only to have her pull away from him. Paul walks toward the front door and he then exits quietly.

While walking into the village, Paul looks towards heaven and asks quietly, "I am your servant, oh Lord, but please give me a sign that what I do is right and in your will." As Paul walks a little farther he notices a fellow believer walking towards the village as well and Paul invites him to join him.

"So, by now I will assume that you have heard that there is a new ruler in Rome, Paul?"

"I have heard, Simeon, but I know little of him."

"He is a relative of the last emperor, Claudius, and I do not know much as well, yet I have heard that he is a pagan and has on occasion even referred to himself as a god."

"Do they not all live under this illusion, Brother Simeon?"

"That is true, Paul, but if only once there was a ruler in Rome who instead of believing that he was god, actually served God?"

"Yes, that would be a joy," replies Paul and then he reflects back to a time when he first entered Rome and thought that he might witness to Caesar and once a believer how things might be better for all men.

"Think of it, Paul, a Christian Rome, what could be impossible then, my brother?"

"Well, let us then pray that the Lord soften Caesar's heart and that he might not only hear the good news but that he also receive it, Simeon."

"Who would ever be brave enough to approach Caesar and have the nerve to tell him that not only was he not Devine but that he had to fall to his knees and serve the one true God, Paul?"

"Who indeed," asks Paul quietly as the two men approach the village square and sit among some of the other men talking nearby.

"So, tell us brothers, what were you two whispering about just now?"

"Whispering, I assure you sir, I have never found the need to whisper," replies Paul with a smile.

"Have you not heard, there is a new ruler in Rome," responds Simeon. The men all turn towards Paul and Simeon and take notice. "Our new ruler is the nephew of Claudius, and his name is Nero," continues Simeon.

"What do we know of him?" asks the men as they begin to talk quietly among themselves.

One man looks at Paul and says, "I fear that this could be bad for us as I have heard that he is cruel and somewhat deranged."

"Well, he is in charge and we must render unto Caesar my brothers," says Paul a little bit cynically.

"Perhaps he will not remember us on the extreme reaches of his empire, questions another man?"

"We pay taxes do we not, so he will not over look us," whispers another man?

"Just once I wish we could have a ruler like the ones of old, someone like David or even Saul," says Simeon.

"Yes exactly; someone who respected the Lord Most High and followed his laws," says an extremely elderly man.

"Or someone who knows Christ as his savior," adds Paul. Part of the men raise their hands in disgust over Paul's mentioning of Jesus being the Messiah and then begin to argue. Paul and Simeon do not stay to debate and head to small inn to relax and discuss business.

After a time, Simeon asks Paul, "Why have you been so quiet, brother?"

"I am sorry, but I have been preoccupied this morning, Simeon."

"So, I noticed, brother," says Simeon with a chuckle, "Anything you wish to share?"

"Rome," replies Paul.

"Rome, what about Rome?" queries Simeon.

"I may be going back to Rome and sooner rather than later, brother."

"But your wife is with child, Paul, why Rome and why now?"

"I will share with you in confidence that when I first entered Rome all those years ago I was certain that the Lord was going to work a miracle in Rome and that Caesar would undergo a conversion and enter the household of the Lord."

"A pagan Caesar coming to know Christ, how could that ever be, Paul?"

"Caesar is Caesar, but he is only a man like any other man and subject to the Lord's will as are all men. If I could only share the good news of Jesus Christ with him, perhaps the Lord would soften his heart like he did Pharaoh's all those years ago and what miracle that would be, Simeon."

"You are not serious, Paul. He would most certainly put you to death even if by some incredible circumstance you would were to even get an audience with Caesar in the first place."

"To die is gain, brother," replies Paul.

"This is madness, Paul, madness."

"Get behind me, Satan, for it is the Lord's will, not yours," states Paul strongly as he rises from the table and leaves the room without saying another word.

"Thank you for coming to see me on such short notice, Brother Paul." Paul looks up and sees that he is being addressed by a young man in royal robes sitting on a throne and a crucifix hanging from his neck.

"Yes, my lord, I am at your service as always," replies Paul.

"I have been seeking the Lord and believe that he wants me to make Jerusalem the eastern most capital of Rome and I would like to place you there in charge as my Proconsul," says the young ruler.

"If that your wish, then it is of course my command Caesar. Please pray and ask the Lord if it is his will for you as well as for Rome, and upon learning the Lord's answer I will then either move forward with these plans or seek God for another path."

"I thank you for understanding my need to seek our Lord and Savior Jesus Christ on this great matter and will reveal to you what the Lord has born witness unto me as soon as I know myself."

"Amen, brother," replies Caesar. "So will you stay and dine with us this evening, Paul?"

"I am honored at your request, highness, but my work of feeding the poor might suffer should I not be there to encourage those who assist me."

"I understand, so I will await your answer and I again than you for your courage in sharing the gospel with me and allowing me to come to the knowledge of Jesus Christ, my brother Paul."

"Praise God, for it is the Lord who raises up a leader, not I," testifies Paul.

Paul leaves the royal palace in Rome during a light rain and is escorted by his own personal guard, who of course is Titus himself. People are scurrying from place to place as Paul makes his way back to his quarters. "I must see to the needs of the poor and feel unworthy to take on such a position as Proconsul, my dear friend Titus," grumbles Paul quietly.

"It was a miracle what the Lord did in Caesar's heart and it was a great healing that quieted the voices which maddened our Emperor. And when two of the generals refused to yield to Caesar once he gave his life and will over the will of the Lord, it was I who engaged and defeated these generals in battle but only by the Lord's grace did I win these battles. I was out numbered three to one and the Lord was mighty in battle and went before us striking our opponents with fear and they fled at our approach."

"So why would the Lord not want to have you there in Jerusalem keeping watch over the Holy Land?" asks Titus. "Have not the injustices stopped in the land, and are the crucifixions no more," continues Titus? "You must be willing to seek the Lord and as you always say, the Lord desires obedience over sacrifice," says Titus laughingly.

Paul suddenly stops walking and pauses for a moment, then looks at Titus and says, "That is written in the Book of Samuel, and he does desire obedience over sacrifice, brother Titus, so his will be done, not mine."

At this time, Paul opens his eyes and realizes that he has been dreaming, but the message of obedience over sacrifice echoes quietly in his head and noticing that he has not awaken his wife, he closes his eyes and drifts back off to sleep once again.

It is early in the morning the following month and Raffella is even more noticeably pregnant but not yet ready to give birth. Paul looks at Rafaela, hugs her, and just sits next to her on their bed for awhile looking at her and their unborn child. Rafaela begins to cry faintly and Paul hugs her more closely. "Why do you have to go now, Paul, why now", she asks repeatedly?

"Now we have been all through this before, my love, and we both agreed that it is God's will that I go to Rome," says Paul.

"I know, husband, but I do not wish to have this child alone, nor do I wish to raise him or her alone, Paul."

"Now, now, what is all of this talk about raising him alone, my wife?"

"I have heard the women talking about this new Caesar, this Nero, and they say he is insane and even defiles his own sister."

"Nothing new under the sun, my wife, and the Lord will guide my path whatever may come," replies Paul. Raffella sobs more intensely. Paul attempts to comfort her and then slowly rises and makes his way over to his traveling pack which Rafaela has helped him prepare and then sits down to put on his sandals and binds them tightly on his feet and legs.

"Why must it be you who goes to Rome, Paul? Why not someone else, like Timothy, or even Barnabas?"

"Because the Lord has called me, my wife, so I go and do the Lord's will."

"How do you know he has not called one of them, possibly Timothy or even Silas? It has been so long since you have heard from any of them, Paul." Both sit quietly for awhile with Paul almost motionless while Raffella nervously fidgets and squirms. "Sometimes I wonder why you ever married me, Paul."

"You know why I married you, Raffella; what a silly question."

"I loved you from the first time I saw you, Paul, but I never felt that was the case with you." Paul remains quiet. "Why did you marry me, Paul, why?"

Paul moves closer to her and looks into her eyes. "When I first realized that you might be interested in me, I tried to avoid you."

"Avoid me? Why on earth would you do that, Paul?"

"It never dawned on me that as the man who once ministered to you, that I should one day marry you. I guess I was just tired too, my wife."

"Tired," Raffella asks?

"Yes, tired. Tired of yearning for a woman, any woman other than my long departed wife, and for me to do that would be to dishonor her and even more so, to dishonor God. I thought that with age and time my need for companionship would just go away, but it did not. I needed to be touched and it sometimes almost made me go mad. I saw singleness as a gift and though I asked the Lord for this gift, it never came. I just could not elude this, this thorn in my side and decided to marry so that my soul would not be in jeopardy."

"Luckily I was available," replies Raffella cynically.

"That is how our life began, but it soon changed and I found myself more and more dependent on you and that eventually quieted the memories of my first wife and I was finally able to love you, and love you I have."

"Love me, Paul?"

"Yes, I love you with all of my heart, and if I did not know for certain that the Lord was calling me to Rome, not even a hundred well armed men could make me leave your side, even if for only one day."

"Then do not go, my husband, it may not be God calling you to Rome, but a trick of the Devil." Paul sighs and then Raffella begins to weep.

"What is that you are wearing around your neck? asks Paul. "Is that part of that old garment I once tore and gave to your father so the Lord might heal you?"

"Yes, it is." She replies.

"But I thought that the senate ended up with that," he questions.

"Before my father was forced to give his report on you and the garment to the senator, he decided to tear it in half and hide it away, even if it meant his own death for doing so," she added, "and gave it to me before just before our wedding."

"I see," replies Paul.

"You know that old saying, 'something old, something new…"

"Something borrowed, something blue', Rafella added.

"You have bestowed a lot of sentimental value to this I see, my dear," says Paul. Rafella smiles.

"Now enough of this talk, please dry your eyes and hug me good bye and I will be to Rome and back before you know it," says Paul with a forced smile.

"No quick scripture off of the top of your head, Paul, to dissuade my anguish?"

"No, I believe that most likely you already know them, my love," says Paul. He hugs her and more importantly she hugs him, tightly.

"I will pray for you and this Nero, and you come back to me as soon as the Lord will allow, husband."

"I will Rafaela and thank you for your prayers, as I am sure that they shall sustain me through my journey."

"The ladies have said that they will look in on you and be here at the time of birth. "How I would love to see our baby take its first breath as it enters this life."

"I will tell you every detail upon your return; you will miss nothing, husband," says Rafaela with a smile. "Now go and get this thing over now, husband and worry not, for I am in the hands of the Lord as well." Paul smiles with joy. "Besides, you would not be the man I married if you did not go and attempt this great thing, my husband. Do you have enough food for the trip, she asks?"

"Yes, I do," he replies. "A piece of cheese, a hard crust of bread and two oranges in your pocket is most certainly not enough to keep anyone alive," states Rafaela. "Let me fix you something to take with you."

"The Lord will provide," says Paul, and then he hugs her, kisses her one last time and departs for Rome as the sun now begins to rise. "And do not eat too much before you get on the ship; you know how sea sick you get when you eat too much," Rafaela calls out. Paul nods his head in acknowledgement as he makes his way down their steps. Rafaela watches him leave as long as she can and then goes back into their home and drops to her knees and prays for his safe return.

"I do not agree with you Lord that you take my husband away from me even if only for a short time, so close to my time of birth. By faith I will trust in you, oh Lord, for your grace is sufficient for me. I will trust in you, heavenly father." She prays again as angels, unseen, come and minister to her while she weeps.

The weeks come and go and a baby is born to her. She wraps the little girl in warm clothing and sings to her as she feeds her. Each morning she walks to the window facing Rome and looks for her husband's return, yet he does not. The baby grows up to be a little girl and she sits sometimes daily with her mother as they both look out the window hoping for Paul's appearance on the horizon as she tells her daughter of the great task her father has taken on and how he has gone to Rome to meet with Caesar and how she is never to forget what a truly blessed man is. Rafaela tells her of her father's meeting of the Lord on the road to Damascus, of his travels around the world, of the times he spent in prison for the sake of the gospel, and of his love for her.

"Your father serves the Lord Most High and has surely found favor in his eyes, Paulette, and never forget this so that one day you may tell your children as well," says Rafaela to her child.

Chapter Seventeen

The winter's day was cold and a young priest reads the engraving above the church doors which says, St. Julian the Poor. Upon entering the edifice, the priest notices a figure kneeling in front of the church. The light coming through the windows keeps the young man from making out clearly just exactly who is praying, but the figure soon stands and hails to him saying, "Bonjourno"! "Bonjour,

to you as well," replies the young priest.

"Please forgive me, my son, but I sometimes miss the sound of my native tongue," replies the figure. "How may I be of service to you, father?"

"I am Father Beauvais and have just completed my studies at the seminary and have been told that I have assigned to this church to be the assistant pastor."

"I knew another Father Beauvais at one time in San Gimignano, Italy; is there any chance you might be related, father?" asks the man.

"He was a great uncle if I am not mistaken, your Eminence," replies Beauvais, as he moves closer and realizes that he is addressing an Abbot.

"Yes, I see the resemblance now, but it has been many, many years since I last laid eyes on him, my son."

"You have his eyes most assuredly," replies the priest with a smile. "I am Father Thaddeus, the Abbot of St. Julian the Poor. I will take you to meet the Prior, Father Hugo, and then you can get settled in."

"Thank you, your Eminence," replied Beauvais.

"What do you parents call you?" asks Thaddeus?

"They named me Gabriel, an old family name handed down through the generations."

After a brief pause, Thaddeus continues, "So I guess that you are eager to start your duties then, father?"

"Yes, I am, your Eminence."

"Please call me father. Do you speak French fluently, my son?"

"Yes, father, as I was born and raised just west of Paris near Orne."

"Excellent, for as you most likely already know the French love to hear their own language, replies Thaddeus." "And why not, it such a beautiful language when spoken correctly… something I have yet to accomplish in all of my years here. I think you will like St. Julian with its gardens; it has become a place of reflection and spiritual retreat in an otherwise hectic world, or so I have found it to be," reflects Thaddeus. Beauvais smiles and listens intently. "Now, follow me young man and I shall introduce you to the Prior, and of course welcome to St. Julian."

A few miles away in a modest hut that has seen better days, a small man with facial hair, struggles to rise from his nightly slumber. His right leg is bent and of little use to him, his hands heavily calloused. He reaches out to finely crafted wooden crutch, and with it finally stands semi-erect. His breathing increases as he struggles to move away from his sleeping pallet. An old mirror hangs in one corner of his living room and with great care he runs a comb through his unwashed hair. He notices that his last bit of bread has fallen victim to a thieving rodent sometime in the night, so he makes his way out the door wearing the same clothes he slept in (one of two he owns), in hopes of finding breakfast almost spilling his night jar which eventually sees its way outdoors as well. A neighbor walks his dog past the hut and announces a hardy, "Good morning," while his dog barks excitedly and pulls at leather leash around its neck.

"Good morning, sir," replies Jonah as he closes his door behind him.

The day starts out overcast and there are only a few snowflakes on the ground, a hint of wood smoke was present from a distant fire and there was a familiar bite in the air. After several hours of laborious walking, Jonah finally finds himself near the River Seine and hears a familiar voice from behind, a voice that had been noticeably absent. As Jonah turns he recognizes a familiar face, and he smiles.

"Is it you that we have to thank for this weather, Jonah?"

With a slight laugh, Jonah replies, "Ges indeed, Gabe. Yes, indeed."

"How are you old friend," asks Beauvais?

"And it is Father Beauvais as well, my son," replies Beauvais with a smile.

After a brief hug, Jonah asks, "Father Beauvais, is it? That is quite an accomplishment a man of your age."

"Alright, that is enough of your flattery, Jonah, and if I am not mistaken, you have not yet eaten today?"

"Well, I was going to eat this morning, but I had such a large dinner last evening when I dined at the king's palace," retorts Jonah.

"The king's palace, Jonah? asks Beauvais.

"Yes, poor chap, cannot make a move without me it seems."

After both men chuckle, Beauvais suggests that his friend join him for a meal at his newly assigned post and his friend accepts his gracious offer. The meal is simple, made up of bread, cheese, and a few sausages with only water to drink.

The day passes slowly and as sun begins to set, Jonah makes his way back to his abode, humble as it is, it is home and most assuredly it is all he has. When he finally reaches the door, the sun has already set and there is no moon light for him to find way through the house. As Jonah gropes for his small dining table, he is relieved to finally bump into it, but now he knows that his bed cannot be far way. As he lies in his bed he hears what sounds like a mouse rustling around in one corner and addresses him as a welcomed visitor. "Have you come to see Jonah tonight and keep him company, my friend? What is our name, my little friend?" The mouse says nothing in response and quickly ceases stirring at hearing Jonah's voice. After a brief chat, Jonah begins to think about his day, the meal that he had with his friend Beauvais, and how his stomach was already growling again with hunger. Pulling an apple from under his jacket, Jonah eats it as if it is a meal prepared by gourmet chefs and once finished, tosses it in the direction of where he had heard the mouse stirring and says sympathetically, "Bonne appetite," before shaking off the cold, rolling over and falling to sleep.

The morning arrives along with an empty stomach and a chill in the air. A small fire is eventually going in a small hearth and one problem for the day is solved, if only for a short while. Jonah makes his way out of his door as usual and misses the little dog that once accompanied him on his daily quests for food. In the distance bread is baked and the aroma could not be denied and Jonah's growling stomach refuses to quiet itself, so towards the bakery Jonah begins his day closing a small gate behind him. A gate that was more for look than security, yet it did give him some sense of reassurance. Jonah makes his way past a very large family living in a small building near the Seine, a family which has more mouths to feed than resources. He overhears the couple arguing over their lack food and the children he noticed were not well bathed, yet Jonah says nothing and minds his own business as he makes his way down the cobblestone lane. A rabbit suddenly appears in Jonah's path and just as quickly disappears with two children in hot pursuit in hopes of making him a well earned meal. The children are dressed in rages and have most likely have no idea what bathing is presumes Jonah, and he contributes that most likely to poor way the children were raised. Soon the source of the smell of fresh baked bread is apparent and a middle aged man is carrying baskets of bread out to a horse drawn cart while a small boy stands close by waiting to depart with him. The man moves in and out of the bakery side door and while the boy waits calmly. Upon what looks like his third departure, Jonah finally gets up the nerve to approach him as he has on occasion in the past and asks for a job of him. "Get out of here, you beggar, and never show yourself again or you will feel the back of my hand, now be gone with you!" the man roared! With that, Jonah scurries as best he can back across the street. The man and the boy depart upon their route and Jonah begins to think of other ways he might earn his breakfast when he hears a quiet voice summoning him from the direction of the bakery. He turns and sees an older white-haired man in the door way holding a few croissants in one hand and a broom in the other. Jonah moves quickly towards the man only looking briefly over his shoulder to make that no trouble might return suddenly and then smiles at the old man.

"Here, please take these croissants as they are too old to sell and dispose of them for me and in so doing I will reward you with a piece of cheese," says the old man.

Jonah agrees quickly and the old man thanks Jonah and then reaches into pocket and produces some pieces of cheese wrapped in cloth and then hands him a small piece of cheese which is received eagerly. The man smiles and discusses the weather, the clear skies, and the crispness of the morning and begins to sweep the stoop of the doorway. Jonah quickly eats the croissants and cheese and then gently takes the broom from his new found friend and insists upon sweeping the doorway himself. The old man then excuses himself and goes back into the bakery at the beckon call of an angry woman inside, where Jonah can hear a brief argument begin. Once the porch is cleaned, Jonah sets the broom inside the door and departs for the center of Paris. Jonah tries not think of the charity he just accepted and decided to think of it as the old man had suggested, wages paid for services rendered. As he gets closer to the river area of Paris he suddenly notices the smell of smoke in the distance, a smell he has known before which usually signaled someone losing their home to fire. Most unfortunate was the person or persons on the receiving end, which surely meant necessity of most to begin the struggle to begin again in an all too unforgiving world.

"Father Beauvais, you will be assisting the sisters giving out soup this morning to the needy?" asks Father Hugo.

"Yes father, as you had requested," replies the young Beauvais with a nervous smile. "The 'corporal works of mercy.'"

Hugo smilingly nods in the affirmative. "The sisters have prepared the soup?" asks Hugo.

"I was going to see to that now, father," says Beauvais. "And the man with the bread has already arrived and I have paid him as you instructed, father," says Beauvais.

"Excellent," replies Hugo, and do not forget to say the blessing over the food as well before you serve it."

"Yes, father, I will remember." Hugo departs and Beauvais makes his way to the front of the church where a large crowd has already arrived and the sisters stand ready with a large kettle of soup and a few baskets of assorted loaves of bread. Three monks also stand nearby as they had cooked the soup during the entire morning as they awaited the sisters from the convent and the new priest to finally arrive. Beauvais asks the sisters quietly if all is ready to begin serving and with the sister's reassurance that all was ready, the priest nervously began to address the crowd. "Shall we pray?" asks Beauvais loudly as he raises his hands over the people there. "Oh, heavenly father, we pray that you bless this bounty we are about to partake of, and pray that it nourishes our bodies as well as our souls and gives Glory to God. We ask that Mary the mother of our blessed Savior, as well as the patriarchs look down upon us and protect us, in the name of the father, and of the son, and of the Holy Ghost, amen." With the last word of the prayer uttered, the crowd now begins to line up single file to receive their soup this day.

"Father Beauvais, please come and dine with me this evening, as I wish to talk with you and see how you are settling in," requests Thaddeus.

"I am honored father, and will look forward to it. Until then, father," replies the abbot with a smile and he departs for the gardens near the monastery.

"Heavenly father, I thank you, as always, for your giving me life and shelter in this world and the world here after. I thank you for intrusting these people here in this outpost of Christendom, and I do not wish to seem ungrateful as you and you alone truly know my heart, but I do long for Italy. Oh Holy Father in heaven," prays Thaddeus quietly. "I thank you for this fine, cool, and sunny morning, the serenity of this garden, all which you have provided, yet something is missing, Lord, something is missing." In the distance, Thaddeus notices the approach of the Prior, Hugo, and ceases praying to welcome him.

"Am I disturbing you, father," asks Hugo humbly.

"Not at all, and I of course as always welcome your presence," says Thaddeus. Hugo walks towards the bench where Thaddeus was not sitting and then sits down beside him. "I love this garden, Hugo, even in the winter."

The winter birds dart around in the leaf bare trees, and look for food. Thaddeus reaches into his pocket and pulls out a crust of bread and begins to break off small pieces. He then throws the bread to the birds which eat and then dart away; that is until another crumb is tossed their way. Hugo looks around and then asks, "Is that not an apple tree, father?"

"Yes, indeed it is, and it makes the best cider each fall," replies Thaddeus. "I believe that the Lord created this for a purpose, or purposes, and one of those purposes, Hugo, is for our pleasure, even if only for our viewing pleasure." Thaddeus continues to feed the birds and almost solely concentrate on them.

"I am sorry, what did you say, Hugo?"

"I was saying that I find peace in this garden, father, as I once did that small farm near San Gimignano," responds Hugo.

"Ah yes, the farm with the spring water and a dog I believe, if memory serves," says Thaddeus joyfully.

"Yes, father, he was the best dog and could find a truffle like none other," says Hugo.

"I remember him well, Hugo, and that was many years ago, and through your hard work and God's grace you have come a long way from that farm," replies Thaddeus.

"Yes, father, thanks to you," says Hugo, "for if it had not been for you I would have never become a monk and later gone to seminary let alone become a Prior."

"And why not, Hugo, you are as worthy as any man to receive God's goodness," states Thaddeus firmly." Both men pause in silence.

"San Gimignano was not an easy place after the plague arrived and ravaged the town folk, Father Hugo, and with so many dead. The Church needed good men on conscious to rise up and serve God… men like you, yes, we needed you, Hugo, and never forget that. Some days I long for Italy, and for Musit, along with Cardinal Beauvais," reflects Thaddeus.

"Please forgive me, Eminence, but I am of a different opinion when it comes to San Gimignano." Thaddeus looks a bit puzzled.

"I have to confess that the majority of the time I was afraid there," replies Hugo.

"Afraid?" inquires Thaddeus.

"Yes, very much afraid that I might unknowingly sin and God might punish me with the sickness and I would most surely die. I was very careful to say my prayers and search my heart before God in hopes that I might find favor with him and see another day." Thaddeus listens empathetically to his friend. "And when I had to bury the dead, I would hold my breath for long periods of time so that I would not inhale the vapors which rose from the bodies. I was only too happy to see them disappear under the soil," said Hugo.

"Those were maddening times, dear brother, maddening, and it was only by God's grace that any of us ever made it out alive," says Thaddeus.

"Now how is young Beauvais fairing in his first post?" asks the abbot after a long pause.

"He is doing well and seems to have made a friend," says Hugo.

"A friend?" asks Thaddeus.

"Someone named Jonah, a man with one bad leg and he walks with an odd gate, father."

"Poor as a church mouse and rarely baths?" inquires Thaddeus. "Asks theological questions as well?"

"Do you know him, father?"

"I believe so and his name is not Jonah, or at least that is not the name he was given at birth, Hugo. Jonah, as you call him, was once in regular attendance here at St. Julian, but I have not seen him in attendance for several years now."

"Shall I have a word with Father Beauvais and dismiss this man who calls himself Jonah, father?" ask Hugo?

"No, I see no reason to do that at this point, but I suggest that you keep a careful eye on this man and see what comes of it, Father Hugo.   And who knows … some good may come of it."

Chapter Eighteen

A monk walks to the door of the abbot's study and knocks lightly. "Yes, come in," says Thaddeus.

The monk enters and says, "There is an official communication for you, Eminence."

"Thank you," says the Abbot as he takes the letter and opens it.

The monk withdraws from the room and Thaddeus begins to smile as he reads. He then rises and goes out to the cloisters and sees Prior Hugo there saying his prayers. "Father, may see you in my study after morning prayers?" inquires Thaddeus.

"Of course father, right away," replies Hugo.

In about an hour's time, there is a knock at the door of the study to which there is a reply, "Come in father," and with that Hugo enters.

"Yes, father, you wanted to see me?"

"Please sit down Hugo as I must make some things known to you so you can continue the business of the Church here in Paris. Hugo looks puzzled, yet does as instructed by the abbot. "I have been writing to the Vatican and have finally been given leave to preach the gospel, much as St. Anthony of Padua was, and shall be leaving my post here in the spring."

"You are joining the Franciscan Order, father?"

"Yes, Hugo as I have heard the call and wish to further the Lord's work much as St. Francis did just a few, short years ago."

"If I may ask, father, who will be replacing you as abbot?"

"Why you of course, Hugo. As the Prior you are the only logical course and told the Cardinal as such." Hugo looks stunned and bewildered. "Take heart, Hugo, for you have been through much more difficult assignments in the past, and you will make the adjustment more easily that you might know. This is the letter from the Church ordering your installation as Abbot, and I am to stay on as advisor until we both feel that you are ready to take on your responsibilities at St. Julian. Please call a special mass to inform the people of your promotion," says Thaddeus. "And congratulations, Abbot Hugo!

"Little did I know that when I made you a monk back in San Gimignano that you would one day rise to the office of abbot. I am glad that I did not abandon you there on that small farm you found and when you came to me ten years ago seeking a place as a monk here in Paris, that I insisted that you go to seminary. God does move in mysterious ways Hugo, mysterious ways indeed," states Thaddeus.

"To where will you be going once you leave here, father?" asks Hugo.

"I will be heading back to Italy and have been appointed Abbot of Santa Croce in Florence," replies Thaddeus. "There is a great deal happening there and also much unrest with the people of Florence, even wars with their neighbors, and perhaps I can help be a calming effect on them by sharing the message of Jesus Christ," continues Thaddeus.

"Is that not the church which was founded by St. Francis himself?" replies Hugo.

"Yes, that is what I have been told," says Thaddeus.

"Is the church complete, father?" asks Hugo.

"I am not certain, but most likely not, Hugo, and perhaps I will live long enough to see the completion before I die."

"May you live a long life, Eminence, and congratulations on your appointment in Italy. May God continue to bless you even more as well as all who serve the church," announces Hugo, joyfully.

"And may the Lord bless you as well, Father Hugo." Both men then raise a small glass of wine and salute one another before they drink a small toast to each other's health.

Later that month, Thaddeus decides to walk through Paris and take in its life one more time before his departure. He looks around and tried to memorize some of the people he has come to know in the twenty-six years of service. All the places he has walked amongst the people, and most of all the River Seine. He stops momentarily to look out over the river and to partake of a small baguette he had with him when he noticed a figure down next to river's bank. The figure just sat there looking into the current as is sped along and then he figure looked up at him and said, "Hello father," and then waved toward him. Thaddeus waved back and the figure slowly made his way up the bank and to the street above where the father was standing.

"You will most likely not remember me, father, after all of these years," said the figure.

"Of course I do, Milton, or is it Jonah now?"

"Yes father, I do prefer Jonah, for like Jonah I spend much of my time in the belly of the whale surrounded by heathens."

"I see, Jonah. So how are you today, my son?"

"I am finally at peace, father, for today is an important day."

"Important day?" Thaddeus wondered, had he forgot some day of importance in his old age?

"Yes, this is the day that I will go to meet God, as I can no longer waste any time here in the terrible place, father."

"What on earth are you talking about, Milton?"

"I have lost my family to disease, my home to the fire, and now I have lost my hope to weariness, but the one thing I can control is my own death, so I shall enter the river and become one with the Lord this very day." Thaddeus looks shocked and is not quite sure what to say to him. I was about to jump when I saw you, Father, and did not want to leave this world before saying good-bye."

"Interesting that you should say, good bye, Jonah, for I will be leaving Paris and St. Julian in the morning and will depart for Italy, to begin a very important task for the Church."

"Italy, Father? That does sound important," replies Jonah.

"Yes, Florence, the city of terracotta roofs, to be exact where I have been appointed the new Abbot there at the Santa Croce."

"Congratulations father," says Jonah.

"If I might impose upon you briefly, Jonah, I will be making a very long journey there, and seem I have been unable to find anyone to travel along with me and assist me on my way. My job in Florence will involve doing the corporal works of mercy and the church here has no one to spare to assist me in getting there. Would you happen to know of someone who would be willing to make the journey with me, Jonah?" Jonah looks stunned. "I would of course be willing to pay, but I could not pay much nor do I travel very fast anymore now that I have entered my fifth decade of life."

Jonah's voice cracks and responds, "I am available, Father."

"Well, then it is settled my friend. Would you please accompany me back to the monastery so we can eat and prepare the morrow's journey?"

"The river will wait, Father, I am at your service." The two slowly walk away from the Seine and Thaddeus tells Jonah of the wonders of Italy as Jonah listens to every word.

Later in the evening, Thaddeus and Hugo sit and go over any last details before new Franciscan's departure to Florence. ",Well, it has been a long time coming and I can barely believe that I will actually be seeing Paris for what will most likely be the last time." Hugo listens and only smiles compassionately. "Now you will remember to have Father Beauvais plan and prepare the meal for the poor on the right days as well as have him contact the sisters so they can be ready as well?"

'Yes, father, it is all written down as you have instructed us," replies Hugo calmly.

"Jonah has been properly bathed, has clean clothes and any items he might need to join me on this pilgrimage (of sorts)?"

"Yes, father," replies Hugo calmly.

Thaddeus decides to have a rare brandy before he retires for the night. Hugo sits in a large comfortable chair and joins him in the brandy.

"Father, I would like to ask you a question if I might?"

"Yes, Hugo, certainly you may ask."

"Why have you invited Jonah to join you on your journey?"

"That is very complicated, as I had no intentions of inviting him or anyone else for that matter, and then I saw him there never to the river, preparing to take his own life and before I knew it I was employing him to assist me in my journey."

"I see, father," replies Hugo.

"I met this Milton, or Jonah as you know him, many years ago shortly after I first came to St. Julian. He was just entering catechism classes, and I was to instruct him in the ways of faith. Jonah was a little older than most of the other children and he never quite fit in. His mother had recently died (or so I heard) and the man who took him in was a Catholic in good standing, and so I met Jonah."

"How did his mother die? That had to be hard him at such an early age?" asks Hugo.

"I was told that she was a very beautiful woman at one time and had come to Paris as a child with some Gypsies, and they apparently fell to the sword, all but her and only because she could faster than the men pursuing her at the time. Her father was apparently a Gypsy and her mother a non-practicing Jew. The child only knew wildness and lived by her wits. Later on, as she matured, the local men took notice of her and would pay her for her company, one being the man who eventually raised Jonah."

"Does he know this about his mother, father?"

"No, Hugo, thank God, and I am not going to be the one to tell him. He has been through a lot in life, especially having a crippled limb," says Hugo. "He has had it since birth, a very difficult one it seems as it took his mother's life. The baby would have surely perished that winter of his birth had it not been for the fact that one of her prior customers was old and without an heir and could not help but wonder if Jonah might not be of his own loins."

"Where is this man today, father?"

"He died about five years ago, Hugo, and none too soon for Jonah's pleasure if you ask me," replies Thaddeus.

"You mean that Jonah hated the man who saved him from sure death?" asks Hugo.

"Apparently the man had begun to resent the thought that perhaps he had acted impulsively when he took Jonah in especially when rumors began to be bantered about that other men thought they might also be his father as well. He began to beat Jonah at the littlest provocation and over time they became more and more severe."

"It is getting late father, and you have a long trip tomorrow."

"Yes, yes," replies Thaddeus.

"I will leave now and allow you to get your rest and will see you in the morning for prayers."

Hugo leaves and closes the door quietly behind him and Thaddeus begins his prayers for his new journey which lies ahead of him. Upon rising early the following morning, he is surprised to find that a late winter snow has blanketed Paris and then decides to postpone his trek until the weather has cleared.

Chapter Nineteen

"Good morning, eminence," says Beauvais.

"Good morning father," replies Thaddeus.

"I see that the weather is detaining your from proceeding on your journey," states Beauvais.

"Yes it has, and I have decided to see it as God's way of letting me know he is still in charge," says Thaddeus with a chuckle.

"If I might have a word with you in private, father. Would you please step into my study?" requests Thaddeus. Beauvais complies with the request and enters the room and then sits down in a large chair at Thaddeus's direction. "Father Beauvais, it has come to my attention that you are shying away from some of your duties, not bathing as regularly as one might, seem lack luster in your prayers, and seem to rush through mass as if you had some place else you would rather be." Beauvais sits with his head down and dangles a small cross on a metallic chain in a circle above the floor below. "Normally I would let Father Hugo attend to this, but he has been so busy with his other duties. I have asked that he allow me to talk to you and he has graciously consented."

After a long pause, Beauvais replies, "Eminence, do you think it is possible to make a mistake, a mistake like hearing one's calling from God?"

"Mistake; whatever are you talking about?" asks Thaddeus. "What mistake? Your calling?" asks Thaddeus again.

"I am not certain I was actually meant to be a priest, father, and that perhaps I might have made a mistake," Beauvais mumbles in a forlorn matter.

"Speak up, son, I am not sure that I heard you correctly!" commands Thaddeus!

The young priest sits and says nothing more. His hair dirty, his clothes wrinkled, and his appearance unkempt, he just sits there dangling the cross and chain in small circles as he stares towards the floor.

"Father, I believe that I should leave the priesthood," says Beauvais.

"Leave the priesthood? Why would you want to do an insane thing like that, my son?"

"Because I am no longer worthy to be God's servant, father."

"None of us are worthy when you come right down to it, my young friend, it is only by the Lord's good graces do we either stand or fall in this profession," says Thaddeus calmly.

"But I have failed to keep my vow of celibacy and can no longer look at myself in the mirror, or my parishioners either, Eminence."

"What happened… ?"asks Thaddeus.

Beauvais says nothing at first, "The first time was with the baker's wife."

"The first time?" interjects Thaddeus quickly. "There were more, Beauvais?"

"Yes, shortly after that with the prostitute, Yvette."

"How many people know about this, Beauvais?"

"As far as I know only four of us know, father."

"Well, the baker's wife will not want to lose her comfortable position in her husband's family business, so she will never utter a word of it, you can count on that."

"Yvette, on the other hand presents a problem," remarks Thaddeus.

"How so?" asks Beauvais.

"She will most likely want something in return for her silence. She will want to torture you for awhile and then when she thinks it is to her advantage, she will make a demand, or demands, upon you wanting to see what she can extract from you in return for her promise of silence."

"If I give it to her, will she then go away?" queries Beauvais.

"Not very likely, but you leave her to me. The important thing here is that you not give up on yourself, nor God," encourages Thaddeus with a large smile.

Beauvais tearfully nods his head in agreement.

"Father Beauvais, if you would regale me with the story of how you decided to become a priest?"

"Actually father, I never really wanted to be a priest," replies Beauvais.

"No?"

"No, Eminence, it was my family's decision and with my uncle's contacts with the diocese. I was able to get into seminary and now here I am at St. Julian's. I guess the church felt like they owed your uncle something, father," says Beauvais.

"More likely they saw something they liked about you," retorts Thaddeus, "As do I."

"Frankly, father, I never liked most of the priest I met very much," says Beauvais.

Thaddeus says nothing in response.

"In all honesty I found that most of the priests I have met were a little bit angry, mostly arrogant, and incredibly self-righteous."

Thaddeus cannot help but chuckle when hears Beauvais description of his fellow clergy. Beauvais drops his head again and closes his eyes.

"Now what is wrong, asks Thaddeus?"

"I fear that you mock me, father."

"Mock you, no, I commend you for your candor as I have found most priests to be exactly as you describe, my son," replies Thaddeus amicably. "The important thing is that you are still willing to serve the Lord, and serve him you will, you just wait and see," states Thaddeus.

After pouring himself and Beauvais a small glass of brandy, Thaddeus stands up blesses the young priest. "Now, I have heard your confession and by the power invested in me by the church, absolve you of your sins, Gabriel, now go and sin no more."

"Agreed, father," mumbles Beauvais.

Thaddeus then makes the sign of the cross and kisses the crucifix which is around his neck and then extends his ring towards Beauvais who then kisses the ring in reverence.

"You are going to love Italy, Father Beauvais, absolutely love it."

Beauvais looks confused and says, "Italy, Eminence?"

"Yes, Italy."

"I think it would wisest if you accompany me on my voyage to Florence and then in time return here, that is if you still desire to be a priest, you Gabriel?"

"Yes father, I do."

"Well, then as soon as the weather allows us we will do a sort of pilgrimage together."

"Like Paul and Silas, Eminence?" Thaddeus chuckles and then says, "You will soon forget this easily as one might the heat of summer after a fall rain. Along our journey I will also tell you several wonderful stories of your uncle and our fight to overcome the all of the death in San Gimignano not all that long ago." Thaddeus begins to go to small drawer in his desk and remove the cloth that he had found clutched in Cardinal Beauvais hand that mournful morning, but decides to wait. Thaddeus decides that the cloth belongs to the boy as Diego long gave up his claim on it. Who else but this young man should have it he asked himself? But this was not the time.

"Now, Father Beauvais, would you please ask Jonah to come to my study at his behind him."

The day starts out clear enough but soon clouds over and without any warning the sky begins to snow once again. It would be another three days before the weather was clear enough to attempt the long voyage to Florence, but that day had finally arrived.

"Father Thaddeus, I am packed and ready to begin our journey," says Gabriel eagerly. Father Thaddeus sort of nods and continues to check to see if he has everything prepared and seems to be quietly talking to himself.

"Shall I have the carriage brought around, father?" asks Beauvais.

"Carriage, why would we need the carriage brought around? asks Thaddeus.

"So that we might begin our trek, father," replies Beauvais.

"And begin our trek we shall soon enough, but not in a carriage, but rather on foot," replies Thaddeus.

Beauvais seems stunned for a brief moment and then asks, "On foot, Eminence? All the way to Florence?"

"Yes, on foot, my son."

Beauvais uses all of his strength to feign a smile for the aging abbot, and then says, "Well, then I will not be needed all the things I have packed, so I will go back to my room and leave a few things there, Eminence."

"A wise decision, a wise decision," mumbles Thaddeus as he continues to check his belongings.

Beauvais goes back to his room and then returns a few minutes later to find Father Thaddeus gone. At this point he is not sure as to what he should do, and decides to go and look for him. Eventually Beauvais finds Father Thaddeus outside in front of the monastery with Abbot Hugo and several of the monks. As Beauvais moves closer he can see the look of concern on the faces of the men as their whispers become slightly louder.

"I will simply have to postpone my journey once again," states Thaddeus.

"No, Monsignor, please do not worry for I will handle the situation, besides it is my job now," replies Hugo. Thaddeus says nothing as Hugo gives him a reassuring smile.

"Of course you are correct, Father Hugo; they are in very capable hands here."

"I will make sure that no harm comes to them, God willing," continues Hugo. Hugo's face saddens momentarily and then he says, "I thank you my brother and my friend for all that you have done for me. You could have left me out in the wilderness to die a broken man, but you did not give up on me even when I had surely given up on myself."

"God did not give up on you and he never will, Father Hugo," replies Thaddeus. "Now remember that the vineyards are behind schedule on their pruning as well as the apple trees. And someone will of course need to say mass for the nuns at the convent as needed, as well as tending to the sheep, for their wool and cheese," continues Thaddeus.

"Yes, of course father," replies Hugo with a faint smile. "All will be taken care of I assure you." There is a long pause and a moment of silence, and then both men briefly embrace and then step back uncomfortably. "And from this point on you are officially assigned by the Church to assist the Monsignor in his duties and as for as long as he requires you, so do a good job," say Hugo. "Furthermore, if possible, come back here in one piece some day as well young man."

Beauvais smiles and nods in agreement. Hugo and the monks then turn and head into the heart of Paris to see what might have become of the elder monk, Amos, and the neophyte, Jonah.

With that, Thaddeus now turns to Beauvais and with a smile says, "Shall we depart?"

The two priests, dressed in their winter clothing and with walking sticks in hand, turn towards the south and begin their journey. Once out of ear shot Beauvais asks what has happened.

"It seems that the chief of police along with another policeman and a soldier came up to Brother Jonah on the street this morning and without so much as a word took him away."

"Took him away asks Gabriel, why?"

"I do not know why, but one of the monks, Brother Amos, who was walking with him, was taken away too."

"Should we go back, father?" asks Beauvais worriedly. "And in my short time here I have learned not trust Chief Harold."

"No, my son; I am certain that they are in good hands with Father Hugo, so there is no need for us to worry. Besides, the Lord will protect them," says Thaddeus with a smile.

"I have heard that the olive trees in Provence are extremely old and majestic looking," says Beauvais.

"Have you never been there?" inquires Thaddeus.

Gabriel says nothing, and Thaddeus quickly chimes in, "Then this will be an additional treat for you on our journey. And lavender, the most incredible lavender lies ahead."

"I have heard of stories of the lavender planted in fields as far as the eye can see," replies Gabriel.

"It may not be in bloom when we pass by, but who knows, it may yet be," shares Thaddeus.

Chapter Twenty

"How long to you intend to keep me in here jailer?" questions Jonah? "Hello, is anyone out there?" There is no response. "How about some food," I said, "how about some food?"

After about an hour's more wait, Jonah hears someone walking towards his jail cell and realizes that he is too short to see through the small opening in the door to see who is approaching. "Hello, who is out there, shouts Jonah?"

"Quiet down in there or I will give you something to shout about," replies the voice of Paris Police Chief Harold.

"Can I at least have something to eat?" requests Jonah a little bit quieter now.

"Yes, of course. What would you like, your majesty? We have a nice pheasant broiled to perfection or perhaps your delicate pallet might prefer some nicely prepared snails smothered in butter and wine sauce," replies Harold?

"I would settle for some bread or even an apple right now," states Jonah.

"I think that can be arranged, provided that you brought some money in here with you, Harold. I would of course be happy to go and purchase some food for you."

"I am a simple monk and of modest means, the only thing that I had of value you took from me when you arrested me," replies Jonah.

"To what are you referring, my good man?" questions Harold snidely.

"Never mind," retorts Jonah. "I guess I am not all that hungry after all, besides the Abbot will be here soon and hopefully seek my release."

"Not even the Pope himself can help you this time, as you have apparently caught the attention of someone very high up with your habitual thieving and pilfering," says a smug looking Harold. "Neophyte monk or not, this time you will most certainly enter the dungeon Brother Jonah, and for most likely for good."

Harold walks away laughing in his now undersized policeman's uniform with all of its glory. Harold is a short man of somewhat stocky build, in perhaps his late fifties. He is also balding and has squinty eats which sort of puts Jonah to mind of a rat, and worst of all his breath always reeks of garlic, stale garlic.

After more than an hour or two, Jonah could hear the voice of the Abbott, Hugo, arguing with Chief Harold but as to exactly what he cannot quite make out, but he knows hit has to be about him and Brother Amos. Soon Jonah can hear the voice of Amos coming from the outside window telling him to hold on, it will only be a little while longer.

Shortly before nightfall there is the sound of a large carriage approaching the jail house, as well as a couple of people on horseback. One of the other prisoners is able to get a brief glimpse outside and notes that the carriage looks like it belongs to someone of either great wealth or importance, or both. Then there is the approach of foot steps towards Jonah's prison door, it is a guard and he stops outside the cell door and seems to just wait.

"When am I going to get something to eat?" inquires Jonah again.

"Not until the chief decides to feed you and not a moment sooner!" barks the guard.

"When can I get out of here? I have duties to attend too!" demands Jonah.

"You will be out here very soon and off to places less inviting than here," states the guard. "That carriage you heard outside is most likely for you," smirks the guard.

"Me? Why me?" questions Jonah.

"You will find out soon enough. Most likely it will not be to your liking," laughs the guard.

"But I have done nothing, nothing!" exclaims Jonah and then he begins to quietly sob as well as pray.

Then a short time later, Jonah hears the approach of several people from within the jail and notices that they are getting closer. Surely this will mean his end and decides it might have been better if he had not acknowledged Father Thaddeus's hail and instead ended it all there once and for all in the River Seine.

"Open the door at once commands!" Chief Harold. The guard nervously goes through the keys until he finds the right one and eventually opens the door.

"I would talk to him alone," snaps a woman from outside.

She enters the cell and stands over Jonah who is almost lying down on the floor. She is extremely well-dressed, her hair in immaculate, she is tall and thin, bordering on gaunt. Her skin is pale as if she rarely saw sunlight in contrast to the bright jewelry that she wore as well as a cameo, and she was lightly scented with the scent of fragrant perfume. "What is your name?" she asks.

Jonah says nothing in response.

"What is your name?" this time asking a little bit louder.

Again there is no reply.

The guard kicks Jonah swiftly and shouts, "Answer the lady!"

The woman quickly turns towards the guard and points her finger directly at him, saying, "If you do that again, and I will personally see that suffer greatly."

The guard looks confused and nods his head indicating that he understands her. The lady then stoops over and with her hand holds up Jonah's head slightly. She briefly looks into his face and calmly asks, "Is your name Milton and was your mother a bar maid who is no longer among the living?"

"She is dead as is my father; do as you wish to me, for I grow tired of this little game," replies Jonah.

"You have his look," says the lady with a bit of joy in her voice.

She then stands back up and says to Chief Harold, "Release him."

"What, my lady?" replies Harold?

"You heard me! At once!" snaps the lady.

"As you wish," says Harold. He walks over to Jonah and helps him to his feet. Jonah just stands there and looks bewildered. By now two other well-dressed men are peering into the jail.

The lady then turns towards the two well-dressed men and says, "Mister Mayor and Mister Alderman, my cousin and I wish a moment alone." Jonah looks even more confused and has all sorts of wild thoughts of peril running through his head by this time.

"Yes, of course, my lady," replies the mayor, who then gives orders to the police to vacate the cell immediately and all depart to the inner chambers except for the Jonah and his new found cousin.

"I know this may come as shock to you, but the man who raised you is not your father, but instead another man."

"Another man," asks Jonah?

"Yes, he was my uncle, and brother to the king."

"Brother to the king?"

"He died only this past week and left no male heir, and was at risk of losing his title and estates, and then on his death bed he revealed that he had an heir, and that is you, my cousin," says the lady quietly.

"Shall we depart this dreadful place and return to Versailles, where things are most certainly more dignified for a man of your stature?"

Jonah wonders if he might be dreaming, but slowly walks along with the lady towards the outer doors. "I will of course have to get permission from the Abbot to leave my duties for awhile," says Jonah.

Hugo is already standing near him, looks at him and with head slightly bowed, says, "Yes, my lord, as you see fit."

All the men in the room bow their heads upon seeing this and step back a few steps. Milton stops suddenly when he reaches the outer door where he can see two soldiers, a beautiful gold incrusted carriage, and a footman awaiting him.

"I am not dreaming?" asks Milton?

"No, not at all, cousin" she replies.

"And I am of the royal blood line?"

"Yes, you most certainly are, cousin."

"Then I would like one thing before we leave," says Milton.

He turns towards Chief Harold, and says, "I believe that you have something of mine?"

Harold almost freezes and does nothing for a second, and then reaches into his pocket and produces a small golden locket with Milton's mother's initials inside of it, along with a second set of initials. Milton's mother had given this to him while she was awaiting death and told him to never depart with it. The chief slowly hands it to Milton and then drops his head as if preparing himself for the worse. The mayor then snaps his fingers and points at the chief and says to the guard, "Arrest him!" And the guard does so and begins to put restraints on the now disgraced chief.

"Cousin, if I may be so bold, what will become of him?"

"Nothing that you should worry yourself over," says the lady, "most likely he will be put to death for the shame he has brought this city by his corruption and thievery."

Jonah then turns towards the mayor and says, "If I might, instead of taking him away, perhaps you could release him into my custody and he could make himself useful by perhaps cleaning out stalls and running errands for me?"

"Are you sure, cousin?" asks the lady?

"I am," says Milton with a nod.

The lady looks at the mayor and the mayor says, "Yes, my lord, as you wish."

The former chief can almost not believe his ears. "You are released into their custody," says the mayor, "and I advise that you do as you are told."

Harold turns towards Milton with his head bowed and thanks him repeatedly. The royal party leaves, Milton, the lady, the soldiers, and the footman and Harold running along the side the carriage, with Harold having an extremely difficult time keeping up.

In the seaside city of Genoa, the seaport is lined with merchant vessels of all shapes and sizes and it appears that there are a number of war ships present in or about the harbor as well. Beauvais periodically looks to the sky to watch the seagulls as they almost circle about and making their ever present call as they continuously search for food. Having rarely ever seen a seagull, Beauvais is quite captivated with them. Thaddeus coughs and almost stumbles but quickly regains his footing as the two priests near the city.

"Is Genoa larger than Paris," asks Beauvais.

"No, but both cities are centers of great powers and Genoa is no place to be under estimated, as their navy is one of the best in the world, if not the best, and the Genovese possess great wealth as well," says Thaddeus. "There is a great church in Genoa that is said to hold the ashes of the head of John the Baptist," says Thaddeus.

"The ashes," father?

"Yes, and they are said to have come from the Holy Land itself."

"Incredible," replies Beauvais, "but how can this be?"

"They believe that these actually are the ashes of John the Baptist severed head and we will not tell them otherwise, my son, if we are wise."

After a long pause Gabriel asks, "Can we go and have a look at them, father?"

"Have a look? asks Thaddeus almost scornfully.

"I mean, may we go and pay our respects, father?"

"We shall see," says Thaddeus, "Perhaps, perhaps."

"On occasion they war against some of their neighbors."

"War?" asks Beauvais.

"Yes, but most likely there are no hostilities in this city today and I for one am looking forward to a nice, comfortable bed for a change," says Thaddeus.

"Agreed, father, for how it has been at least a month or more since we stopped at that convent and performed mass, and the sisters were kind enough to supply us with a most satisfactory bed and the best croissants as well," replies Beauvais.

"Yes, I do remember Sister Mary Agnes' croissants, and I can almost taste them now," says Thaddeus.

Thaddeus is near enough to the coast to notice that several of the great warships moored in port are badly damaged are undergoing repair. "Must have been a great sea battle recently," says Thaddeus as he points to the harbor.

"How do you know father? asks Beauvais.

"Notice those war vessels, my son. Anything odd about them?" Beauvais stops momentarily and shields his eyes from the sun and then he too notices the damage to the ships.

"Looks like there was a great battle indeed," says Beauvais.

"Who were they fighting with, father," asks Beauvais.

"Mostly likely either Venice or even Pisa, and if so, it could go badly for us if they think us spies," whispers Thaddeus to Beauvais between coughs as the two approach the city gates.

Now upon arriving there, the guards notice that the travelers are priests and allow them access to the city with very little questioning and it is at this time that it begins to rain and a cold rain at that. Thaddeus begins to look a little pale and one might even describe him as almost drained of life, for the sickness which lay heavy in his lungs was beginning to take its toll although he kept insisting that he was fine. Finally they see an inn which is serving food from the smell of it and so the priests enter and soon find a table at which to rest.

"Good-day my good man," says Thaddeus as the inn keeper responds in like. "My young friend and I will have the special of the day and ale if you please." The keeper turns his back and goes behind a small bar and says something through a window into the back room where an older woman is cooking, he then begins to poor the ale.

"Father, how much further is it to the local parish church?" asks Beauvais.

"Oh, not far," says Thaddeus as he begins to sip the ale which has just been sat before him.

"I am sure they might have provided a meal for us at the church, father," says Beauvais quietly.

"Yes, of course they most certainly would have indeed, but I am not completely sold on the idea of us stopping there yet," replies Thaddeus, "Besides the food smells good here."

Thaddeus takes off his outer warm garments and hangs them on the back of a chair next to him and suggests that Beauvais do the same. After a short while the inn keeper, a tall, unkempt, and dirty man brings some bread to their table along with looks like a sort of porridge, as well a small amount of cheese and two pears, slightly over ripe. While they eat, other patrons enter the establishment and order food and drink as well. Most carry on conversations, but only one conversation in the far end of the room catches the attention of Father Thaddeus. Carefully turning his ear towards them; he is able to hear just exactly what the men are saying as they speak of two wars with both Pisa and Venice, which seems to being going badly for Genoa at the moment. After the other men eat and leave, Thaddeus turns his attention towards Beauvais and states with a look of concern.

"We shall rest here a little while longer and then be on our way."

"Yes, we should be getting to the church soon, father," replies Beauvais. Thaddeus shakes his head slightly and quickly from side to side and puts one finger up to his mouth to indicate that nothing more on the subject should be said. Gabriel understands the look of concern in his mentors face and remembers the words of caution which were shared with him briefly before they entered the city and begins to finish his meal and not draw any attention to himself. About an hour passes before Thaddeus motions for the inn keeper to come to their table and he then settles their bill and begins to put on his outer garments which have almost dried by now. Thaddeus looks up to see that Gabriel is already standing and walking stick in hand begins to start towards the door when another priest walks in and says gives greeting to them both.

Beauvais slightly nods his head towards the what he know recognizes as a monk and then goes just outside the door, but Thaddeus stops to engage him. "I am not familiar with your order, father," inquires Thaddeus.

"I am of the Cistercian Order, from a monastery much to the west of here near the village of Narbonne, in the south of France."

"Interesting," replies Thaddeus and then begins to explain that he is they are of the Franciscan Order and on a pilgrimage from Paris. "My young companion with the poor manners is Father Beauvais, and I am Father Thaddeus."

"It is a pleasure to meet you as well your aide. I am Father Dominic, a lowly priest in the service of the Lord."

"As are we all," retorts Thaddeus.

"Pity all that recent trouble in Paris," comments Dominic. "What do you make of it, father?"

"Trouble in Paris? What trouble?" asks Thaddeus.

"I thought you knew," replies Dominic, "or I would have not mentioned it, after all it is the talk of the local parish."

"Please enlighten me," requests Thaddeus. Dominic sits down and looks up at both priests with obvious grief in his face and says nothing. "Father, I must insist," demands Thaddeus softly.

It is at this moment that Dominic first notices that Thaddeus is wear a right which signifies that he has achieved the station of Monsignor. With that Dominic says, "Yes, of course, Monsignor."

"Well, it is a truly a tragic story and I am sorry to be the one from who learn of this dreadful thing," starts Dominic. Thaddeus then moves closer to Dominic and gives him his full attention as Beauvais stays back by the door unaware of the details of their conversation. "From what I know, the Paris City Police Chief had two monks arrested from just outside one of the monasteries there," continues Dominic.

"Yes, I know all about the arrests, they were in my Order at the time, but I am confident that Father Hugo quickly straightened it all out," and the look of relief reenters Thaddeus' face.

"Forgive me, Monsignor, but do you mean to imply that the death of one of your own does not bother you then in the least," asks the Cistercian.

"The death of one of my own?" questions Thaddeus.

But Dominic says nothing and only looks down at the floor.

"Who died?" demands Thaddeus, "I urge you, father. Tell me who died1"

"Why one of the monks died, neophyte, and they say he was a crippled man who had once been homeless in the city and now," states Dominic quietly.

Thaddeus sits down at the table and begins to cough slightly again. The room is silent for awhile, when Thaddeus breaks the silence. "How did Brother Milton die?"

"I am not sure, but some of the priests have claimed that he died from the cold in his jail cell as he had no fire to warm by, nor any food, and the worst part of all is that he was arrested for another man's crime." When the authorities learned of their mistake and opened the cell door to release him, they found him dead. There is an uproar in the city," continues Dominic. "Apparently this man who meant so little to the people in Paris while he was alive, means a great deal to him now that he is, well gone."

"I beseech you, please do not tell Father Beauvais as I do not believe he has heard our conversation, and I will wait until the right time to tell him."

"I understand, father, and my condolences on your loss," says Dominic. "If it is of any consolation, the police chief died from an accident a couple of weeks later," reports Dominic. "Apparently his carriage slide off of the road and he was thrown out and head on into a tree. Apparently the whole matter was dropped by the church there and then, Monsignor."

Thaddeus rises from the table and starts once again towards the door, when Dominic suddenly calls out to him. "If I may, father?" asks Dominic. Thaddeus stops and looks at the Cistercian and listens. "If you are heading back towards Paris, perhaps we could travel together for awhile as there is always safety in numbers."

"If that were only the case," interjects Beauvais, "as we would love to hear all about your Order, but we are headed towards the east and..."

Thaddeus interrupts him quickly saying, "And to Rome." The Cistercian and the Franciscan smile at one another and the men then part company leaving Dominic at the inn.

The rain had become a light drizzle and they make their way across the vast city, deciding to err on the side of caution they follow the less traveled streets and alley ways as not to be noticed if at all possible. Eventually the two of them arrive at the eastern most gateway, only stopping off shortly to purchase a small amount of supplies. They now exit the city and attempt to make the most of the light they have left to put some time and distance between them and the City of Genoa.

Chapter Twenty One

It is an early and sunny morning in the small, fishing village of Portofino, and Beauvais finds himself sitting at a small table just outside the area of the church which is still standing that he and Thaddeus commandeered for their living quarters. Gabriel sat and watched the small hand full of little, brown birds hoping around just out of his grasp upon the ground and ate whatever that might find or perhaps anything he might discard. The seagulls that Gabriel once found fascinating just a few short weeks ago, he now tried his best to ignore. That early spring in which they left Paris had now moved into late summer and fall could not be far behind, and Beauvais wondered just how he had ended up here, with a man he really did not know, and in a land he was not familiar with. "What would happen?" He thought, " if his mentor died... Was he expected to go on to Florence, or should he return to Paris?" Neither prospect appealed to him at the moment. If he returned to Paris, then his sin which led to his departure might make itself public and he would have to return to the small village in which originated, not as a hero, but most certainly as a failure. Should he go on to Florence, he might get caught up in all of the turmoil and squabbling that he had heard was present there and might find himself at the mercy of strangers, with no one like his mentor to protect him. Gabriel liked Portofino and the local parishioners were friendly enough, and with a little effort the church could be restored to an acceptable point so that the daily masses could be held without fear of rain falling upon their heads. Lucky for them it had been a more or less dry summer, but fall usually brought the rains, cold rains, and things could quickly change, as well he knew. Perhaps Father Thaddeus might make a full recovery and then it would be out of his hands, but for now, it was all very, very much in God's hands and Gabriel knew he would have to content with that, for better or for worse.

"It is time for some coffee, father; do you feel like having some coffee this morning?" asks Beauvais. Thaddeus shook his head indicating he did not want any coffee, as he lie there unshaven, his eyes sunken and dark, his skin was ashen in color, and he, on occasion, wheezed when he took in a breath.

"Some of the ladies from town have brought beard, fish, cheeses, and an assortment of fruits for you, father, would you care to eat a little something?"

Thaddeus did not answer him. The ladies will be by later to change your bedding and they said they would make a fresh pot of stew as well, father. Thaddeus struggles and eventually sits upright in bed, and then utters the word, "Florence?"

"No word from Florence," replies Beauvais as he makes his way over to the bed with a bowl containing small pieces of bread and cheese. Gabriel sits on the side of the bed and attempts to get his mentor to eat, and he does but only a little.

"How long?" asks Thaddeus in a raspy voice.

"Let us see now, the letter went out almost two months ago, father, but there is a war going on and that would have most assuredly slowed down the speed in which it was dispatched."

Beauvais could not help but notice that Thaddeus seemed to be clutching on to an old piece of cloth and rarely did it ever leave his side. Perhaps it held some sentimental value, or was some family heirloom, perhaps, or maybe it was what was handy when his mentor went to wipe the perspiration from his own brow?

"Gabriel, it is time that we spoke about what may or may not happen," says Thaddeus faintly.

"There will be plenty enough time for that later, father, once you have regained your strength," retorts Beauvais.

"No, this is the proper time, Gabriel, as I am uncertain how much longer I will still be able to communicate with you."

"I understand, father," says Beauvais as he now sits quietly on the edge of the bed. Thaddeus then points at some scrolls of paper which lie on a table near his bed next to a small candle stand. Gabriel reaches picks them up and sits them on the bed next to him.

"As we both know, I am most likely not long for this world, and despite my best prayers, as well as those of this parish, I will most likely going to be with the Lord soon," whispers Thaddeus. "I can also assume that should that happen, you will not be wise for you to go back to Paris, nor on to Florence either."

"Yes, father," says Gabriel respectfully.

"Now, what is that you would like to do in the event I cannot continue this journey, Gabriel?"

"I am not sure, father. What is to become of me?" asks Beauvais. "My hands are not used to hard labor. I am not a carpenter, a stone mason, nor a fisherman, and my hands do not know the art of war? May I never be forced to steal and disgrace God in doing so, father. Whatever shall be come of me, father? Gabriel asks in all earnestness. "What shall become of me?"

After a short pause, Thaddeus speaks up. "Well my power is somewhat limited, but I do have me some authority and influence with the Church as a Monsignor and shall use it to the best of my ability as long as I am able to hold pen in hand and have breath in my body, so fear not," says Thaddeus in a voice he has used so many times in his career, a voice of compassion and comfort as only a pastor might.

"Do you like it here, Gabriel?"

"I do father," he replies.

"How so, my son?"

"I like the people here, and the food is incredible as well, especially the white truffles," replies the young priest. "Go on," says Thaddeus with a smile on his face. "In Paris I felt like I was just small cog in a very large wheel having little effect on much of anything, but here, well here I can perhaps make a difference," says Gabriel. "The people here seem hungry to learn more about the Lord, not either indifferent or forced into going to mass like many often did in Paris," the young priest continues, "and there are rumors of food riots amongst the people in Paris as well this past winter. Yes, Eminence, I do like being here very much."

"Now as you well know the church could use a little shoring up, but there are more than enough hands here to make the work go quickly should a shepherd decided to stay and tend the flock," says Thaddeus.

"And I would be that shepherd, father," asks Gabriel? "If that is your wish," replies Thaddeus, "but do not decide this too quickly because you would be making a very sacred commitment by doing so," says, Thaddeus.

"If I might ask, father, why there is no priest here presently?"

"The war is most likely the cause, Gabriel, and with both sides taking and giving up ground so to speak, it appears that this little one (Portofino) somehow got lost in the process."

After a long pause, Gabriel stands up and taking an obvious deep breath says, "Then it is settled, father, I will continue as your assistant and continue to help tend the flock here until you are ready to travel, or should the worse happen, I will stay on here until the Church sees fit to place me elsewhere."

"Are you most certain, my son?"

"Yes, father, I am, and I just hope that I can live up to your standards, father," replies Gabriel.

"You already have, Gabriel, you already have. Now, if you will hand some parchment to me and then ask Mrs. Florentino to come in, I will begin my letters; that is her voice I hear outside is it not?" asks Thaddeus.

"Yes, father it is."

"One letter I will want dispatched to Santa Croce in Florence, immediately requesting funds for the rebuilding of the church here, and in it I will explain my calling to stay here and preach the Gospel in Portofino with you as my assistant, as well as my regrets for not being able to become the new abbot there. The second letter will be for you restating all of these things should I die and anyone come here to challenge your right to be here as pastor. Now, you have a church to rebuild and a flock to tend until I am stronger," says Thaddeus with a slight smile on his face.

"Yes, Monsignor," replies Gabriel with a term he has rarely used for his mentor.

"And on your way out would you please ask Mrs. Florentino to prepare something hot for me eat as I believe I will have something before I begin my tasks after all," adds Thaddeus.

"Yes, father," says Beauvais and he leaves the room feeling a little more ready to face the world than he did a few brief minutes before.

Summer turns into fall and then comes winter, and Father Beauvais continues to see to the needs of his aging and health stricken mentor. Good days come and go and Father Thaddeus plans to do the daily mass, but is not able to venture very far from his room. The cold of winter does its best to hinder the aging priest, but it is far much milder than the winter might have been in if he had still been in Paris. The church building is slowly making progress in its repairs, but it is slow progress and although there are many willing hands, there are so few funds with which to buy the necessary materials required to complete the task. Beauvais has become quite comfortable in his duties with in the parish and the people there are beginning to trust him, yet there is still no word from Florence. "Why is there still no word from Florence," Beauvais wonders to himself as he sits outside Thaddeus' room and waits.

It seems that the same, small birds still show up every day to be fed crumbs and such, Gabriel ponders on whether or not he should give each one of them names. His day dreaming is suddenly interrupted by a long, harsh coughing spell delivered by Thaddeus just beyond the wall nest to where he is sitting. Gabriel begins to go and check on his friend, but then hears Mrs. Florentino and a couple of the other ladies tending to the now feeble priest. The father had seemed bear death so many times the last couple of months, but had somehow managed to hang on to life, perhaps a miracle in itself? The ladies of the church had been wonderful and exemplarily in their care for him, even as his need to keep warm was becoming harder and harder to accomplish. If only we had a nun or two to assist us, Gabriel thought to himself, how they might truly be helpful in the Abbot's time of need.

While Gabriel returns to feeding his feathered friends, he hears the sound of hooves in the distance coming towards them from near the rocky cliffs above the seashore. He squints into the morning sun and tries to make out who be approaching them this winter day and he is only able to make out one rider, and then a second and even a third. Gabriel now stands and straightens his shirt and collar so that he might look his best upon the visitor's eventual arrival, which now appears to be four people, one who from her size and stature is most likely a woman. Gabriel starts to alert Father Thaddeus to presence of the strangers approach, but being so new to the area himself he still had a hard time distinguishing between who was a stranger and who was simply a neighbor from just down the road a ways, so he says nothing. They will most likely want food should they be from afar, and that we can oblige them, and some may need prayer or perhaps confession, he went over in his mind. He knew his prayers well enough by now and was certain he could handle whatever spiritual need might present itself to him, and at that he decides to sit back down and to pretend to have not noticed them as they continue to approach.

"Greetings father," Gabriel hears from just over his shoulder. He slowly turns to see who is addressing him and smiles.

"Greeting to you as well, sister," replies Gabriel, noticing her nun's attire.

"I am looking for Father Thaddeus and would like to speak with him if possible," says the nun.

"Oh, he is quite ill and does not see many visitors these days, I am afraid," states Beauvais.

"But I am on here on behalf of my order and I am willing to wait," replies the nun. Beauvais stops and thinks for a moment, had he not just been wishing for the assistance of a nun to help with his mentor's care?

"Upon further thought, sister, you will please follow me through this door and assist the ladies in the caring for him, but your friends will have to wait out here," says Beauvais in his sternest voice trying to look priestly.

The nun acknowledges his request and begins to get down from her steed as the others just look at one another as if they cannot believe this priest's rudeness and ill-manner behavior which came incredibly close to a personal insult which they are not sure they wish to endure after such a long trek. The nun follows Gabriel into the priest's room where they find two ladies changing his bedding and upon noticing the father and then nun, the ladies depart carrying a chamber pot.

"As you can see, sister he is not well," says Gabriel, "and he rarely talks to anyone these day. (He just lies there clinching that rag of a cloth which he holds tightly in his fist.)

The nun stops for a moment and then begins to approach the infirmed priest, and unannounced to them one of the men from outside quietly enters as well.

"Father Thaddeus are you awake?" asks the nun, but she gets no reply. Again she tries and still there is no word from him. Thaddeus just lies there almost motionless and then recognizes a voice from his past, a voice that cannot be possible. He decides that he must have died and that his old friends have come to take him home to his reward, and then he hears the voice again calling to him and with that he opens his eyes widely and at last responds to the voice with a question, "Musit?"

"Yes, I am here, father. Sister Rosa and I are here to assist you in your recovery."

"And how, how can this be?" inquires Thaddeus. "Am I dead?"

"Not unless I am too," sounds a deep voice from the back of the room.

"I know that voice as well," says Thaddeus.

"Don Fernando Cristobel Diego Bedoya, Esquire, at your service," the voice responds respectfully as he takes off his hat and bows ever so slightly.

"Then it is Diego, Diego my old friend, how can?" asks Thaddeus in sheer amazement and yet joy. Gabriel just stands stunned as he has no idea who these people are or exactly why they are there. Yet the father seems to know them which meant this was most likely a good thing, a very good thing indeed as he observes the father for the very first time in a long time, smiling.

"Please do not take this question the wrong way, but what are you doing here? And how did you know that you would find me here?" asks Thaddeus.

"Your letter made its way to Florence and with your work with the Franciscans, the church decided to forward it on to our order, being that we are dedicated to the memory and service of St. Francis," replies Musit.

"Of course!" exclaimed Thaddeus.

"Once your request reached the Mother Superior, she made the decision to send Sister Rosa and myself to assist you in your recovery here in Portofino," continues Musit. Sister Rosa was a younger woman, very short with a very pretty face, and yet most of all was very noticeably deaf. It was not easy to understand her replies, and she did try very hard to be useful along the journey. How she ever became a nun confused Father Beauvais completely, but he kept those thoughts to himself.

"And naturally," interrupted Diego, "once I learned that my very good friend was in need and that these two sisters would be making the trip here alone..." I said to myself, "You must not allow the sisters to travel in such dangerous company alone, and that I, Don Diego, must, must escort her here and assist you in any way I could."

"I can hardly believe my eyes," says Thaddeus tearfully.

"There is more, father, when the people heard you were attempting to restore the church here in Portofino, they immediately took up a collection and have sent a tidy sum of gold to help you get this holy venture underway," states Diego as he takes the palm of his hand and carefully cups a bag of what sounds like coins which is tied to his belt, near the sword on his side.

"Bless them, bless them all," says Thaddeus. "And bless the two of you most of all." Musit smiles at the sight of life returning to the father's face.

"All that we ask is for your permission to begin, father," shares Diego joyfully.

"Yes, yes, of course" replies Thaddeus, "but first you must eat something."

"My son's and I are well and his sons help them become familiar with the project at hand."

"Father Beauvais," asks Diego suddenly, "but how can this be?"

"He is the Cardinal's nephew," says Thaddeus.

"Yes, I see the family resemblance," says Musit with a smile, "I truly do."

Chapter Twenty Two

The door to the room where Thaddeus lay in his bed was suddenly swung open and in came Diego carrying one of his sons in his arms and the young man looked almost lifeless. There was a sense of urgency in Diego's pace and the look of fear about him. Beauvais and Musit followed close behind them as well as the second brother.

"Oh, my God. What happened?" utters Thaddeus.

"Help me father!" exclaims Diego as he lies his son down carefully in the corner of the room on some bed linen lining there that the ladies of the parish had not picked up yet for laundering. The young man's face was pale and his breathing shallow, and Diego then dropped to his knees and beat himself with his fist on his legs and looked towards heaven, eyes closed he cried out, "Why, God why?"

Then Beauvais says nervously, "Please let me through, as I must administer the last rights." Diego wailed louder upon hearing those words and Musit begins to weep. Beauvais leans over Giovanni's almost lifeless body, which was dirty and slightly bleeding as if he had had a great fall, and begins to pray and then says nothing. Beauvais begins to whisper to himself, and it quickly becomes apparent that the he is in some distress. Musit stops and takes notice that the young priest is not saying anything, and she cannot understand why he is performing his sacred duty?

Just then, Beauvais, speaks out, "I cannot remember the words; oh Lord, I cannot remember the words," when he then notices a frail Father Thaddeus standing next to him. Thaddeus puts his hand on Gabriel's shoulder to both comfort him and to support his attempt to kneel next to Giovanni on the floor. Thaddeus then begins to pray silently and extends one hand towards the boy and begins to pray for him.

"Diego!" exclaims Thaddeus, "I require your assistance on this."

Diego quickly turns and after moment's pause realizes what it is that he is to do and extends his hand to his son as well, his hand resting on the hand already there, and both men pray in earnest as do all who are in the room. The young man's breathing then begins to slow, and the pigment returns to his skin. For this day he would most certainly not die and everyone in the room was now very much aware of that and all looked on in astonishment, except for the young man's father and the aging priest, Thaddeus. And those standing dropped to their knees, made the sign of the cross, and began to worship God.

About an hour passes before Giovanni awakens from his long sleep and asks his father where the angel came from?

"An angel?" asks his father. "To what angel are you referring, Giovanni."

"The one appeared to me in my sleep, I suppose," replies Giovanni.

At this Beauvais again approaches the young man and asks, "What is this about an angel?"

"Yes, father, an angel," says Giovanni solemnly, "an angel and she spoke to me as well."

"Spoke to you?" the priest asks.

"Yes," she said, "I would not die today and that the Lord would use me to bring the message of the gospel to many," Giovanni replied.

"My son," asks Diego, "exactly what do you remember about this day?"

"I remember walking along the rocky edge with Jose and then seeing the angel before I woke up here in this room with you looking over me by my side."

"Well, today was a great miracle, Giovanni, and the Lord spared your life as you took a great fall and we feared you dead, that is until the Lord healed you."

"Healed me, father?" asks Giovanni?

"Yes, you were badly injured and the Lord healed you."

"When we prayed for you," interjects Beauvais, "a true miracle before our very eyes and we must tell the people of this great deed."

"Yes, we must," said Giovanni.

Then a weakened Father Thaddeus spoke up and said, "No, we shall not."

"No, Father? But this was a great miracle and you were a large part of it," asks Beauvais.

"No," says Thaddeus calmly, none of us should speak of this miracle outside of this room.

Thaddeus looks at Musit and she nods in obedience, and Diego simply smiles, nods his head in agreement. "Neither I, nor my sons, will speak of this; I give you my word, father," says Diego.

"But, why father?" asks Beauvais disappointedly.

"Because if this gets out, the Church will get involved, and even though what little funding we receive comes through Florence, we are still officially under the authority of the bishop in Genoa."

Beauvais looks confused.

"If Genoa gets wind of this then they will come and investigate and if they find this miracle to be credible, then they will insist on having any artifacts for themselves, and in turn the Vatican itself will most likely then go and take possession and any miracles which might continue to happen here, would most likely cease."

"Artifacts? What artifacts, father?" asks Beauvais?

"Never mind," says Thaddeus.

Beauvais' face soon becomes very long with disappointment.

"Gabriel, I remember having a very similar argument with your uncle many years ago, an argument he was right about as I am right now," says Thaddeus in a kind tone. "All will all be made known to you in time, now do as I say and keep your silence," says Thaddeus. And with that ailing priest rolls over in his bed away from everyone and closes his eyes so he might sleep.

"Come everyone, the father needs his rest," insists Musit softly. So they all depart the room, even Giovanni as he is he is now back up on his feet.

Later that evening there is a noticeable chill in the air as Diego and his sons build a camp fire next to the spot where they have been bedding down the past few nights. There is a small cooking pot above the fire in which they cook their evening meal. The three of them then sit by the fire and watch as the sunlight is slowly replaced by firelight. They sing songs and laugh as they make merry in their joy of Giovanni's miracle.

"May I join you this evening?" asks Beauvais as he approaches the men from the church after checking on Musit and Thaddeus.

"Of course, father," says Diego, as the men rise to greet him. "It would be an honor." Beauvais sits down on a log and then seems quietly subdued, but after a couple of promptings joins them in eating the evening meal. "Father, Jose and I were just discussing how proud we are of Giovanni and his decision to go to seminary, should he be accepted of course," states Diego.

"Yes, wonderful," says Beauvais sounding preoccupied.

Diego and his sons sit quietly and eat noticing that something is bothering their new found friend. "So, how is Father Thaddeus?" asks Jose.

"He is still with us," replies Beauvais somberly.

"Have I ever told you how I met Father Thaddeus, my sons?" asks Diego.

"Yes, father, many times," reply his sons in unison.

"Well I do not believe the good father has heard my story, so you will indulge me while I share it with him." Both sons simply roll their eyes and smile at one another as Diego begins his tale, when suddenly Musit comes out to the fireside and motions for Gabriel to come with her.

"He is asking for you, father," says Musit.

At this, they all stand up and both Beauvais and Musit reenter the dwelling and see a weaker Thaddeus motioning for the young priest to come closer. Musit stands over by the door as Beauvais quickly approaches and asks softly, "Yes, Monsignor, how may I be of assistance?"

"I would like to for you to see to the needs of my burial should that become necessary, Gabriel, and you must be strong and continue the mission here."

"Yes, Monsignor, of course."

"A flock must have a shepherd, Gabriel, it must not be scattered by the wicked one," insists Thaddeus.

"I understand, Monsignor," replies Gabriel.

"Thank you, father, now I would speak with Musit if you please."

"Certainly," replies Gabriel, as he slightly bows towards Thaddeus as a sign of respect, and then departs.

Musit, who could not help but over hear the previous conversation slowly walks towards Thaddeus with her head slightly bowed, and then sits in a chair close to his bed.

"He will need a lot of help with this mission, and he will specifically need your help, Musit," states Thaddeus. Musit briefly smiles and nods in the affirmative, but she says nothing. "I have prayed for him and you as well, and I ask that you help him as you would me, Sister." Musit still says nothing and listens patiently. "Musit, please promise me something," requests Thaddeus.

"Yes, father, I promise," replies Musit. "If anything was to happen to me, that you will quietly see that this cloth here in my hand, a very old relic, is passed on the Gabriel as it once belonged to his uncle, Cardinal Beauvais and it is only right that he inherit it, Musit."

"Of course, father, as you wish," she replies.

Thaddeus then smiles slightly and lies back in his bed briefly only to once again turn towards Musit to address another topic.

"I only wish that there were more sisters here to assist the father," complains Thaddeus.

"Ah, but perhaps soon there will be," says Musit happily.

"What do you mean, Sister?"

"I was able to make one friend in my time in the convent, and she is partially of Sicilian heritage as well. She was sent to serve in Rome two years after she entered my Order and then was allowed to go and see her dying father in Genoa, as her father was once wealthy French merchant there, and her mother is from the old city of Palermo, and her mother from some far off place unknown. Well, as you see," Musit continued, "once I learned I was being reassigned to work with here, I asked and received permission to write a letter to her, Sister Solena, and requested that she come and join us here as well."

"I see," replied Thaddeus.

"Now if the Mother Superior in Rome will permit her to be reassigned, then she may be joining us soon."

"We can only pray that Lord manifest this addition to our mission here," says Thaddeus in a weakened voice.

"To be honest father, if the Sisters there want to be shed of her as much as they were with me in San Gimignano, then it is only a matter of time," laughs Musit. "Besides she loves the water, always have and I spoke of Portofino being near the water."

"That is awful that you were treated shabbily," says Thaddeus. "And they should be ashamed of their behavior, but yet we must forgive them and pray for their souls. Both make the sign of the cross as they bow their heads in quiet prayer.

"There is something else I would like to ask you to forgive as well, Sister," requests Thaddeus.

"What is that, father?"

"It concerns my confession."

"But should you not be giving that to Father Thaddeus?"

"Normally that would be true, but in this case, for this part of my life, I think that it would be best if I shared it only with you."

"I will go and get Father Beauvais," says Musit as she starts to get up from her chair.

"No, please, I beseech you, please stay and hear my confession, Musit, please." Musit nods in agreement and relents nervously to the dying priest's request, forces a nervous smile and she sits down again. "Thank you," says Thaddeus and then he begins. "I will make this simple and to the point and will not weigh you down with a lot of formality, Sister, for I have sinned in my heart over my desire to, for lack of a better word, posses a woman that I knew long, long ago."

"Are you sure that Father Beauvais would not be better equipped and versed to deal with such a matter?" asks Musit.

Thaddeus continues as if he does not hear her, and continues his bedside confession. "I would often attempt to purge the thoughts of her from my heart by hours of prayer and days of fasting, or would attempt to keep the thoughts at bay when in her presence by placing one of my fingers in the fire of a nearby lit candle. But always would they return and I not wanting to lose my integrity, or to break my vows, I would simply put time and distance between she and I and hope for the best. I would take long walks and pray and ask God's deliverance, but much like St. Paul, I would conclude that God's judgment for me was that His grace must be sufficient for me, and so it had to be. Over time I would find myself thinking of her, wondering about her, what she was doing at the moment. On occasion I would take and early even stroll along the Seine and would happen by and young couple holding hands and making tremendous eye contact with one another, both obviously very much in love and would think of her. I might see a woman with a child and would wonder what our children might have looked like, but still I could not tell her. I could not even give her the least hint as I had already made a commitment to another, that one being God, and so I eventually learned to live with my pain, my longing. I figured it was just my lot in life." With that, Thaddeus' voice begins to weaken even more, he coughs and wheezes with every breath now and Musit then insists that he rest now and he eventually agrees but only after she agrees to absolve him of sin.

Soon Thaddeus falls fast to sleep, but yet a restless sleep. Musit sits by his side well into the night, when she is suddenly awaken in her chair by the sound of a man's voice. It is that of Thaddeus talking in his sleep. "I have always loved you and could not tell you. How many times I wanted to tell you and did not dare, not even the flame of the candle against my skin drove my love for you away, and now it is too late, Musit, much too late."

Those were the final words the Monsignor spoke as he exhaled for the last time and never spoke again. Musit, now in tears quickly departs for Gabriel to administer that last rights, and still she cannot believe that he is gone, nor that it happened oh so fast, nor that he had been in love with her, a love never spoken of, a love which she would always keep buried deep within her heart.

Just before dawn, Diego is awaken by the sound of Father Beauvais quietly leaving Monsignor's dwelling and as he passes what is left of the light from the fire which burned throughout the night, Diego notices the pain and grief present in Gabriel's face. Soon the young priest makes his way over to a small group of trees overlooking the seaside and it is there that he begins to cry aloud and grieve he does as the dawn breaks in the distant skyline between the darkness and the morning's light. Now his friend and his mentor are gone, an event which he knew was coming, one he that he had prepared himself for, or so he thought. No one dared disturb him as he wept and they simply bowed their heads and wept silently for both the father that was gone and the one who would soon assume his burden of his mantle.

The burial of Monsignor Thaddeus went almost unnoticed by anyone who might have been considered important to the Church, yet the parishioners of the small, fishing village of Portofino turned out to pay their farewells to a man they had barely known, but to a man who brought them a place to worship in as well a renewed hope that their desire to serve God had not been forgotten. Father Thaddeus got through the funeral with a hint of alcohol on his breath, and by his side were the people who loved the Monsignor most, which included a late arrival of one Father Hugo. The winter had made the ground hard to break, but Don Diego braved the cold weather and a chilling wind from the sea and made sure his old friend had a place to rest until that one day when they would all meet again in the great hereafter. Jose and Giovanni departed for home now that spring had arrived, to fields which needed to be planted and Giovanni had much preparation as well before the autumn and his upcoming studies at the seminary. Diego decided to stay awhile longer in Portofino to see that the reconstruction of the church was completed and was most displeased that the church could not be named St. Thaddeus Church as the recently departed Monsignor had not been declared a Saint officially by the Church, but was agreeable to the name of St. Paul's. A plaque had been engraved on a large rectangular piece of wood and would soon be attached to the church above the front door. At last the church was to be complete, but still there was a since of loss without the presence of Father Thaddeus, as well a chill in the night air.

So back to his fire Diego went, to sit and warm his hands and feet awhile which too quickly now grew cold as his years had begun to advance. As Diego sat and looked on occasion away from the fire and out towards the sea, he remembered the words of his now departed mother who said, "That we either get older or we die," and he took some comfort in her words as he looked briefly at the wrinkles now present on his hands. It felt good to sit and see the outline of the soon to be completed church and to smell the salt in the air, "For tomorrow would take of itself," he thought to himself. Plenty of time to worry about tomorrow then, as for tonight his work was done.

Still Diego could not help but to notice the well worn cloth that now lie partly tucked under the young priest's belt that day, and even more so, did he know exactly what it was that he now possessed? "Should I tell him?" reflected Diego. "Did Father Thaddeus tell him?"

Soon Diego decided that this was not the time for revelation, for this was a time of mourning and mourn they did. It was also during this time that Diego decided that if he could not see the church named after his now departed friend, that the next best thing he could do would be to come back one day and build a monastery here in this place and dedicate it to his memory. Diego knew he was no priest, but had longed for awhile now to do something pleasing in the Lord's service and this all seemed right to him. And he would see that Giovanni went through seminary and even more so, that Jose would continue to mature into a man of God; he would now become a father to Gabriel as well. Diego, for an instant, remembered a time after Cardinal Beauvais died and shortly after Father Thaddeus moved on to Paris. He recalled how he had tried to minister to a few of the people who were most needy in San Gimignano, but how the new priest scolded him into not doing so claiming that Diego had not enough education for such a task and was better suited to being a farmer. He remembered the words of love the spoke and the look of anger upon the priest's face, and no, he knew he was not a priest nor even a monk, but much like a priest he now had his flock, even if for the majority of the time it would only be a flock of one. This time there would be no self-important priest to stop him, which suited him just fine. With that, Diego dropped to one knee and made an oath to the Lord to head the call which had been revealed to him this day.

Chapter Twenty Three

Many years had now passed since the miracle of God saved the life of his son, Giovanni, and as well as the time of the passing of his friend, Father Thaddeus. Diego was now well into his years and most of his hair was now silver, rather than the jet black that it once was, hair that he once saw as his pride and which the ladies take notice, was nothing more than a memory in time lost. He was to make this trip to Porto Fino alone after the passing of his wife and yet his linage was strong and thriving through Jose, his oldest. The vineyard was doing very well and Diego found himself feeling less than useful, so he would make the trip to the coast and see this monastery which he financed, and make sure that Father Beauvais had all the help he needed.

Even more so he would see that his son, now Father Giovanni, was settling in there as well now that he had finished seminary and had taken his oath of poverty, chastity, and obedience. He could hardly wait to see Giovanni and to hear him perform his first mass, so wait no longer would he and he prepared his horse and his provisions and made his way westward and to the sea. And although Jose had insisted to join him on his journey, he knew that Jose was needed more by his own family and the son he was only now teaching the secrets of the grape and the mysteries of the sun and soil, along with the rain make the grapes grow. Young Don Diego, his namesake, was not yet four years of age, but already Diego could tell that when it came to having an eye for good grapes. The boy was sure to one day excel, and Jose would be staying here in the shadow of San Gimignano and tend to that education as a good father should. Diego stopped briefly to look back and to wave farewell with his hat to his family that morning, if only for a short while that crisp September morning. And so his trek began.

In Genoa, the archbishop summons a priest to his office and asks him to sit down in a stiff, wooden chair across from him. The archbishop then dismisses his aide and begins his inquiry. "Monsignor Benedetto, it has recently come to my attention that two Franciscan priests are holding mass and staying at one of our now defunct churches."

"I see, Excellency."

"This would present a problem," replied Benedetto.

"We cannot allow these Franciscans to hold mass in a Byzantine Church. I require that you go to this parish and seek out these priests and ascertain exactly what it is that they are up to," states the archbishop.

"May I inquire as to where this parish may be found and exactly what it is that I am to look for there?" asks Benedetto.

"This is of the strictest of confidence, but there are rumors that some kind of miracle took place there and a relic of great age was used in the process," replies the archbishop. The archbishop now has the monsignor's full attention. You will proceed to Porto Fino on a ship named the Agostina."

"But the Agostina is a warship, Excellency."

"You will depart at once for Porto Fino and with all pleasantries you will gain their confidence and then discern the nature of this supposedly miracle and as to whether it ever did happen. Moreover, if it be true, then you will learn if there truly is a relic and then confiscate it for the church here in Genoa so that it can be better... administrated."

"Of course, Excellency, at once," replies Benedetto. "If I might ask though, will not a warship in such a small harbor draw attention and raise suspicion? asks the monsignor.

"You will tell the priest that you were on ship to when it was attacked by pirates and that the ship needs to take on provisions and to make repairs before departing for the long trek to Amalfi, and then on to Egypt," instructs the archbishop.

"Yes, Excellency."

"It is an easy enough story to believe, monsignor."

"Do you have any more details on what this, this relic, might be, Excellency?"

"I do not, but it was relayed to me to be of great age and most of all of great power.... said to have possibly come from even from heaven above."

"I see," replies the monsignor, and if there is no truth to this miracle, or of the artifact, what are your orders?

"Then if you find this to be the case, you will instruct them to stop saying mass in a clearly Benzyntine Church and evict them both immediately and take whatever wealth they have acquired while there."

"Yes, Excellency."

"But I wish to make this perfectly clear, that if you do find that there is anything to this story you will bring the item back, is that understood Monsignor Benedetto?"

"Of course, Excellency," replies the monsignor. "Also, in three months time I will send a priest, Father Nuncio, to take assume the duties of tending to the flock in Porto Fino, and you need not reveal this to the priests not squatting there."

"Yes, Excellency," replies Benedetto.

"Very well then, I shall keep you no longer, my son," and with that Benedetto stands up and heads for the exit. "The ship's captain awaits you and only knows that you are on very important business for the church, and that is all he needs to know," barks the archbishop.

Benedetto nods in agreement and then goes to gather a few necessities and soon departs for inner harbor. Once out to sea, all the time wondering if the archbishop will send him on any more of these quests for so called relics in the future.

"Other than receiving my meals I do wish to be disturbed my good captain, if so please, as I shall be in much prayer and meditation upon the scriptures," announces the monsignor.

"Of course, Eminence, as you wish. May I inquire as to the exact nature of our voyage?" inquires the captain.

"No, you may not," replies the monsignor without so much as a smile as he suddenly closes the door to his cabin in an abrupt manner.

Truth be told, the monsignor hated the sea and he especially hated sea travel of any kind, yet he served an archbishop in a great port city and such travels could sometimes not be avoided. He viewed this trip as just another thing he must endure if he too ever wanted to have the office of bishop one day bestowed upon him, and possibly even archbishop might one day await him. But first, he would run this little fool's errand for this all high and mighty archbishop and soon would return with the usual findings. No relic, no miracles, and of course fictional soon to be fabricated stories of how he had come to these great conclusions. Yet, if by the slimmest chance that a there might actually be a relic in of all places, Porto Fino, what an accomplishment it would be for him to bring it back in triumph. Certainly then the archbishop could deny him nothing. Benedetto soon lies down on his bunk trying not to think of the boat swaying back and forth on the waves. He looks about the room for a nearby bucket just in case and eventually manages to fall fast asleep.

On the following morning there is a knock at the door and a quick announcement alerting him that the ship would be entering port soon and with that Benedetto opened his cabin door and in almost one fail swoop takes his breakfast from the yeoman and then again closing his door.

The breakfast, other than small amount of fairly fresh fruit was unpalatable, so he decides to simply leave it on the plate and prepare himself for the charade he was about to begin on a surely clueless and most likely unseasoned small town priest, or at least he hoped this would be the case.

"Shall I send some men with you, Eminence?" asked the captain.

"No, just have someone row me to shore and I will attend to things myself, thank you very much," replied the monsignor. "Having a warship in a small harbor will most likely frighten most of the people away, so there is no need to send armed men as well into the village," directs Benedetto.

"As you wish," replied the ship's captain.

Benedetto made his way down to a small boat which had been lowered down the side of the warship and along with two other men somehow made it into the craft safely. Benedetto hated traveling in these less than steady small boats almost more than he did the bigger ships, but he knew he would soon be on dry land again, if only for awhile. As his stomach begins to churn, the monsignor looks back up to the ship and says, "And keep your men on board as well, captain, is that understood? I will send these men back with whatever provisions you may take on and then will signal you when I am ready to leave; is that clear, captain?"

"Crystal", snaps back the captain in a less than hospitable manner not being used to taking orders from anyone while on the deck of his own ship. But the captain knew his place and knew that they were all on some mission for the church, and disobeying the church had its consequences. So he would endure this humiliation and hope he would not have to endure it much longer.

The small craft made its way with the monsignor and two sailors passing a small fishing boat and two fishermen preparing to go out to obtain their daily catch. The two fishermen greeted the priest as he sailed by them, but the monsignor barely acknowledged as if they were no more than a bug to be swatted out of the way. Several men who were preparing their nets on small fishing boats near the shore begin to notice the activity in the harbor now that the sun has ascended enough to greet the day. There was still a slight fog which had settled on the water and the sea gulls were beginning to move about although there was still a noticeable chill in the air. Having never been here, Benedetto eyed the small homes on the hill side and made out what he believed was most likely the church on a flat place overlooking the village. There was a small building not too far from the small dock which the landing craft was headed were a few people were going in and out of most assuredly some sort of inn or possibly a store he surmised. So far he had not seen anything even resembling a priest, and the natives seemed friendly enough, although cautious. Not very impressive this Porto Fino, the monsignor thought to himself, little more than a pimple on the map of life really. Yet, he still had a job to do and it was at this point that Benedetto prepared a very warm smile in preparation of his duty which lie ahead of him, and so being the cynical man he was, Benedetto thought, so let the charade begin. And smile he did.

His dark brown and silver hair, the finely fashioned embroidered red shirt, black hat, pants, leggings, shoes and cloak, along with the modest cross which hung from his neck, indicated that he was someone most assuredly of great importance. His face was roughed, yet his hands were soft, his voice distinct. Trappings which were guaranteed to intimidate almost any peasant he might cross paths with simply at the mere sight of them. At last they had reached the dock, and small as it was, it was a very welcomed sight to the monsignor especially once the boat was securely moored and he had once again set foot on dry land again. "Welcome children, welcome, extolled Benedetto with arms opened wide, and do not be afraid for I have come to the good news of the gospel of Jesus Christ with you this day!"

The fishermen who had been mending nets and patching boats slowly began to remove their hats and make way towards the priest, and one before him the all bowed one by one and kidded his ring as he extended his hand to each and every one of them. None of the villagers dared to speak; most wondered exactly who this man could be, and even more so, why a priest would arrive no less vessel than a warship which was not only bearing men, but cannon as well? Some of the older villagers recognized the monsignor's garb as that of the Byzantine Church, yet it had been so long since any of them had seen anything like this. Finally one of the eldest villagers, a very old man with hunched back begins to slowly speak to Monsignor Benedetto and then points up on the hillside towards the church. The old man offers to walk with and guide the priest up the hillside, but Benedetto will not hear of it but eventually and reluctantly accept a younger guide and the two of them begin the slow climb through the rocks and up the path towards the church.

It was at this point that Father Thaddeus notices a ship resting in the harbor, and then there were two men coming up the path towards him. One was wearing an expensive cloak, the kind of cloak he had not seen since he left Paris the year before. At this Gabriel begins to say a quick prayer under his breath, over comes his fear and retires inside the church to begin his daily prayers, and await whoever this stranger might be who had come on such a large ship to visit such an even smaller church in the tiny fishing village of Porto Fino. "Hello, father," greets Musit while Sister Rose looks on suspiciously.

"Hello sisters," replies Benedetto.

"How may we be of assistance, father?" Musit asks.

"I am seeking the two priests who are caring for our church so well out here in the wilderness, sister," he replies.

"Two priests?" Musit questions.

Benedetto looks puzzled and says nothing.

"You must mean Father Thaddeus and Father Beauvais, but I am sorry to report that the Monsignor is no longer with us as he passed on to his reward recently and all of the duties have now fallen to Father Beauvais and to ourselves," replies Musit.

It was at this time Gabriel approached the three of them and asks, Musit, "Who is our honored guest?"

At this point he steps up and says, "I am Monsignor Benedetto, a Marionite Priest of the Byzantine Order, and I have the pleasure of overseeing the spiritual needs of the flock in this lovely village." Gabriel stands motionless for a brief period as he tries to absorb what the Monsignor has actually just said to him as well as to what his next move might actually be concerning this stranger and it was at this point that he missed his mentor, Father Thaddeus, who would most certainly handle matter s of delicacy such as this with much more ease. Yet, Thaddeus was not here and it would now fall to him to deal with this situation, whatever it may be, thought Gabriel.

"Also father, I wish to express my deepest sympathy for your recent loss of Monsignor Thaddeus and shall beseech the Lord on your behalf ask that he guide and comfort you in this time of unsettlement in your lives," says Benedetto as he now looks around at all three of people present there in front of him.

"Thank you father, and we very much appreciate your kind prayer this day for our continued comfort and further guidance," replies Gabriel. "And please, allow me to introduce everyone. This is Sister Musit and Sister Rosa of the Order of

San Francisco, as Gabriel motions towards each sister individually, and I am Father Gabriel Beauvais, formerly of St. Julian the Poor in Paris, and now temporary overseer of this humble church that you now see before you.

"How did you come to this position as caretaker, father?" asks Benedetto.

"As you well know, father," paused Gabriel, "the Marionites are not in communion with the Papacy…"

"Yes, I understand all that, but I am here only as an observer, not here to make any demands of you, father, but there are a few questions if I might," replies Benedetto.

"Perhaps you would like a tour of the church and the grounds to see what repairs have initiated in the absence of any shepherd, father, and there we can walk and chat further? " Gabriel motions with his left hand towards the church and gently puts his right hand towards, but not on Benedetto's left elbow.

"As you wish, my son," replies the monsignor with an almost disarming smile on his face and the two men leave the nuns and make their way towards the church.

Later that afternoon, Sister Rosa walked up the clearing on top of a hill overlooking the city and then harbor where she would often sit and soak up the sun and enjoy her lunch time meal. As she sat with her feet dangling over the edge of the rocks, she could not help but notice the dark haired man she had met earlier in the day now standing down near the waterside. She watched as he seemed to have sent one of the fishermen out the large ship which rested in the middle of the harbor. Soon the ship raised sail and turned to leave as the man walked over and disappeared into the inn. She wondered about the large ship and what it might be like to travel on one, having never actually seen one before, she could not help but be impressed by it. How many wonderful places it (the ship) must have visited in its time and all of the interesting people and exotic languages the ship and crew must have encountered. Perhaps one day too she might take an ocean voyage upon the high seas and possibly see Venice, or Barcelona, or even the holy land itself? To walk the steps once walked by her blessed savior, to see the place where he was crucified, and if possible the Garden of Gethsemane where had once prayed, or perhaps even the empty tomb. Maybe she would be asked to help establish a Sisters of San Francisco Order there, yet that was almost too much to hope for? But all these things were too much to dream upon, especially with the work there was to do. For now she must settle for viewing grand ships from a distance and she could live with that, yet, still maybe one day she thought. Sister Rosa looked back towards the church and noticed Sister Musit hard at work sweeping the main entrance, so she decided that she too would make herself useful and start cleaning something too.

  The days grew a little longer and warmer as well. Spring was in the air and the mornings seemed sunnier somehow. On one of these sunny mornings both Musit and Rosa took their baskets and headed down into the village to shop for some poultry, a little seafood, and of course any fresh fruit and vegetables that might be available from the local vendors. Friday was market day and many of the locals would be there looking and buying, and most of all talking, something the sisters were not about to miss out on. So off they went, basket in hand, to shop and perhaps get out of their room for a little while. They had taken over the only bedroom connected to the church, one which was made available when Father Thaddeus passed on to his reward. Father Gabriel (the name he now went by) seemed quite content in his new quarters, a small room in the far side of the church that had most probably been a closet of some kind, yet all had adjusted and seemed to be settling in nicely. The sister looked for Father Gabriel, but he was nowhere to be found on this morning. It was not until they almost reached the market place did they sisters notice him buying nice round loaf of bread from an elderly lady who had set up shop there just that morning. Musit knew that the bread she made was at least as good as the bread Father Gabriel was purchasing, but the woman looked as if she truly needed the business so Musit decided to keep silent in this matter. Sister

Rosa walked slightly behind Sister Musit and always had a big smile on her face. It was at this time that the sisters notice the man in the black robes depart from the end and make his way towards Father Gabriel.

The young priest could hardly hide his being uncomfortable around the older man of the cloth, and seemed like he wanted to get away from Benedetto, yet Gabriel never quite did and a polite discussion would once again begin. It was at this point that Sister Rosa would alter her course to avoid the older man and would wonder ever so slightly to the edges of the market place as she smiled and nodded to any local women who might be present. Yet never would she venture out of eyesight of Musit, at least not until today. In one of the narrow alley ways Rosa could not help but notice some sort of commotion going on and her curiosity got the best of her, so investigate she did. Upon glancing she noticed a small songbird standing in a somewhat dazed form in the middle of three cats, (who most assuredly hung around the water front cleaning up whatever scraps which were left over from the fishermen's catch of the day), who were watching the bird carefully to see what its next move might be. Upon closer examination, Rosa notice the bird was slightly bloodied and some of the poor dear's feathers were somewhat disheveled. The bird was surely a goner, when the mother instinct in Sister Rosa got the best of her and with that she stepped in between the bird and the three cats, who had hardly noticed she was even there and with one motion reached down and scooped the bird up and placed it in her a small pocket and out of the reach of the cats. The cats looked astonished as if they could not believe what had just happened and looked on her to see if she might produce the bird once again like some sort of game they might all play. But Rosa turned and stepped back into the market area and looked for a small cage to purchase for her new found friend to convalesce in at least for awhile.

Rosa eventually found a small cage made of twigs and twine, which she purchased for little or nothing, and soon the sisters began their short trek back up the hill towards the church with neither Sister Musit nor Father Gabriel the wiser. Rosa thought about how they would soon be breaking ground for a vegetable, a task which would most certainly provide plenty of earth worms and bugs for her little friend to eat. Yet what to call her friend, she wondered? Was it a boy bird or even a girl bird? And even more so, would it survive its wounds, wounds which could have been much more devastating had the cats been more hunger than bored that morning.

Soon the sisters reached their room and once inside Rosa produced her little friend who still seemed in shock, so she placed it inside the cage along with a small piece of soft cloth in order for the bird to rest upon. Musit eventually discovered the small bird that Rosa had rescued and could not help but come to the conclusion that it would most surely die in a day or two and break Rosa's heart. So, Musit would stay still on the matter not wanting to add to Rosa's awaiting grief which would soon come a calling. She simply took Rosa's hand and bowed her head in prayer and with a warm smile, Musit, departed the room and went about her daily chores. She would also not tell Father Gabriel of the guest that was staying in their room, for as far as Musit was concerned the room the sisters occupied was their equivalent of a convent for now and what happened in the convent fell under her domain. Besides being the baby that he often was he would begin to complain about the bird and any bugs it might have roaming around on it, but that would most certainly infest the church and everyone who entered it. Some things are just better left unsaid she thought, and with broom in hand, Musit, swept the church, inside and out that spring afternoon until the evening meal which Rosa was most certainly preparing.

The following morning Rosa got up to find that her bird had died in the night and she wept quietly. Nothing much was said the rest of the day, with the only real words being spoken were those of Father Gabriel when he noticed the sisters burying the poor creature near the resting place of Father Thaddeus under an aging olive tree on the grounds of the church just a few yards outside his bedroom door. None of them had known this bird long, but it deserved a decent burial, and decent burial it got on this overcast and somber Saturday afternoon.

The summer was slow to approach but once it did so, was warmer than the summers before. The Marionite, Benedetto, tarried about the village buying dinner and drinks for anyone he thought might lead him to what he wanted to know, yet after his three month stay, he left upon the same ship he had arrived on with nothing more than a few rumors, a few innuendos, and a few less coins in his purse. The warship which had arrived just as unannounced as it had the spring before more trouble this time in the form of another Marionite as well as four Genovese soldiers who walked up to the front of the church, a church which had been abandoned and fallen into disrepair under the Byzantines, was now suddenly their long sought after prize possession. With no more than a few harsh but polite words read from an official looking piece of parchment, the Franciscans were invited to leave, and so they did.

Father Gabriel wanted to protest but knew saw that it was a waste of time, and so he watched as the soldiers waited for the sisters to pack their things and vacate as well. The three of them moved up the road to the newly established Franciscan Monastery which was not in use and waiting for the return of Father Giovanni. The sisters temporarily took up residence in the Spartan like facility while Father Gabriel slept and took his meals outside under the open sky. It was soon decided that once Father Giovanni arrived to take on his duties in the monastery, that the father and the sisters would make their way to Florence to seek guidance and most of all direction on what was to be done now, and that is if anything was possible. None of them liked giving up and leaving the church the way that did, but with the authorities on the side of the Byzantines, there was little else they could do. Rosa was especially displeased that she not only had to leave her garden behind which she had worked so hard to plant and care for, but she also left behind the small friend that she had buried there just a few short weeks ago.

Benedetto reflected upon his stay in Porto Fino and his search for the relic his city so very much desired. He had heard the strange story of the young man who fell from the cliffs onto the rocks below him but who later showed no apparent ill effects to such a fall. The Franciscans were most assuredly hiding something, something which was most likely derived from heaven above, yet for some reason they kept it quiet. They did not use whatever it was for power, or glory, or even for riches, something Benedetto could hardly expect his own kinsmen to do if they acquired such an item.

The Franciscans had brought neither war nor the threat of war and that, the Marionite found honorable, both in his eyes and God's as well. He was very skilled at his duties, but Benedetto was also a man of conscious and so the Franciscan's mystery would remain just that, or so his report would reflect and the leadership back in Genoa would be none the wiser for it. The launch had now reached the ship, and Monsignor Benedetto made his way carefully back on board and to his room while he waited for the warships' departure. He thought he might like to retire her one day, should the opportunity present itself, the Marionite thought to himself, but first a nap, a very long nap which might find Genoa once again waiting up the arrival of morning of course, solid ground.

Father Giovanni was alarmed to learn of the situation in Porto Fino upon his arrival four days after the eviction from the church. Don Diego was displeased with the ouster and planned on presenting the Marionite with a bill for services rendered upon the church, but he decided that it could wait until he made the trip to Florence with the others. He had met up with Giovanni a day's walk outside of Porto Fino and looked forward to a long rest in the sun above the waters, but this was not to be the case. With Father Giovanni now stationed in the monastery, the other four would depart on the morrow and would soon hopefully return with some sort of resolution in their hand that would return to them what they felt they had earned through hard work and the sweat of their brow. Only time would tell and Florence was not an easy place to navigate, and it was also full of treachery if one was not very, very careful.

Once in Florence, the sisters were reassigned to their Order in San Gimignano, and Gabriel was sent on to Assisi to complete his vows as a Franciscan. Don Diego was thanked by the bishop for his assistance in this matter and was offer and accommodation for his troubles in which he could rest and renew his strength after a long journey, but nothing little else. It seemed that no one was willing to declare war on Genoa over a small church and both Gabriel and Diego decided in private not to reveal the miracle involving Giovanni's injury back in Porto Fino.

Gabriel did not know the whole story associated with the strange cloth that Monsignor Thaddeus had left to him, but he did see the effect it had on Giovanni and knew it was too important to part with, least of all to that arrogant, Marionite rival. So off the relic went, tucked inside the garment of a relatively young and inexperienced priest was it to stay and make its way to Assisi as so many other pilgrims had over the years before. Ten days of rest came and went and Diego once again took to his mount and made his way once again to Porto Fino and to his son, Giovanni.

Chapter Twenty Four

Spring was again approaching Umbria and Father Gabriel had completed his vows in presence of the brothers in the church at Assisi. He was beginning to feel at home in his new order and wanted to make the best of it in honor of his dear departed mentor. Gabriel was even more pleased to be going back to Porto Fino where he is to join the monastery there and oversee operations there until an abbot can be appointed to formally take charge in the near future. Yet until then, he would be in charge and pretty much be run things as he pleases.

Gabriel had seen something in Assisi that he had never witnessed before, a nativity scene which was set up by the brothers with assistance of the town's people in order that they might reenact the birth of the holy baby Jesus. There was a manger, oxen, sheep, assorted chickens and geese, as well the holy family and even a babe supplied to be the baby Jesus. Often some of the town's people would bicker over whose child would be used that particular night to represent our King of Kings, almost to the point of ruining the whole idea in the first place. But eventually the monks would come out and begin their roles as shepherds, soon followed by three priests which were to represent the magi which had followed the star that ever so holy night. The people soon forgot about their differences once all had assembled except for a few grumblings oh whose baby had acquitted itself in a more Christ like matter than the others.

Overall the nativity scene was a success and Gabriel could not wait to get to Porto Fino and suggest it to the people there for the upcoming Christmas season still several months away. A manger of some type would have to be erected along with some sort of shelter to receive those wishing to join the festivities, all things that could be worked out at a later date. Perhaps even Don Diego, if still present might even consent to playing one of the magi if properly approached?

Father Gabriel would depart for his new assignment the following morning, and with a short stop off in Florence to rest and pray, he envisioned the journey as being a pleasant one now that the grief (which had weighed so heavily upon him) of losing his friend, the monsignor, had at last subsided.

Giovanni watched the church below him from outside the monastery he and his father helped rebuild, the hand full of people went in and out of it for daily prayers. The neophyte priest had been holding mass outside the monastery near a rather large olive tree, that is when the weather permitted and the parishioners actually showed up to participate. The change over in the church leadership had obviously confused and frightened the town's people; Giovanni was sure of it. The four soldiers camped nearby did not help to ease those fears either. The village went on though as it had for centuries before; fishing, visiting family and friends, planting harvesting, tending to olive trees, making olive oil, selling goods, raising families, and enjoying the fruits of their labors. Father Gabriel had been right when he said that Porto Fino was a wonderful and peaceful place to live.

Soon Father Gabriel would return and with perhaps a whole Florentine army and perhaps even a navy to take back the church that was rightfully theirs, thought Giovanni. Soon we would no longer have to suffer such humiliation at the hands of these interlopers. And if only his father was here, the great Don Diego, would those soldiers fear him or they would most certainly feel the edge of his sword, a sword fit for king. Giovanni reflected as he imagined his father dueling with all three of four of them and of course, besting them all.

Now it was time for a nap in the shade of the Olive tree until the mid day sun had passed. A few figs to nibble on would quiet his stomach until he was ready to build a fire and prepare his evening meal. Yes, Porto Fino was a wonderful place and he prayed to God that he might not ever have to depart from it. In the distance Giovanni could hear the waves lapping against the rocky shoreline, the sound of children too restless to sleep running just outside their mother's grasp as they wanted desperately to play, and he could also not help but hear the grumblings of the soldiers below who did not want to be posted in such an unimportant place as Porto Fino, and least of all to play nurse mate to an unimpressive and insignificant rat hole of a village's church.

Father Gabriel finally arrived back in Porto Fino and began sharing his ideas with Father Giovanni on the idea of a nativity scene for the upcoming Christmas season. But it was not to be, as one month later an older priest arrived at the monastery and upon becoming abbot decided a nativity scene was too new to share with these simple villager folk and that they might better wait until a more appropriate time.

Father Adelfo, was a short older man who was balding, walked with the help of a cane, and who would sweat profusely at any hint of physical exertion, so he avoided the mid day sun as much as he possibly could. He always seemed to carry a small handkerchief with which he repeatedly used to wipe the perspiration from his furrowed brow. Adelfo, being of Greek origin was sent to Porto Fino by the church mainly because he had some previous dealings with the Byzantine Church in his country of origin and it was believed that he might calm the situation and possibly even bring it to an advantageous solution for the Catholic Church in general. The Marionite rebuffed any attempt by the Franciscans to be sociable.

Two years passed by very slowly for the three priests and little was done to add a chapel to the monastery itself. Most days were filled with monotony and frustration. The villagers got to where they ignored the two warring parties for the most, or at least that was how they were viewed. Soon, so few people even attended services that the soldiers were ordered back home to Genoa. One man who lived in a sort of small settlement in the hills just outside of Porto Fino did inquire about becoming a monk at the monastery, but upon his asking a few basic questions, he left and went down the hill to the Byzantine Church and presumably asked the Marionite the same sort of questions without joining either that day. The man would leave and then reappear a week or so later and ask more questions of the Franciscans and Marionites without ever joining either order, and soon he was just dismissed by all concerned as most likely a half whit and more likely some sort of trouble maker up to no good.

On the third year after Aldefo's arrival, a drought set in and the food crops which had been so plentiful before were now quite scarce. There was still an abundance of seafood, but one could only eat fish so many times a week before despising the very sight or even the smell of it. The sea gulls that Gabriel once took great pleasure in when first arriving had now for the most become a nuisance by their constantly stealing of whatever they could in order to feed their empty stomachs, which surely appeared to be bottomless by most accounts. The droppings that the gulls left behind were as far as the eye could see and without the sisters there to clean up after them, the gull's presence became an unwelcomed one around the monastery.

In town, the people hoarded what little goods they had and shared very little with the priests and by the second year of the drought, things became even harder to acquire as were the donations. The drought seemed worse than the year before and no one could remember when there had been a decent rain in or near the village. Animals died, and the people began to grow thin as were their patience. The small garden that Giovanni and Gabriel attended to brought in very little and for the most withered long before there was any hope of harvest. People seemed to lose hope and some began to abandon the village all together with some moving in with relatives in other parts of the continent. Some took to ships and some to the highways, and yet some just settled in and planned to endure. Giovanni was eventually reassigned to Assisi which left only Gabriel and Adelfo, the abbot.

Don Diego had purchased a small villa on the edge of the village two years earlier and was rarely seen anymore except for an occasional outing to the market place to purchase whatever he might find there to eat. On one occasion a merchant ship sailed into the small harbor in need of repairs and was willing to trade any food goods it could spare in exchange for their needs being met. The ship's captain brought some Valencia Oranges, (directly from Spain), into the village square and Don Diego bought all of them that he could, where he immediately took them home and sitting in his favorite chair, he began to eat them. Diego would savor each orange and slowly ate one at a time in hopes of making them last as long as he could. Diego missed home and as his years began to reveal themselves more and more, he thought less of San Gimgnano and more, and more so of going home, home to Catalonia. Often the town's people would hear Diego playing his guitar in the quiet of the day. The melodic notes would resonate with their hearts and at this point any break from the monotony was a pleasant distraction indeed to the town's people. No one dare complain for soon his guitar music became as loved by the villagers as one might come to love the sound of bells ringing from a church near the center of the city square. Yet, poor Porto Fino did not have a church bell to its name, but it did have Don Diego and his melodic guitar, and that was exactly how they wanted to keep it.

Don Diego had primarily come back to Porto Fino to grieve the loss of his beloved wife, yet he had considered alternative places. On occasion, Diego would consider running off to Granada and finding a beautiful young woman there, where he would marry her, make passionate love to her and then they would lie on the bed together for hours feeding one another ripe dates and of course Valencia orange slices. He would impregnate her and raise a child with her in order that might feel young and most of all alive again. Don Diego imagined, that he and the boy might make trips to the sea where they would both fish the days away as his wife looked on, but Diego always decided against going at the last second. And then without so much as a word of regret, Diego would stop his day dreaming just long enough to remember to thank God for his goodness and then to pour once again from his wine bottle. How fortunate he was to be alive this day even if his body did ache from the ravages of time, Diego reflected as he continued to play his sweet melodies upon his guitar for all to hear.

One hot afternoon Gabriel went to check on the old gentleman and pay him a visit only to find him dead in his chair, his long and now silver hair pulled back behind his head, and his three cats milling about his feet. A half-filled wine glass one the table next to his chair, two small Valencia oranges in his pocket, and of course his guitar by his side. Gabriel for a moment considered taking the relic from within his robes and applying it to the old man as he lie motionless, but then decided not to, for more than a year now, Don Diego had not looked physically well, yet he now looked like he was finally at rest and most of all feeling no discomfort.

Upon learning of his death, the whole village mourned. A letter was dispatched immediately to his family, and a simple funeral soon took place as he had previously requested. All of the town's people were in attendance in lieu of any family and not a dry eye could be seen within miles. Most did not know really know him nor had even met him, although many claimed they did. As the town's people walked by his casket to pay their last respects, it was even said that some quietly deposited a Valencia orange or two into his casket as sort of a farewell gesture to him, because they knew he loved them so much. Gabriel wanted very much to speak at his friend's funeral but was not asked to by the man in charge of the ceremony (Father Adelfo). Within six months of the funeral, Aldefo retired and soon went back to Assisi to live out the remainder of his years. Moreover, Father Gabriel assumed the role as abbot in the absence of anyone else coming to take charge.

In the days to come there was such was the outcry of the people in the village that Giovanni was soon sent for by Gabriel. Upon arriving, Giovanni stayed in his father's grotto, where he eventually learned to play his father's guitar far better than Don Diego had. Giovanni became so popular with his music playing that the Church even sanctioned his performances as being good for the moral of the people. The Marionite looked on with disdain at all the fuss being made over something as trivial "guitar music". Yet it was rumored that Don Diego, (now buried high on the hill overlooking the Spartan like monastery that he had built which overlooked the sea that he also grew to love), could on rare occasion be heard playing his guitar at night, when there was a full moon among the ancient olive trees. His legend quickly grew and soon he became known affectionately as "Don Diego, the Troubadour of Porto Fino". Eventually there was a small chapel built by the villagers just outside the monastery in Don Diego's honor; he was sorely missed.

In the days to come, Father Giovanni was lax in his duties at the monastery, but Gabriel did not press him on these matters deciding it was far better that Giovanni be allowed to grieve and would most likely sooner or later return when he was able. So, it came as a total surprise to Father Gabriel when he received word from the bishop a couple of weeks later that Giovanni had requested to be relieved from his duties as a priest and the letter which Gabriel held his hand granted just that, with no hint of when a replacement might arrived for if one was even be considered. Gabriel was not quite sure what to make of this sudden change in young Giovanni's life, but if the bishop had approved it, who was he not to go along with it? Gabriel went to the villa and knocked on the door a few times, but no one answered, so he left the letter tucked away near the door and figured that Giovanni would eventually find it.

The days became little more than a battle to fight boredom and with the exception of a small number of older ladies, few attended mass on a regular basis there. Holidays were always the exception and the thoughts of a nativity scene once again peaked Father Gabriel's interest, but only briefly as there was a drought going on in the land and with food being scarce the town's people had more important things to attend to than a nativity scene, so the idea was quickly dismissed by Gabriel. The thought of food shortages reminded him a little of Paris and the soup lines there, yet that was under totally different circumstances.

Soon the people began to come to the church in search of nourishment, and not necessarily spiritual nourishment either, with which the church had little to offer in the way of bread, nor cheese. Gabriel did what he could and wrote to his bishop requesting assistance and yet the Church remained strangely silent only replying with vague promises of soon, soon help would arrive, even if that help was only in the form of rain. Yet, Gabriel knew the few that had petitioned for his help would not be alone in their search and that the numbers could grow daily. As much as Gabriel disliked even the thought of Paris and the soup that he served there, he knew that was exactly what he must do and so he went into the village in search of a large cooking pot and items he might put into it. Before the week was through the smell of fish stew could be smelled from a great distance and the people came, heads down, shoulders slumped, and bowls in hand. Father Gabriel, along with the assistance of two of the local ladies began to serve the soup and with it, hope. "Welcome, welcome," Gabriel would say," Welcome," as they made their way up the hill. In two months more time the Marionite packed up and left for presumably Genoa and was never heard from again. S

  Soon afterward Father Gabriel moved back into the old church building and began again where he had in the beginning. He dispatched letters to both the bishop in Florence and to the Sisters Musit and Rosa telling them of their great fortune to have the church back. He also told them of them of the drought, the poor in need there, and of the despondency which seemed to hover like an unwanted cloud on an otherwise sunny day. Gabriel hoped that they might return to assist him in his quest to feed to the people and only time would tell. Eventually two monks were sent to Porto Fino, yet neither were priests, yet they would have to do. The monks settled into the monastery and the Father into his small room in the back of the church. The room that Father Thaddeus had once occupied, as well as he sisters, was left untouched for now in hopes that one day the sisters might one day return. The winter was a particularly cold one and some people died from a combination of disease, little food, and the bitter cold. There was always the cold. Soon the spring would return and if seed could be found there would be a garden, a garden that would most certainly produce such delicacies as tomatoes, cabbage, and even peppers. So when Gabriel was not in prayer, or caring for the sick, he mostly spent his time dreaming about the spring time and the food they would all soon eat.

On more than one occasion, he questioned whether or not he was actually doing any good for the people in his care; after all they did look to him for guidance. Who was he, only as lowly priest just a few years removed from seminary and now trying to care for an entire village? Perhaps they would be better off without him, and a more seasoned man placed in his stead? But eventually those thoughts would pass and he never did tell the people how he felt in fearing that they might lose hope, if not in him, in God, and that was not something he wished to have on his conscience. So, Father Gabriel got up every morning, dressed in his one of two frocks and after preparing for his day with prayer, went out the great the parishioners with a big smile on his face, and there were often times he had little more to offer them. But he stayed in Porto Fino in fulfillment of a promise he made to a friend a few short years ago.

The people needed a shepherd and for better or worse, Gabriel was going to see that they had one. Gabriel knew that he was not perfect, but he was there and humbly at their service. When he looked into the mirror he began to see himself no longer as a boy, but has a man and would wear the mantle of Father Beauvais well. Suddenly his time of reflection was soon to be interrupted by a man entering the church carrying a child who was on the verge of death, exclaiming, "Father, father can you please help her?"

With that the priest gathered himself and grabbing a blanket he put it around the child and asked them to come in and stand next to the fire to warm themselves. "Here my son, here is some soup for you and this child, as I have little I cannot offer you more, but you are welcome to what I have."

"Bless you father,""the man replied, "Bless you," as he took the bowl of soup with his one free hand. "What church is this father, as I am not from here and walked a great distance on our way to Genoa finding ourselves here?"

"The church has not been officially named yet, but I am Farther Beauvais and I welcome you to God's house, you and your daughter." With that the man sat his child in down beside the fire and began to sob.

They stayed with Father Beauvais for three days before they began their journey again. Father Beauvais had hoped that they would have stayed until the child was stronger, but when he awoke that third morning he noticed that the sun was shining, a note thanking him next to the altar, and that they were most assuredly gone.

Each day of the winter the people showed up at the church for their daily bowl of soup and Father Beauvais as well as the two recently arrived monks made sure all who wanted had a least something to eat and did not go home hungry. Each night the pot was empty and each morning Gabriel would awake to find it filled with soup again. The people never asked where all the soup came from and the clergy did not bring the subject up to them. The only thing that Father Beauvais could figure out is that when he was purchasing the kettle that he used the hem of his robes to wipe the dust away in search of any cracks that might be present and noticed that he has inadvertently used the cloth relic to wipe the pot as well. He never imagined that such a thing would create such wonderful results as to feed the people through the hard winter and into the summer to follow.

The rains returned to Porto Fino in the springtime and crops were sown as well. The soup pot remained filled each morning until the need was no longer there and just as mysteriously as it appeared, it vanished. "This was truly the Lord's handiwork", something Beauvais wanted to shout from the mountain tops, yet he did not nor did the monks who attended him for they had vanished too. What had just happened here he marveled? But what if the famine returned he wondered? It was at this time that Beauvais remembered the words issued to him by his mentor, Monsignor Thaddeus and the warning that the Church might take the relic if they ever got wind of it. So it would be another miracle kept silent and Gabriel was certain that there may be more miracles to come. No, he could not risk the risk that someone might take this truly blessed item from him and his flock in Porto Fino, he reflected, as Father Thaddeus had cautioned those few, short years ago.

Father Beauvais served the flock in Porto Fino another twenty one years as the unofficial abbot of both monastery and church as. It was about this time two middle-aged priests arrived and relieved him of his burden. A relief that he neither asked for not wanted, but of he did anything well it was that he obeyed orders. Gabriel was being reassigned to Florence to become Pryor of Santa Croce and it was a highly coveted spot within the Church Hierarchy, but first he was to have a respite, a sabbatical of sorts for the period of one calendar year. Gabriel learned that he could take this "rest" any place he pretty much saw fit, so he decided to go to a monastery in Rome, a place he had never been to and a place that sounded exciting and wondrous to him. And so he went to begin the next chapter in his life and with that he bid Porto Fino, farewell.

Chapter Twenty Five

"Thank you for coming to see me, Father Beauvais," said a visibly weakened Sister Musit, as she tried to sit up her bed in the room at the far end of the hall in the convent while Sister Rosa looked on.

"When I received word in Rome of your request, I came immediately, sister."

"I heard that we got the church building in Porto Fino after all," Musit almost whispered.

"Yes we did, and the garden was almost as lovely when I left there a month ago," replied Beauvais cheerfully.

"And how is Giovanni?" she continued. "Any hope that he will return to the priesthood one day?"

"Of that I am uncertain, but I never give up on the goodness of God, sister."

"Yes, of course," she replied. "I was saddened to learn of the death of our dear friend Don Diego, father. How did he go? In his sleep I hope?"

"Yes, in his sleep and he looked quite peaceful when I found him," Beauvais reflected.

"First Monsignor Thaddeus, then Don Diego, even your uncle the Cardinal, are all gone, all except me and Father Hugo. And soon I will be gone too, Father Beauvais."

"Nonsense, Sister. You are going to be fine, just fine."

"Well, father, I never like to disagree with a priest, at least not publically, but age is the one enemy that none of us mortals have ever been able to escape." Beauvais just sits quietly with his head partially downcast as he gently holds Musit's hand.

"Did I ever tell you the story of how I met them, father?"

"Who, Sister? Who did you meet?"

"Diego, the Cardinal, Father Thaddeus, and of course Hugo," Musit continued.

"No, you have not," he replied politely.

"And Hugo is not even his real name;" she comments with a slight hint of laughter in her voice, "I gave him that name if you must know."

"Father Hugo?"

"No, then what is it if I may ask?"

"I cannot remember exactly, but all I know is I could not pronounce it properly and so the words sort of came out something like "Hugo" and so it became his name here in San Gimgnano."

"I see, sister."

"Cardinal Beauvais was not yet a cardinal when I arrived; Hugo came here about the same time, and later Father Thaddeus showed up with Don Diego not far behind him."

"I see," said the priest.

"It was all happenstance, or so we all thought. By the way, do you still have the relic, the fringe garment that Father Thaddeus left to you upon his death? she asked.

Reaching with one hand to his waist belt, he replies, "Yes, I do."

"Excellent, then it has not gone by the way side, father."

"I know that this relic had something to do with the healing of Giovanni back in Porto Fino, but I have never understood how that happened nor why," Beauvais inquires.

"Then I must tell you the secret of the relic that you now use as a sort of sash about your waist, and you must listen carefully as well for I shall not repeat these words before my death," Musit stated.

"I did not learn the exact details until years later that a man working for a monastery up north near Fiesole was cleaning out the home of an elderly woman who had no heir and had left her property to the church, when he found some scrolls with writing on them hidden in some old Roman clay pots which were left behind by a previous occupant of the house. Inside these scrolls was the very relic which you now hold in your possession. This man knew that he had found something of importance and decided to use it to make a comfortable position for himself in his later years and thus ended up in the service of then Abbot Beauvais, your uncle." Beauvais sits quietly and listens intently. "He had visited a couple of other places in an attempt to secure a position, but to no avail as no one had enough sense about them to notice just how valuable they relics were, but that also meant that the word was out and soon others began to seek the relics as well. Cardinal Beauvais needed someone to help translate the treasures he now possessed and so he bullied the young Father Thaddeus into staying and assisting him in the discovering the mysteries which they held. Diego it seems arrived all too innocently in search of a missing uncle that apparently did not exist."

"So, why was he there sister?"

"He was there for the relics, namely the one, being this piece of cloth you are now holding."

"Whose garment is it, sister?"

"It is known as the hem of Paul's garment and it was originally torn from his own robe many, many years ago, blessed by him and then used to heal the daughter of one of his followers."

"This cannot be, sister!" exclaims Beauvais.

"Ah, but it can be and is true.

"Then that would make this relic well over millennia old," Beauvais retorted.

"Exactly, father, that is exactly right. It seems that Diego heard of the rumors of the relic being discovered and decided to go and investigate it himself. The Cardinal wanted to keep the relic a secret and somehow benefit from its powers to heal, but he eventually died and it then became to be in the possession of our friend, Father Thaddeus."

"So that's how I ended up with it?"asks Beauvais.

"Not exactly, for the father at one time offered the relic to Diego after he learned who Diego was, but by then Diego no longer wanted, nor needed it."

"Who was Diego then, and why did he no longer want it, sister?"

"Diego was a descendant of the Apostle Paul himself and believed he was the rightful heir to the relic and all the power which it possessed. Upon arriving in San Gimgano, Diego was an angry and bitter man, but somehow he had changed and no longer felt the need to own it nor to weld its powers and left it in the hands of Father Thaddeus, (who always seemed content in life and never really needed a personal miracle), who then passed it on to you and here we are today sitting in this room now telling of these events."

"This all seems too incredible to be real. Is there any more proof as to what you say, sister?"

"You want more proof, then I shall give you proof."

"Was Hugo there on a mission as well, sister?"

"I have not heard that he was, but I guess that anything is possible, father."

"Then how are these things possible?" he asked?

"There was another who was seeking the relic in their midst as well, and that someone was never suspected nor revealed that is until now," she continues.

Father Beauvais looks puzzled as he awaits her explanation.

"The other seeker of the relic was also a descendant, but not of Paul, but of one his followers." Musit pauses and then says, "A one-time slave known as Onesimus."

"Was he not the black slave which ran away from Philemon and the same slave which Paul pleaded mercy for fleeing?"

"Yes, father, the same one and he was also my ancestor as well."

"So then you were the other seeker, and yet when you had opportunity to take possession of the relic right after Father Thaddeus died and did not?"

"I had many opportunities prior to that and did not take it, father."

"Well then why not, Sister? Please explain."

"Oh, that is very simple father, as I, like Diego, no longer needed it or the power which it wielded."

"I see, you wanted it enough to travel a great distance to acquire it, yet when the opportunity presented itself, you did not take advantage of it."

"Strange behavior in my opinion, sister, strange indeed," the priest exclaimed.

"It is not strange at all, father, for our hearts had been healed by the one and only true God. He is the one who you, and I, and even the Apostle Paul serve, the Lord Jesus Christ, our savior."

Beauvais looks puzzled.

"There was never any real power in the cloth at all; it only served as a focal point for one's faith in the Lord. All the miracles came from heaven above and not from the relic on the earth below," replied Musit with a large smile.

With this, Father Beauvais understood the words Musit shared with him that day. It is said that she died later that night, and it was a peaceful death as she went in her sleep.

Father Beauvais presided over the burial of a very elderly nun from a far off land. It is also said that being the last one to depart her grave that day that he dropped something looking very much like an old and tattered cloth in with her before the earth covered her remains. With the only possible witness to this act being Sister Rosa, but who would she ever tell?

Beauvais took his leave and departed for Rome the next morning to continue his well earned rest, but could not help but think of Musit's words and the of the miracles performed, the body that was raised from the dead, the soup kettle which did not run empty, nor the hearts that were healed. He thought of the writings of the prophet Joel when he spoke of a land ravaged by plagues and locust. Of a people devastated by trouble and pain and how these people were very much like the ones he had know and yet had been healed, by a God who did after all care in a land that often does not. His next sermon would have an added zest to it he thought once he got back to Rome, much like Paul's might have once been while he was in Rome at one time as well. How it must have been for Paul in those days of trial and tribulation, under a Roman emperor who was no less a monster than possibly Satan himself? Yet this was the modern age and we are fortunate enough to be able to worship freely in this great city called Rome. Upon arriving to his abode, Beauvais ate a light meal and then took a long deserved nap where he began to dream.

"You there, young man, why do you flee?" asked Paul of the boy no more than six or seven years old.

"The soldiers have killed my parents and now I fear that they will kill me," the boy replied.

"Killed your parents?" Paul inquired. "What on earth ever for?"

"Because they dared worship the one true God, and not the emperor," said the boy as he tried to skirt around Paul on the vacated Roman street that night.

"Here, here now, you are safe with me," Paul stated. And with that the boy relaxed and stopped running. "Please now, where are the soldiers are that did this awful thing to your parents, young man?"

"They are only up the lane and to the right, sir."

"Will you please take me there?" Paul asks.

"I will take you as close as I can and then no farther." Paul agreed to this and the two walked a short distance up the road until they could see fires burning in the streets and upon closer investigation Paul discovered that the torches were actually people who were apparently killed and then dipped in some sort of pitch and set fire to and left to light the way for any who ventured that way.

Paul decided that he would ask no more of the boy as he could hear the approach of soldiers in the distance. About a stone's throw away, Paul noticed a man lying dead in the road way and with that he said, "In the name of Jesus of Nazareth, rise and walk! And with that the man rose and so did a woman who had been lying dead hidden behind the man as well."

"What happened, how am I here?" the two of them asked?

"I do not have time to explain, but this boy is now and an orphan and I trust him to your care," cried Paul, "so please see to it that he gets safely out of the city for he is now in your care." The couple hearing the approach of the soldiers decided not to stay around for further explanation when they began to leave. All at once a solder called out for all of them to halt. The couple halted momentarily as the boy began to cry.

"Take him and flee at once! Do you hear? Flee now!" Paul commanded as he began to walk towards the soldiers in a quickened pace, saying under his breath, "Greater love hath no man than a man lay down his life for his friends."

The couple only looked back briefly to see soldiers stopping to interrogate this man who had somehow helped them escape sure death under Roman justice.

"Greetings gentlemen, I am Paul, a Jew by birth, a Roman citizen by right, and now a bond servant of the Lord Jesus Christ who I once persecuted, much like you do here as well this very evening," he announced to the approaching soldiers gleefully! "Not only to do I preach salvation just to the Jew but to the gentile as well, as His work upon the cross was complete, my brethren."

And with that being said, one of the soldiers struck Paul in the face with the butt of his sword, knocking Paul to his knees and then he was taken off in custody to meet his fate. "How dare you treat a citizen of Roman like this? I demand to see you superior at once!" Paul demanded as he looked back to see that the couple, along with the boy were now safely out of sight.

Once before the centurion in charge, Paul made his case before him and claimed his right to appeal unto Caesar, and so before Caesar once again he would go.

Paul spent three days and nights in a dungeon awaiting his appeal to the emperor. It is said that as he was beaten by the guards that Paul often sang hymns of praise to the Lord and quoted much scripture as well. It is also said that Paul left the dungeon under guard and in chains on the third day, looking quite confident with even a smile on his face as he might know what awaited him.

"The LORD is my rock, my fortress and my deliverer; my God is my rock, in which I take refuge. He is my shield and the horn of my salvation, my stronghold." They say Paul continued to quote scripture all along his way to stand trial, which is a quote out of the Book of David's Psalms.

The majority of the latter part of Paul's life was as a bond servant unto the Lord, and he most assuredly died that day as well. The couple and the child told of the miracle that happened to them in the city of Rome and that the man, whoever he might have been, and how encouraged the believers where ever they told the tale of their salvation. "And the man," the couple said," was never heard from again. God rest his soul."

Paul was a rare one man indeed, one who started out as a persecutor or the church and then as a martyr for that church.

Father Beauvais served out the majority of his service to the church as an abbot in Florence and then once he reached his sixtieth birthday, he was replaced by a younger man and then sent off to Rome and given an honorary title and a small place to live in a small place, inside the walls near the garden adjacent to a small church, where he mostly walked, prayed, and meditated upon the holy scriptures. But most of all, Beauvais just waited to die. He no longer said mass, rarely if ever heard confession anymore, and had not been given this assignment of solitude as a reward, but more likely as a punishment for his outspoken behavior as abbot of Santa Croce in Florence. Here the church could at last shut him up, or at least if he railed against the greed of the wealthy and the agony which fell upon the poor, there would be no one of substance to hear his complaints. The birds that happened by most days were of course fed by him, and he tried his hand at writing poetry, but nothing eased his tortured soul.

After a while, Beauvais began to question God's compassion and even started rationalizing the miracles he had once witnessed back in Porto Fino. The healing of Giovanni, the pot of soup that remained day in and day out during that terrible drought, and the two monks who came to help and just as mysteriously disappeared, perhaps all just happenstance with a touch of imagination he wondered. The priest considered leaving the church without so much as a word to anyone, perhaps to some place where they never heard of priests, or sacraments, or rituals. But did that place even exist in the civilized world, he wondered. With little or no wealth, the task seemed even more impossible. Perhaps he would just take his own life, yet that seemed as if it might be painful, and Beauvais knew one thing for sure, he was not fond of pain. So about the gardens he walked, eventually not being able to even feign interest anymore, he fell into despair and wondered just how long he could endure this, this exile?

Often he would skip strolling through the gardens at all and with his long face and down cast appearance, he would reside to just sit on a bench and feed the birds which always seemed to be hungry. On occasion someone would happed through the gardens on their way to and fro conducting church business and sometimes people would either stop to view the gardens or might happen to ask him for directions? These opportunities rarely presented themselves, but they did allow Beauvais the chance to chat and even more rarer, he gave some unsolicited, fatherly advice. Or perhaps he would pray for one of the visitors loved ones in abstention. The best people he discovered to talk to were those who were grieving the loss of a loved one, for often they were vulnerable and especially desperate to talk to someone, anyone.

But after awhile, not even this was enough for Beauvais and was certain that would eventually have to take his own life rather than to stay here and lose what was left of his sanity. No longer did he talk to God, no longer did he care about his appearance, and even the very thought of bathing seemed like a monumental task to overcome. Yet he did bathe, as every good Frenchman knows, that if he must die, he would most certainly die clean. Beauvais often found his mind wondering to back to France, to a different place and time, a loved lost, and the heart break he once endured there. Surely she is married and with child by now, even grown children, but Belle has once owned his heart and he was too young to appreciate her. He began to second guess his entire adult life and the path he had chosen which made him all the more miserable. And even though he had never been to Portugal, the very idea of going there, standing on the seashore with the sun warming his face seemed very, very appealing to him.

Maybe he would steal some of the church's gold and make his way to Lisbon or possibly Oporto, live the remainder of his life under an alias? Once there, Beauvais would rid himself of this collar, make the acquaintance of a beautiful woman, and they would spend hours and hours just enjoying the seaside, living the simple life, and most of all just laughing. How he missed the sound of laughter these days, especially the laughter of a beautiful woman. He also missed the sound of Don Diego's guitar which had not dulled in the recesses of his mind over the years. And even though the music was Spanish in origin, it still spoke of Portugal to Beauvais and better times. But reality, as always, found its way back into his thinking and Beauvais knew none of it was to be and so he had better get used to and stop such dangerous thinking as this. And so he did.

One morning as he was sitting in the gardens, a letter came address to him from a friend had known many years ago when he was first abbot in Florence. Father Reinold was a Dominican and served at Santa Maria Novella and unlike himself, had not been passed over for promotion and now worked as some sort of bishop in Rome and was very well connected with the Vatican. All that the note said was that he had recently returned from a sabbatical in Spain and was hoping that Beauvais might have dinner with the bishop and allow him to tell all about his adventures in Spain. This was the first invitation Beauvais had had in recent memory. He and the bishop had been close friends years before but lost contact over the years, with the exception of a letter here and there to bring one or the other up to date. Reinold was a few years his elder and had always claimed to be of French extraction, but being French himself, Beauvais knew that was not the case. More like German, he had always thought to himself, besides, no self-respecting Frenchman would have a name like Reinold anyway. But Beauvais always kept this point of view to himself not wishing to offend his friend, and had even gone as far as to the bishop as an honorary Frenchman instead.

Upon reading the letter, Beauvais sent word that he would accept his friend's kind hospitality and then prepared for the evenings social event. The walk across town was not a long one and it would be nice to see his old friend as well as any new faces that might be in attendance as well.

"Yes, Father Beauvais, please enter as the bishop is expecting you," said the priest at the entrance way. Once inside the grotto, and down a long hallway, there stood his friend Reinold. Beauvais was always on the short and stout side, where his friend was a tall and gaunt as ever.

"Welcome, welcome, my old friend, welcome," said the bishop as they retired into the study and waited upon the evening meal which was still currently being prepared.

"Thank you, Eminence," replied Beauvais as he reached out to kiss Reinold's ring.

"Now, none of that my old friend," replied the bishop, as you are among friends here.

"So, you have been to Spain and back and lived to tell about it I see," said Beauvais.

"Yes, Gabriel, I did and I had the time of my life, and I even brought back some items to remind me of the trip as well." Reinold went on and on for what seemed like forever about Spanish artwork and culture. "The culture that the Moor's left behind as well as the influence that some of the Jews had brought there as well."

After dinner, (a recipe from Spain that the bishop insisted that he try), the two of them retired to the study to see the items which were brought back and to hear more tales of Spanish Galleons, a famous flamenco dancer there named Nuria, of course the painting that were brought back as well. Reinold had always taken a liking to paintings of common everyday things, things like a bottle of wine and a partial loaf of bread resting on a table, or items such as an apple or pear resting in a large bowl on a dinner table. Bowls of fruit on a canvas were something Beauvais tolerated to keep from insulting his guest, but for the most he did not care for them one way or the other. This time he had brought back two such pictures, with the first of a lady flamenco dancer dressed all in red and black, and the other of a bowl full of oranges sitting on a patio table under a partially covered roof to give shade.

"This must be Nuria, Beauvais questions when shown the painting?"

"Yes, she is apparently famous and I would have liked to have seen her perform while I was there that month, but I believe that she was previously engaged in Cordoba and was not due to arrive in Granada until a month or more after I left," said the bishop.

"Oh, too bad," replied Beauvais.

"I really should have made the trip over to Cordoba to have seen her, but I just never got around to it," said Reinold. "So perhaps my next visit I will schedule her in advance?"

"Now this painting you may find fascinating, Gabriel, and as you can see it is a beautiful likeness of a bowl of oranges. I bought it at a little bizarre the last day I was there," said the bishop.

"Oh yes, I can see that," says Beauvais feigning interest as he reaches out to take the picture from the bishop's outstretched hand.

"Consider it an early birthday present, Gabriel."

"Oh you should not have, Eminence, it is too kind of a gesture on your part," replied Beauvais.

"Here, please use my magnifying glass, Gabriel, and you will notice the fine workmanship in the brush strokes," urges Reinold.

Taking the glass in hand, he half heartedly scoots his chair closer to the light on the table and begins to look at the picture in more detail when all of a sudden the priest notices something of interest in the background of the painting. There in the background behind the table and the oranges sits a woman at another table. The woman is accompanied by a small child, a girl of about ten or eleven years of age holding something in her hand. What is this he wonders as the woman and the girl look somewhat familiar, and then he notices what it is in her hand and can hardly believe his eyes while the bishop continues on about the different contours of the painting?

"What is that the child is holding in her hand," asks Beauvais?

"Let me look," says Reinold. Upon doing so he returns the looking glass to Beauvais and then announces, "It looks Hebrew to me."

Beauvais silently and says nothing.

"Possibly something from a garment worn by their men, perhaps a hem of cloth," replies Reinold, "but I have never seen such a thing in a painting before, Gabriel."

"It is then that Beauvais remembers the tattered relic that Monsignor Thaddeus had left him, the same relic which helped heal Giovanni all those years ago, the garment which he associated with miracles in Porto Fino, and the same relic which now rested at the bottom of a dead woman's grave he thought to himself. "Then the story must be true," he said quietly to himself.

"What story?" asked the bishop of him.

"Nothing Eminence," replied Beauvais, wanting to keep this to himself.

"That would also explain why the Arab street merchant told me that the painting was quite old and also of Jewish origin. He demanded a higher price for it too," mentions the bishop, "but I held out and did get my price for it."

"Do you happen to know who might have painted it or if it has a name," inquires Beauvais?

"Well, as to who painted it, I have no clue, nor did the merchant. And as to the name, well in Spanish it is 'Las Naranjas de Valencia,'"replies the bishop proudly showing off his skills in the Spanish Language.

"Can you kindly translate, my friend?" asks Beauvais?

"Yes, of course, 'The Oranges of Valencia,'" he replies. It was at this point that Beauvais decides to tell his friend of the story had held inside all of these years and in the strictest confidence begins by saying tearfully, "Father, forgive me, for I have sinned."

Later that night Beauvais thanks his guest for a nice meal and a wonderful birthday gift. The bishop sends a monk along to aid the aging priest in his long walk home and wishes him well. Beauvais cannot help but remember all the words that Musit had told him about the relic, its history back through the ages, and how she and Don Diego had their lives restored through faith in Jesus Christ. Now his faith in God was also restored and freed from the burden of such a secret which he had carried inside all this time. The old priest would now sleep well knowing that his friend, the bishop, would never reveal the things he had heard this night. Beauvais then said his prayers thanking the Lord for his new found faith and settled in for the night. As he lie there remembering the evening, and the words of his friend, the bishop, "Your faith has made you free," still fresh in his mind, Beauvais fell into a deep sleep.

A nun found the old priest dead later the next morning thinking him to be ill when he did not come out to feed the birds as was his custom. The painting lie rolled up like a scroll on the study beside his bed exactly where he had left it. Later that week, Beauvais was buried with only a handful from the church in attendance with his earthly items later being sold and the money then given to charity just as he had wished , all of his property, that is except the painting, which Reinold purchased. And when asked why he purchased it, the bishop simply said,"It was to remember and old friend by," as some secrets were better not shared.

No headstone was ever erected to mark his grave next to that spot in the garden where he once fed his ever present birds. Naked we arrive and naked we depart, and such is the way of the world.